Bear Creek Saddle Cowboy

Sweet inspirational
contemporary cowboy romance

Book 2 in
the Bear Creek Saddle Series

by *NY Times* & *USA Today* bestselling author
Shoshanna Evers
writing as

Shoshanna Gabriel

Bear Creek Saddle Cowboy

Stand-alone 2nd book in the Bear Creek Saddle Series

by Shoshanna Evers writing as Shoshanna Gabriel

A young woman escapes an abusive relationship in NYC, determined to find her independence in the beautiful mountains of north Idaho…until a handsome rancher reaches out to her, and she finds herself questioning everything she thought she knew about relationships and faith.

When Megan Moore leaves New York City to live in the country—far away from the crowds, the traffic, and a controlling ex-fiancé—she finds herself way over her head in the mountains of rural northern Idaho.

Zach Walker runs a cattle ranch with his friends in small-town Bear Creek Saddle. It's not every day a beautiful woman falls into his life—and he's been looking for a wife. He just had no idea the exact opposite of the traditional-type cowgirl he thought he wanted would end up needing his help. What's a red-blooded man to do when he can't get his mind off the wrong woman?

As for Megan, she can't let her growing friendship with the handsome, guitar-strumming cowboy put her at risk for getting into a smothering relationship again. She came to Bear Creek Saddle to prove to herself she could make it on her own—certainly without any help from a rancher. But Zach's solid faith inspires Megan as she works to change her life.

Megan doesn't know anything about country life, so if she's going to make it on her own in Idaho, she'll need to learn fast. Zach is willing to show her the ropes.

Especially when he realizes Megan just might be the wife he's looking for, after all—and that sometimes, God puts a man and a woman into each other's lives for a reason…

Keep reading for BONUS CONTENT after "The End" –
read the first chapter of *The Rancher's Convenient Pregnant Bride*,
Book 3 in the series!

Bear Creek Saddle Cowboy
Book 2 in the Bear Creek Saddle Series
by Shoshanna Gabriel

© 2017 Shoshanna Gabriel

Bear Creek Saddle Cowboy © 2017 Shoshanna Gabriel
The Rancher's Convenient Pregnant Bride (Bonus Content) © 2017
Shoshanna Gabriel

Cover art by Rob Sturtz at SelfPubBookCovers.com
Editor: Therese Marie of ChristianProofreaders.com

Paperback book publication, copyright © 2017 Shoshanna Gabriel

ISBN-10: 0-9992166-3-5
ISBN-13: 978-0-9992166-3-7

All Rights Reserved.

This is a work of fiction. Any resemblance to persons living or dead or
places, events or locations is coincidental.

Shoshanna's Testimony

> "But he was pierced for our transgressions, he was crushed for our iniquities; the punishment that brought us peace was on him, and by his wounds we are healed."
> Isaiah 53:5 (NIV)

I USED TO BE known as Shoshanna Evers, a *New York Times* and *USA Today* bestselling author of steamy romance, from 2009-2015. Why did that end in 2015? In short, I came out in a public blog post as a Christian, and explained why I could no longer write sexy books. My career immediately crumbled.

Everything changed—my writing career, my religion, and my name. In 2014 (while still writing as Evers) I had a "road to Damascus" experience, and I started to think seriously about Jesus as the Messiah, and what that meant for me. I'm Jewish, so that was something I had *literally never* thought about before.

The seeds had been planted as early back as December 2012,

after the horrific Newtown shooting, when I turned to the *Tanach* (Old Testament) for comfort. For the first time, the Messianic prophecies seemed to jump out at me. I noticed something I'd never seen or heard before: *Isaiah 53*. At my Jewish synagogues, from Reform to Conservative to Orthodox, from the time I was an infant through till adulthood, *I'd never heard Isaiah 53 read*. It was always skipped over in the weekly Haftorah readings, presumably because it just didn't correlate with any of the Torah (Pentateuch) portions or any festivals. Reading it shocked me. Even after looking into what the rabbis and Jewish philosophers teach about this chapter (they don't believe it's about the Messiah, but about Israel), I *still* couldn't shake the effect Isaiah 53 had on me.

I can't quote all 12 verses here, so please… check it out for yourself, and you'll see why this Jewish girl nearly fainted while reading it for the first time.

I barely knew anything about Jesus. What little I did know came from the musicals *Godspell* and *Jesus Christ Superstar*. That's all I knew, but I could see the Prophet Isaiah was telling me all about Jesus long before Jesus came to Earth, and I'd never even known it. This started over a year of questioning and researching to find out if Jesus was actually the Messiah I had been looking for all along.

A year later, at the end of 2013, my family and I left Los Angeles and settled in a small mountain town in north Idaho. I attended church weekly for the first time in my life, and I loved it. It felt so right, even if I wasn't ready yet to fully give myself to Jesus. I loved praying in English instead of Hebrew, and I loved the church family.

In 2014, I had gone from writing erotic romance to less-explicit but still very steamy romance (books that came out that year had been written the year before). In 2015 when I bit the bullet and got baptized (despite the extreme disapproval of my secular Jewish family), things started changing for me very fast, from the moment I came out of the water.

I had been getting more and more successful as Shoshanna Evers. Writing sexy stories was very good to me, but it wasn't good *for* me, personally—not when it was keeping me from writing the stories I truly wanted to tell. I found myself writing faith elements into my storylines, only to have to remove them because they weren't part of the Evers "brand." I didn't want to freak out my readership, who hadn't signed on for anything having to do with God. Most importantly, I started feeling weird about what I was doing with my writing. I wanted to use the gift He had given me in a way that would be for His glory.

I'd never felt ashamed or weird about writing sexually explicit stories before—and I won't judge those who do. Who am I to throw stones? But something had changed in me. Writing love scenes was no longer my thing, which—considering I had written and had been editor of the 2011 non-fiction book *How to Write Hot Sex*—was going to mean *a major overhaul* in my life.

When I wrote *I Am Not Your Melody*, which I called "a Bear Creek Saddle short novel" and prequel to an upcoming series, I was already tired of writing sex scenes (after writing them in every book since 2010, I had essentially burned myself out). And my hero, Bill, was clearly (to me) having a faith crisis, but I couldn't articulate that. When the book came out, it wasn't the book I had really wanted to write in the first place. Despite that, I knew the book was good and that it fulfilled the promise I'd made to my readers as Shoshanna Evers: *Sexily *Evers* After.* It sold fifteen thousand copies in the first week as part of the Cowboy 12-Pack, and kept on selling. The follow-up series was bought by a big publisher.

But ultimately, I realized I couldn't sign the contract. I was just...*done* writing secular romance. There was no way I'd be able to write the series the way the publisher wanted me to. Instead, I wanted to write inspirational romance. They were very gracious and let me out of the contract. My agent—who was also very gracious—and I parted ways because she didn't represent Christian fiction. In one fell swoop I had lost a six-book contract and my agent, and though it felt as if I were pressing the career-self-destruct-button, I wrote that blog post entitled "Saying Goodbye to Erotic Romance" (http://bit.ly/GoodbyeErotica) in November 2015, where I came out as a Christian and told my readership what was happening.

The response from readers and many authors was overwhelmingly wonderful, despite the negative effect the move had on my publishing career. A percentage of my most loyal readers assured me they loved the way I tell stories, so they'd still read my books, and the Christian romance author community was so kind and welcoming. For some reason, I'd expected them to keep their distance, since I was "that kind" of author who had written "those kind" of books, and I didn't belong over in the squeaky-clean section of the cafeteria. But just the opposite happened—the inspirational authors welcomed me with open arms. Those ladies really walk the talk, friends.

There have been, of course, some readers who are upset. They've told me they're done reading my books. The day after the blog post went out, I had to step down as the Erotica Captain for a big annual book convention. I had created panels and topics, and I was going to be speaking on them as well. The panels went forward, but without me on them. The decision hurt my pride a bit, but it made sense. I needed a clean break in order to move forward.

Shoshanna Gabriel is my new name for my new genre. No more *Sexily *Evers* After*, now my promise is a *Faithfully Ever After*. Originally, I'd wanted to keep the name Shoshanna Evers, since I'd spent nearly six years building it up and had my "letters" (*NYT & USAT*)—but I have too many sexy books out as Evers, and I didn't want my future readers to accidentally pick up a backlist book and have a heart attack. Giving up my bestseller status to start all over again wasn't an easy decision, but it's one I made after a lot of prayer, and it feels right.

Now that the publishing contract for my new series was gone, I was able to revise the opening book to be how I'd originally intended it to be, as a sweet inspirational romance. I re-titled it *Second Chances for Trampled Hearts* (Book 1 in the Bear Creek Saddle Series) and wrote it under the name Shoshanna Gabriel.

I'm thrilled to have the opportunity to share the rest of the Bear Creek Saddle Series with you in a personal, very real way that I never would have been able to if I'd gone against that little voice whispering inside of me, a voice that said, *God has a different path for you than the one you are on.*

All I want now is to write for His glory, and to do His will. It's not easy. But it's worth it.

Please pray for me, friends, and I'll be praying for you. Happy reading!

All my best wishes,

Shoshanna Gabriel

Chapter One

"Look at the birds of the air; they do not sow or reap or store away in barns, and yet your heavenly Father feeds them. Are you not much more valuable than they? Can any one of you by worrying add a single hour to your life?" *Matthew 6:26-27 (NIV)*

ALMOST THERE.

Megan Moore pulled into the gas station about ten miles or so outside of her final destination, according to the GPS. The place was deserted.

She stepped out and stretched with abandon—it felt good to move around after being in the car for so long. A week of driving cross-country from New York to northern Idaho made her muscles knotty and tight. Around her, the cooler summer-evening air was still warm enough to leave her jacket draped across the passenger seat while she pumped the gas.

With her hand on the pump and her back to her twenty-year-old two-door blue Eclipse, Megan scanned her surroundings. She was accustomed to being constantly presented with a new potential danger to evaluate. But there weren't any people around, and not even many places to hide behind if someone were lying in wait. Everywhere, evergreen-covered mountains towered in the near distance, separated from her by wide expanses of fields.

So different from Manhattan—exactly what she'd been hoping for. There had only been a few vehicles on the road during what would have been rush hour on the East Coast.

One of those vehicles was coming her way now.

Who's this? The keychain dangling from her pocket tapped reassuringly against her thigh, the small canister of pepper spray her backup plan if the driver of the truck wasn't friendly. Or was too friendly.

A beat-up red pickup truck pulled up to the other side of the pump. There was a split second of no sound but the rumble of its engine, then *WOOF WOOF WOOF!*

Megan startled when the big black dog barked at her from inside the truck.

"Don't mind her," a young man said as one long, muscular, denim-clad leg climbed out of the truck, followed by the rest of the perfect specimen of Idaho cowboy.

Megan wasn't sure if he was talking to her, or to the dog, since his handsome face was partially in shadow from the light-colored cowboy hat on his head. A Stetson? That was the only kind of hat she knew the name of. Light stubble covered the strong lines of his jaw. The unkempt brown tendrils kissing the back of his neck could've benefitted from a comb, but this man didn't look like the type to play with his hair.

His striking good looks were so distracting she almost forgot why he was talking to her in the first place. If he was even talking to her at all, that is.

"Wh-what?" Megan asked, setting the pump back in its holder.

She should go—get in her car and leave now that she was done pumping gas. But instead, she wanted to stay. Stay to just…look at him. Heat flushed her face… and she probably wouldn't be able to blame that on the mild weather.

He nodded toward his black Lab. "That's jus' Inky. Everyone knows Inky—she's tamer than I am."

"Oh, that's good," Megan said. "Wait…are *you* tame?"

The man looked at her in surprise at the question, as if noticing for the first time that she was a woman alone, fidgeting with her keys.

"Almost always," he said. "Neither of us bite, anyhow."

He grinned at her, flashing his nice white teeth for a moment as he picked up the windshield sponge and got to work cleaning the dead bugs off the truck's front grille.

"That's good," she repeated, and peered over into his truck at the dog again in an attempt to not stare at its owner.

"New York, huh?" the cowboy asked her over his shoulder.

"What gave me away?" Maybe he could tell by her accent. Her clothes? The fact that she physically jumped a bit when his big dog barked?

He turned to face her, and her attention drifted to his warm, kind eyes. Green with flecks of brown.

"Your license plate," he said, interrupting her thoughts. "New York.... Bit of a culture shock for ya here."

Megan smiled and shook her head. "Well, maybe, but it's a *welcome* culture shock, if that makes sense."

"Sure does." He set the windshield cleaner back in its bucket of murky water and wiped his hands on his jeans. "And here I was thinking you must've gotten pretty lost to end up all the way out here. Middle of nowhere."

Megan smiled at the unexpected pleasure of having a person to talk with, after days of only the radio to listen to.

"I traveled through some mountainy stretches of nowhere to get here," she said. "It's not really nowhere if there's a gas station." For a moment, Megan let herself fall into his gaze, enveloped by the cowboy's handsome green eyes.

"That's a fact," he agreed, his lip curling up in a half-smile of amusement.

His arm, draped over the side of the pump, made him look casual and friendly. As if he were enjoying chatting with her.

Stop. The last thing she needed was to have her thoughts dominated by a man's charms.

"Well, at least I'm not lost," she said, a nervous laugh escaping her throat. The only time Megan had really felt lost was when she was still in New York, trying to work up the guts to make the big move.

Driving here was the easy part.

The familiar safety of her car called to her, and she slid into the driver's seat. "So. Um...see you later."

"You betcha." He tipped his hat in a lazy way that indicated how customary the gesture was to him.

She smiled out her window in response and lifted her hand in what she hoped was a properly friendly "bye-neighbor" wave instead of an "I'm-from-NY-where-we-don't-wave" wave.

The dog barked at her again, but Megan didn't mind. *That's just Inky*. Now she was one of the "everyone" who knew Inky, too. And maybe she actually *would* see that cowboy later. It was a small town, after all.

Wow. Megan shook the silly grin off her face so she could focus on driving back out onto the road without crashing into something.

If he was representative of the type of man who inhabited her soon-to-be new hometown, she wouldn't be as uneasy here as she was around men in New York. All of her ex's colleagues had the same too-slick feel that Todd did—as if their skilled small talk and unnoticed-by-most grabby glances at her were part of a carefully built façade—one that would crumble should she ever stand up for herself, or stray from the herd.

Not so with this cowboy. He felt…genuine. As on edge as Megan had been beneath the friendly chitchat, he still somehow gave off the vibe that he would sooner protect her from danger than *be* the danger. Megan couldn't know that for sure, of course. Their chance encounter had lasted all of about three minutes. It was just her gut instinct talking. But weren't gut instincts pretty much always right? If only she'd listened to hers sooner with Todd…

How crazy was it that humans were the only animal that ignored their instinctual silent alarm bells ringing? If a gazelle did that, if it saw the lion approach but didn't run because it didn't want to make a scene, or look stupid, or be wrong about the lion…well, fortunately for gazelles, they were smarter than she was in that regard.

But who said "you betcha" without irony, anymore, anyhow? Megan grinned out at the road ahead of her, her grip relaxing on the steering wheel a bit. The deeper into Idaho she got, the more different it seemed from New York. Like cutting pieces off of a tart apple and finding a hearty potato underneath. That different.

She was close, so very close to Bear Creek Saddle. Her new home.

And she already had made an acquaintance. Sort of…she didn't even know You-Betcha-Man's name. Or if he lived in town or was just passing through. She should've asked him. Maybe he would've even asked her out, to show her around.

No. Stop.

If she was never going to tie herself down to a man again, then why should she even care who the friendly cowboy with green eyes really was?

And yet she did care. *You betcha.*

* * *

That night, Megan leaned down and gently blew into the struggling fire. "Come, on," she urged the flames softly. "You can do it."

Considering this was her first-ever campfire, it was going much better than she'd dared to hope. *She* was doing better, even. If someone had told Megan even a few months ago that she would find herself sitting in the woods in the mountains of northern Idaho—single—she wouldn't have believed them.

The idea of leaving Todd, leaving New York City and her unexciting part-time job in human resources, had occurred to her, of course. That wouldn't have been the shocker that would have kept her from believing this would happen. There were more than a few moments when his cloying manipulation left her feeling suffocated, times she stared out the window at work and felt jealous of the construction workers laughing and yelling to each other across the street. But if she could go back in time and tell herself that she would actually get the guts to *do* it, to leave him for real and not just in her daydreams—to run off into a brand new life… there was no way she'd have believed it. Not even if it were future-Megan telling her.

So all that considered, struggling flames aside, she was doing all right. More than all right.

The forest itself was an adventure—the breeze flowing through the evergreen trees and the way the wildflowers popped up throughout the clearing excited her senses in a way that city lights never had.

Megan hadn't seen this much nature in all of her twenty-three years stuck in New York. She'd gotten out before it was too late, at least, before she ended up miserably married. This was the last place anyone (*Todd*) would think to look for her, camping alone in the middle of nowhere, as You-Betcha-Man had called it.

The beautiful, awesome, thank-goodness-it's-not-the-city, nowhere. Not even a gas station in sight.

"I think it's time," she murmured.

She didn't have to rummage in her bag too long to find the three-dollar bottle of sparkling cider she'd gotten from the store that sold her the firewood. They'd sold wine, too, but if she was going to start fresh, then she'd be better off letting go of her vices. Thus the nonalcoholic bubbly.

The twist-off cap dampened the ceremonial "pop" sound, but it still launched her into celebration-mode.

"To a fresh start," she told the fire, lifting the bottle. She took a sip straight from it, since she hadn't planned ahead enough to bring a glass.

The sky was filled with stars, bright pinpoints bedazzling the wide expanse above her. It had (presumably) *always* been filled with stars—but in New York City, there were too many lights to ever see them. Stars may as well have never existed for her.

But now they did.

Underneath the tight control Todd held over her, surely Megan had always been there, buried beneath his good-intentions-gone-wrong—just as the stars were too overpowered by the city lights to shine.

She may as well have never existed, either. But now, she did. Now Megan had a chance to shine as well.

"I'll drink to that," she murmured, and took a sip. The taste reminded her of celebrating New Year's Eve with her sister when she was twelve. For three dollars, it could've been worse.

Camping out in the woods imparted a feeling of independence. It was a new feeling. On the long drive from New York to northern Idaho, cross-country practically, she hadn't made use of her brand-new tent once. Instead, she'd stopped at cheap motels along the way, watched their boxy TV sets, and eaten their free continental breakfasts in the morning. It'd been too scary to risk camping for the very first time while on the road.

But Megan wasn't on the road anymore…not now that she'd arrived at Bear Creek Saddle. This small town in the mountains of northern Idaho would be her new home.

Megan laughed and shook her head. Before she'd checked Google Maps, she'd been under the murky impression—despite having a college education—that Idaho was somewhere in the middle of America, like Iowa. Whoops.

Kinda embarrassing when she realized she'd been conflating Iowa and Idaho her whole life (the few times she'd had reason to think of states that started with the letter *I*, that is), but even more so when she found out none of her Manhattan colleagues even knew where Idaho was either. It was like, who cared about any place that wasn't New York or Los Angeles?

"I do," she said, unaware she murmured to herself out loud.

As she'd discovered after a few map clicks, Bear Creek Saddle was a tiny dot right near the top of America, the best-kept secret in the Pacific Northwest. Idaho shared a border with Canada, with the skinny panhandle of northern Idaho sandwiched between Washington and Montana. The photograph she'd seen online while searching for somewhere (anywhere that was nowhere) had called to her, enticing her to click on the picture of this little town and study every bit of it. Such a great mental escape from all the concrete in the city.

It was that one photo—with its incredible mountain peaks, lakes, and evergreen trees—that hooked her. It had been captioned with the location of the town, so here she was.

The whole state of Idaho was sparsely populated—NYC alone had *way* more people. The few who lived in north Idaho appeared to be hardy and self-sufficient, the exact opposite of how she viewed herself.

You-Betcha-Man was probably like that, too. There was something incredibly appealing about a man who knew his way around just about everything. She could just picture him, with that smile he'd flashed her, building a...barn or something...whatever men in Idaho did. He'd know exactly what needed to be done, whereas she had no idea where to even start.

Stop. Megan sighed and pushed the thought of him from her mind. Another man was the last thing she needed right now. If she felt like going the relationship route again, she'd be better off shackling her feet together instead. The end result would be the same. Stumbling on her path to freedom.

A breeze blew over her, and the flames tilted perilously. In her jacket, she was quite comfy, despite the little chill that had crept into the air. Thank goodness she'd decided to run away from it all in the summertime. Northern Idaho was probably not the best place to visit for the first time in winter.

When her pot of Chef Boyardee was ready to be pulled off the flames, she poured the chunky pasta into her metal camping bowl and dug in with the metal spork that had come with it.

"Mmmm." *This is the life.*

Before, it had been a lifetime of waking up to a buzzing alarm, and heading out the door every single day—first to Pace University on the NYC campus up until a year ago, then to work in a low-level, part-time position in HR that her bachelor's degree should be wiping its feet on. After being told what to do and where to go and how to behave, the mere thought of living here in this little rural mountain town, collecting eggs from squawking chickens, milking a cow...doing whatever else it was that homesteaders did (make hay?)...well, the fantasy calmed her.

She could have her own little house; she'd make friends with the people who lived here. Not with You-Betcha-Man though, because he made her too…*interested* to just be friends with.

Getting *interested* was dangerous. She knew that much.

Time would go by, she imagined, and perhaps they'd start calling her a spinster. Megan liked the idea of that. Spinsters weren't tied to a man, spinsters took care of themselves, and then got called spinsters for having the guts to not want to be dependent on *any* man.

"Call me what you want," she said to the townsfolk in her imagination—those who might call her a spinster when they saw how far she stayed away from a wedding chapel. Ha! Or was she thinking of Regency England times?

She took another sip of the sparkling cider.

Thank goodness Todd had asked her to marry him—because the *wrongness* of it had hit her like ice water, and that was what woke her up. If she didn't want to be stuck in the same anxiety-ridden rut forever, she'd had to get away—before it was too late. Living with Todd had been so bad from day one. Surely God had a hand in that. It helped her to wake up to the fact that her life needed to completely change.

If she didn't have such a stubborn independent streak—and a growing distaste for city life—Todd could have been her Prince Charming. Who wouldn't love having a man swoop in and pay for everything and take care of everything… and control everything… and obsess over all the little ways she wasn't doing things exactly the way he wanted her to… yeah.

Every day Megan had spent in Manhattan had the effect of sensitizing her a little more. Each stranger who bumped into her on the street added insult to injury, every siren that howled past her jangled her nerves just a little bit more.

Maybe it was city life that was killing her. Maybe it was being under Todd's thumb. Or the soul-sucking treadmill of going to a job she hated, to make money that paid for a lifestyle she'd never asked for.

Tomorrow, when the sun was up again, she'd find a dumpster somewhere to get rid of her trash. It wasn't littering if she put it all in a garbage bag with every intention of throwing it out, right? Were there even dumpsters in the mountains? Or was that just in all the dark back-alleys in New York? Fun times, back-alleys, where she got to walk with her pepper spray in hand, her head on a swivel, just waiting to get mugged or worse. No, that wasn't utopia to her, not anymore.

Megan took another cleansing breath of night air to clear her thoughts.

If she'd been looking for the exact opposite of New York, then northern Idaho was it. This town encompassed so much land, huge mountains and lakes—but it only had a population of 649. That meant there was a lot of land for each person. A lot of space to find herself.

Bear Creek Saddle was going to have to change their sign to say POPULATION: 650 ...because Megan was staying. This would be home now.

She tilted her head back, letting her long, dark hair fall out of her face, and searched the sky. Beyond the tall trees, diamonds sparkled down at her from above.

Here she would start fresh, and be independent, and *Be. Happy*. No matter what it took, no matter what she had to do to make it happen. They could even call her Ol' Spinster Megan (she sort of hoped that nickname took).

In fact, she was starting to feel better already.

* * *

The sun was barely over the horizon when Zach Walker parked his red pickup truck where the dirt road ran out. He'd go on foot from here. His lips pursed to whistle, when he stopped himself. He was just so used to having Inky with him, but she was sitting this walk out to let a crack on her back paw heal a bit. Poor ol' girl.

Zach walked along the long, twisty trail, a trail beaten down by his feet more than anything else. He'd been taking this route all summer, basically since the last of the snow melted on the mountain. If he wanted to bag an elk when the season started in September, he had to scout out his hunting grounds first.

There were plenty of men who'd just hunt wherever they could drive to, hike out for a few minutes, open up a six-pack, and wait it out. Privately, Zach thought hunters like that wasted their hard-won elk tags. But those men weren't really his competition. His friends at the ranch were all looking to fill their freezers as well, and they were good at it. Maybe they should team up to help each other.

Zach preferred going *au naturel*—hunting with a bow and arrow. He'd been an archer since he was a kid. There was something about the feel of it; the bow was an extension of his body when he pulled that string back, his hand coming right up to his cheek and letting that arrow fly. The gun on his hip was for protection, but not for hunting.

His phone buzzed in his back pocket, alerting him to a text.

It was Paige again. Her text read: *"Good morning, sunshine! Want company for scouting? I'm wide awake!"*

Of course. Who else would want to go scouting for elk at dawn when they didn't even hunt? She was a sweetheart, but every time he texted with her or let her in for coffee when she stopped by the ranch, he felt like he was just leading her on. They'd broken up almost five years ago, officially—after being together all through high school and for a few years after—but she and his mother were still planning on Zach coming around, and settling down with Paige.

It wasn't going to happen.

Not because Paige wasn't a great girl, but because he wasn't in love with her. She deserved to be with a man who loved her properly. And he deserved to be with a woman he was crazy in love with, too. He would do everything in his power to ensure his future marriage was nothing like his own parents' had been.

"Thanks anyway," he texted back. *"I'm already out."*

Zach sniffed the air. Was that... Chef Boyardee? He shook his head. That didn't make any sense. He was in the middle of the woods, in the mountains. But as he had been walking up, he'd only smelled the crisp air, the grass and dirt beneath his feet, and sometimes, the sweet scent of wildflowers blooming along the trail. The evergreen trees had a smell too, that fresh piney scent that was better than any air freshener could ever hope to replicate.

Paige interrupted his train of thought with another text, a frowny face, followed by: *"Don't forget about Bill & Allie's harvest party! Let me know, we'll have so much FUN!! ;)"*

He slid his phone back into his pocket. Yeah, parties were fun—and Zach could eat with the best of 'em—but the "Sadie Hawkins" thing where only the girls were asking out the guys had put him on the spot. Wonder how many guys had chewed out Bill and Allie for putting out those stupid flyers, to celebrate their new deep fryer. Free french fries for every couple. *Couple* being the key word—probably Allie's way of ensuring twice as many people would show up. She was business-smart like that. Crazy thing was, the place was going to be *packed*.

Telling Paige he was too busy to go with her hadn't worked, because she'd just made sure his schedule was cleared (that mainly involved talking to his mom). Now the only way to avoid leading her on even more was by telling her the painful truth—yes, he supposed he could go to the party, but he didn't think it was a good idea to go together. Man. That conversation was going to be uncomfortable for them both. Maybe he could just give her money for french fries and send her on her way without him. *Nah.*

It wasn't that he didn't want to settle down. He definitely did—just not with Paige. There came a time in a man's life when he had to get serious about finding a wife, raising a family. Now that the ranch was on firm ground, he had no more excuses. He was ready for it.

What Zach really wanted, when he thought about it, was a kid. A kid he could be a real father to, someone so different from how his own father was to him. Someone who wouldn't leave his kid, ever. First step to creating a loving family was for Zach to find a wife.

All he wanted was a woman he was madly in love with, who also happened to be a cowgirl who could help him run the ranch, cook up a storm, be well-liked in town and in church, be great with kids, and of course, who wanted to marry him too. And she'd be beautiful, if at all possible. Not too much to ask, or maybe it was.

Paige fit the bill completely—except he wasn't in love with her, not even a bit. He'd already tried to fall in love with her exactly because she was so perfect, but there are some things that couldn't be forced. Love was one of them.

Working the ranch didn't exactly provide too many chances to meet a woman he didn't already know. He'd dated some of the girls from town in the past few years. Zach was starting to think the only way to find a wife would be to leave the ranch and travel some, or start internet dating. Man.

The slightest scent of canned pasta carried to him on a slow breeze. What on earth? His woods weren't the same as they were yesterday morning. Something was different.

Zach deviated off the trail, checking his whereabouts carefully, and followed his nose. He wasn't more than a few hundred yards from the trail when he spotted what had to be the messiest campsite he'd ever seen.

A brand-new tent, clearly never used before, was set up, still zipped up tight. Despite the fact that the sun had been up for over an hour, he had a feeling that the owner of the tent was inside, sleeping in. A long-dead fire had left its ashes in what he could only suppose was meant to be a crude fire pit.

Sitting right out on the rocks around the charred logs was a used dish. Next to that, a tipped-over glass bottle of what had probably been white wine or champagne, judging by the tiny puddle in the dirt around the mouth of the bottle. But that was just a drop in the bucket compared to the worst of it—a ripped-open trash bag, the contents spread around the campsite like confetti.

"Everyone had themselves a party," he grumbled.

Some sort of animal must have gotten into the trash bag that was on the ground, tied up and held down by a stone. They had torn it open, littering the campsite with granola bar wrappers, baby wipes, juice boxes, chewing gum, tissues, and yes… two cans of Chef Boyardee, open. Something must've scared them off, because

Zach could still smell the pasta that reminded him of visiting with his friend when he was a kid.

If he could smell the campsite from yards away, the bears would be able to catch the scent a lot farther off. And the wolves. It was nice of the camper to try not to litter, but obviously this person was a moron. Who else invites bears to their campground like that? They may as well send out invitations.

Something pink and white caught his eye. A lady's socks? Yes. Hanging from a tree branch behind the tent, as if the socks had been washed and left out to dry.

New-York-Girl.

It had to be. The campsite wasn't from a crew of out-of-town teens partying, after all. He hadn't seen the girl's little blue car, but it was probably around here somewhere. What had she been thinking?

For some reason, Zach felt almost…betrayed. He hadn't thought she was the sort to get drunk by herself and pass out in the tent. She must be hurting more than he'd picked up on. He'd seen this before, but only with a couple of homeless guys traveling through.

It's not like he actually knew her, just because he'd spoken a few words with her at the gas station the day before, anyway. And yeah, she'd set up camp practically in his own backyard, but that didn't mean much. It wasn't hard to do considering how much land the Bear Creek Saddle Ranch covered on the edge of town.

The girl was lucky nothing worse had happened during the night, with hungry animals prowling around, looking for free food.

Why hadn't the sun woken her up?

Zach walked right up to the tent and tried to peer inside. All he could see was a bundle of sleeping bag and some of her beautiful dark hair poking out. Was she even breathing? He watched closely until he saw the sleeping bag move slightly.

All right, she wasn't dead. Good. He forced himself to look away. It wasn't…appropriate to watch a woman sleep. She was too vulnerable like this. He should forget scouting and pull up a log, sit watch until she came to.

Should he?

It wasn't his business anyway. It only *felt* like his business because he'd mentally claimed this area as "his" hunting spot, and, if he was honest with himself, because he had really liked her when they'd met. There was a longing inside of her that drew him in.

And she's beautiful. Right. But that didn't matter. Her beauty and one chance-meeting didn't make her his personal responsibility.

In Idaho, people took care of themselves. It was one thing to be neighborly and give a helping hand. It was another to try and police folks.

No one else was likely to come up this way past her tent. She was safe where she was.

Let her do her thing. It wasn't his life, it was hers to live how she chose to. Zach backed out of New-York-Girl's campsite and returned to his hike. He'd check in on her on his way back, just to make sure she was still alive. She was kinda petite to have drunk that whole bottle of…whatever it was.

Zach hiked about a quarter mile up the trail, to the part where it wound down closer to the creek. It soothed his senses to hear the running water as it bubbled over the rocks, past the fallen branches, leaving little white peaks in the water—visible disruptions of the water's motion. He sat on the ground, resting on his elbows, and took a load off his feet.

This was the best. He loved his morning walks in the woods. Even though he lived spitting distance from all his friends, he was glad none of them joined him in the morning. They each had their own routines. It was nice to have this solitude sometimes.

Zach closed his eyes and listened to the water. A vision of the willowy girl from New York smiling shyly up at him flitted behind his closed lids, and he grinned to himself.

Are you tame, she'd asked him... His first instinct had been to joke in response, but the look of resigned fear in the girl's eyes had made him slow down and tell her the truth—she had nothing to fear from him. Or Inky, with her ouchie on her big gray paw pad, poor dog.

The branches rustled down on the other side of the creek. Something was amiss. He sat up, alert, and stared at the area the sound came from.

Zach had leaned up against a fallen log, the same hollow tree he'd used as a backrest for the past two years. Something was different this time, though.

A small patch of brown fur clung to the bark. It looked like an animal had rubbed itself against the log, scratching its back, perhaps? Or maybe even just passing by it. He picked it off and rubbed the fur between his fingers. Bear fur.

Uh-oh.

Zach stood up slowly and looked around the grass for tracks. Sure enough, he saw some stomped-down grass, but more importantly... a big pile of bear scat. Wasn't too old, either, from the looks of it. How could he have missed this?

"HEY bear," he said loudly, to warn the animal he was in the area, and to stay clear. "HEY bear."

Bears in his part of northern Idaho were brown bears more often than not (much more dangerous than the black bears, which weren't exactly friendly themselves), and he didn't want to risk meeting this one face-to-face. He had to get back to the truck, and come back the next day—equipped with bear spray as a just-in-case—and hopefully the bear would have moved on.

What about the girl, passed out in her tent?

"Oh no." He shook his head. *Not good.*

If there were a bear in this immediate area, she was in danger and didn't even know it. If Inky had been there, she would have sniffed out that bear early on and possibly even frightened it off with barking.

Zach searched the area with his eyes, ears, and nose, looking for any sign of the bear. He could kick himself for being so distracted before that he'd forgotten what he was supposed to be doing—scouting. Looking for tracks and droppings. If he'd been doing that after he'd left the campsite instead of worrying about New-York-Girl, he would have noticed signs of the bear long before he got close enough to hear something…big…moving through the bushes.

The more he looked, the more signs he saw…but no actual bear. *Where is it?*

Then—a large, dark shape moved slowly behind the trees, then disappeared again. Yup. That was a bear all right. First one he'd seen in years this close up that hadn't been dead, stuffed and on a stand.

"I'm not dancing with a bear today, my friend," he whispered.

He put his arms up, to appear even larger, and walked backward out of the area, keeping his eye on the trees where he'd seen the bear, until he was back on the trail.

Hikers were supposed to make noise to warn bears off, but at that moment his instinct told him to stay quiet and unnoticed. He rushed back down the trail, his eyes and ears wide open so he wouldn't accidentally sneak up on the bear—or any of its cubs, if it was a mama bear, which would make it even more defensive—and ran back toward the campsite.

This time, he was going to wake that woman up.

* * *

Megan lay in her tent and snuggled into her sleeping bag. Celebrating her independence last night had been exciting—when it wasn't terrifying. She'd stayed up way too late, her mind racing with possibilities for her future. All the things she could do with her life, and all the things she could no longer do, if she was going to try and live right.

Her water bottle called to her, and she gulped some down to rehydrate.

Her first night trying to sleep in the woods hadn't been so bad at all. A little scary at times, maybe. The forest was alive with sound at night, from the crickets chirping to the flapping of wings above the trees. Somewhere in the far-off distance, a train whistle blew, her only reminder that civilization was just a car ride away.

She pulled her phone out of her purse and checked the time. 6:30 a.m., and battery at five percent.

Ugh. That was way too early. Why did she have to wake up at the same time her alarm had always woken her? She'd thrown that stupid thing in the trash, and now for vengeance it was haunting her internal body clock. But she wouldn't mind getting the fire going. That way she could heat up some water for coffee.

Getting a fire going… a lot of work for a little hot water. Ha. Maybe she should've stayed in a motel after all?

No—that was sleepy-Megan-think. This was her home now. And if there was no hotel in town, then camping was the way to go.

It was what she wanted, anyway, right? To live off the land. It was going to be hard enough going from living in New York City to living self-sufficiently in northern Idaho, without adding never-even-been-camping-before to her list of reasons she shouldn't be doing this.

The sound of something moving outside the tent caught her attention. *What is that?*

Then—a voice. A man's voice.

"Hey there," the man called, with just a touch of country twang—

(like You-Betcha's voice)

—the sound deeply melodic while terrifying…simply by the fact that she could hear it at all.

No one else was supposed to be here. How had this man found her? What did he want?

"Hate to wake you up, ma'am, but you need to come on out now."

Oh my goodness. Oh my goodness oh my goodness…

Her heart raced. She'd thought she had escaped the dangers of predatorial men when she'd left the subways and the dark alleys of New York City behind. Now she was alone in the woods, with no one around for miles—except for this man. A man who wanted her to come out of the tent.

No way.

"Ma'am, you okay in there?" the man called, an edge to his voice now. "You need to wake up right now and get a move on—" He interrupted himself. "Can you hear me, ma'am?"

She held her breath, terrified. How did he know she was even inside the tent? She could have left her campsite to go hiking, for all he knew. She didn't answer him.

Just go away.

"I'm coming in to check on you, ma'am."

Oh no. He was going to come in if she didn't come out? *No.* She would not be bullied by another man. This was *her new life*, it had to be different. Jerks like her ex didn't belong here. Her heart continued to race, but her thoughts remained clear.

Time to use that adrenaline. Fight or flight, right? *How about both?*

Megan grabbed her keychain, and readied her pastel-purple cylinder of pepper spray. She gripped it tightly in her hand. If she had to use it, she'd have to hold her breath and turn her face away when she sprayed, so she wouldn't get any of it in her own eyes.

She'd never actually used the thing before. Hopefully it would work.

Please, God, protect me.

A shadow at the front of the tent darkened the inside where she crouched. The man outside the tent was on his knees just a few feet away from her—separated only by a thin layer of material. The opening unzipped slowly before her eyes, from the bottom up, the action as mesmerizing as it was dangerous.

Light drifted in past the opening from the outside. She could see dusty jeans, as the man kneeled on the ground and opened her tent.

Megan wanted to scream—instead, fear paralyzed her and only

a choked whimper escaped her throat. Who would hear her, anyway? The pepper spray was her protection, not some unlikely rescue. It probably only took about three seconds for the man to get that zipper all the way up, but it felt like a movie playing in slow motion before her eyes.

A sturdy-looking young man with a familiar cowboy hat ducked his head inside and stared at her—*it was him*! The cowboy! His grass-green eyes widened with surprise, his lips slightly open, as if he'd forgotten to exhale. The stubble on his jaw, darker than the tousle of brown hair falling onto his forehead from under his hat, glinted in the rising sun.

"Oh, you're awake—" he started to say.

"You *followed* me," she gasped, not having enough air in her lungs to scream the words the way she wanted to.

How could her gut instinct have been so wrong? Why was the gas-station cowboy here, uninvited, in her tent? He was supposed to be one of the good ones!

Or maybe there was a tattoo on her forehead that said VICTIM. Men who wanted to hurt her could see it clear as day. Men like her ex, men like the cowboy she'd been so sure had been different. How had he found her?

Don't mess this up.

Megan aimed the pepper spray right at his handsome (*No! Terrifying!*) face. "GET OUT."

When he didn't immediately move, she pushed the trigger down.

The cowboy turned his head instantly, but OH NO where was the spray? Nothing came out of the cylinder!

"Whoa," he shouted—as if she were a panicked horse—and put

his hands up in defense. "Whoa there!"

"Stupid pepper spray not working I will HIT you, you scary mountain-man-rapist cowboy what on EARTH are you doing in my tent?!"

The words flew out of her mouth at a high-speed rate, all running together in her terror, which admittedly, sounded a lot more like furious anger when she expressed it.

With a desperate howl, Megan wrapped her fingers around the pepper spray instead and slammed her fist into his nose. She'd never hit anyone before, and GOODNESS GRACIOUS it hurt her hand, even with the cylinder taking the brunt of it for her.

The man grunted in a way that sounded as if he were trying to keep from roaring like a lion. Holding it in, holding back. He was quick—he grabbed her wrist on its way down, not letting her get another blow in.

"Let go of me—" she shrieked.

"Stop hitting me!" he yelled. With a quick movement, he threw her own hand back at her and jumped up, standing once again outside her tent.

Blood dripped from his nose, and the man dropped his face into his hand, as if to make sure it was still attached. Why hadn't the pepper spray worked?

"You hit me good," the man said, and pulled his shirt up to wipe the blood away, revealing a muscular abdomen she was too frightened to appreciate.

It was important to notice, though, for the sake of the sketch artist—if she made it out of the mountains. Was this why he hadn't introduced himself at the gas station?

That one punch was her fight, but now what—flight? Could she run all the way to her car in time, before You-Betcha started chasing her? All he had to do to get her now was to lunge…and he'd be back inside her tent, on top of her. And then what?

If all she'd done was anger this guy, what would he do in retaliation?

"Get away," she said. "Go away from my tent." Her voice was high and shaky to her ears. She sounded like someone she didn't even know.

"LEAVE ME ALONE!" That sounded more like she meant it. Oh man.

The cowboy put his hands up again, as if to show her he was no threat. The nosebleed had stopped. "I didn't mean to scare you. It's me! From the gas station. I'm not…seriously, I'm not gonna hurt you."

I can run. I can do it. She just needed to get out of the tent. The door to which this stranger—that's what he really was—now blocked with his imposing physique.

"There's a bear in the area," the man said, gesturing behind him, toward the creek. "We gotta get outta here. That's what I came here to tell you."

A bear? The word filtered through her mind as a potential threat, but she had zero experience with bears. If there really even were a bear, was that more of an immediate danger than a man who had apparently stalked her?

"Move away NOW," she said. "I need to get out of my tent. STEP AWAY."

The keys, now weapons between her fingers, were hot in her hand. They had been cold only a few moments earlier, when she first picked them up to spray the cowboy. He wouldn't want a punch from her spiked fist now, that was for sure.

"Why did you break into my tent?" she demanded, crouched inside, peering out the opening at him—as if the thin material would save her from this man, as if it were a house of bricks instead of less-than-straw.

"Why'd ya hit me?" he growled. He paused, as if realizing her question answered his own. "You remember me, right?" He sighed. "I didn't follow you or...nothing like that."

"Of course I remember you." Her cheeks burned. "This is a *bit of a coincidence*, isn't it?" she asked, managing some sarcasm despite her fear. "How'd you find me, then?"

"You found *me*, New-York-Girl. You're camping right behind my land, on my stomping grounds."

What? How had that happened? She hadn't even known for sure he lived in Bear Creek Saddle, much less where his land was. The look of confusion on her face must've shown through, because You-Betcha-Man smirked.

"It's all right," he said, his lower lip crooked in the half-smile. "I ain't mad 'bout that."

Megan took a breath. *He* wasn't mad at *her*? Please.

"Camp where you want, lady. But we should get outta here." He stilled, cocking his head to listen for...something.

A bear...?

"Explain why you thought you could break into my tent uninvited," she said through gritted teeth.

"We got no time for that—"

"Well," she said, "then I'm not moving."

He sighed. "I'd been hollering for you to come out," he said. "I saw your empty bottle—you were passed out drunk."

"I was *sleeping*," she spat. "Not passed out. And I'm not drunk."

"Well, you sure showed me." He tentatively touched the bridge of his nose and glared in her direction from under the rim of his hat. "Don't worry, you didn't break it."

Ha. Like she was worried that she'd injured him. Megan was more concerned about the fact that her one weapon, the pepper spray, had completely failed her in her time of need.

"Go away then," she said, brandishing her key-loaded fist at him.

"I won't hit a girl, but I will keep you from hitting *me*, you understand?"

"Don't you touch me. I will poke your eyes out with my keys if I have to." The steel in her voice matched her resolve.

"You keep threatening me, ma'am," he said, taking a long stride backward, "next time I'm gonna throw your keys so far into the woods the bear'll find 'em 'fore you do."

"You will not," she gasped, pulling her spiky fist closer to her chest. But he was big, and he looked serious.

"You're setting there arguing when there's a bear nearby and you've got the messiest camp I've ever seen."

Mess?! He was a liar. He was trying to lure her out again so he could serial-kill her.

"I didn't leave a mess," she said indignantly. "I put everything away in the trash bag. You're lying." *For what purpose?*

"I make it a point to not tell lies," he said, as if he were offended. Was he? "I smelled your food when I was walking up the trail," he added. "And if I can smell it—"

"Why can't you just leave?" she interrupted.

She sniffed the air, and yeah, maybe there was the tiniest whiff of pasta sauce. But if there really was a bear, would it really want pasta?

"There is a bear *nearby*, in this area. A big, *brown* bear," he said, emphasizing the word *brown* like it should mean something to her. "It will find its way to your camp just by following its nose. Just like I did. Now stop arguing and come outta that tent 'fore I go in there."

"I don't see a bear." She crossed her arms protectively across her chest. "But I will hit you again if you come in here."

The man shook his head, his lips tight. "And I'll take you out kicking and screaming if I think it'll save you from getting mauled."

Then she noticed the gun, holstered on the man's right hip. *A gun.* He was armed. She'd never seen anyone with a gun before, other than a cop, or in the movies. Was it on him at the gas station, and she just hadn't noticed it under his shirt?

"Okay, okay," she said softly, putting her hands up. "Just don't shoot me."

"What the...? I'm not gonna shoot you—what is wrong with you, lady? We don't have time for chitchat!"

Megan kept her hands in the air and nodded toward his sidearm.

The cowboy scoffed, as if she'd offended him. "These are the mountains. There's wildlife. This is...come on, this is *Idaho*."

This man was clearly a danger. Or was he? The hairs on the back of her neck should be standing up on end right now, the way they used to when Todd would get going on something. Every bit of logic she had told her to keep away from both a stranger *and* a hypothetical bear, but instinctually, she wanted to have that man stand next to her, somehow. Maybe even slightly in front of her, in case the bear got in their path.

"I get why you reacted that way to me," he said, tentatively touching his nose, wincing. "Why you punched me. No hard feelings—and you don't need to look at me like that. I ain't gonna hurt you. But we need to go. Now."

"Why should I believe that?" she asked. "Or believe that I'm camping practically in your backyard. You could even be making up the bear."

The words were barely out of her mouth when she heard...something. A growl. Not even quite a growl, but definitely a bear sound. Or a...monster. It didn't sound too close, or was it? *Stop.*

"Wh-what was that?" she whispered.

"Well," he said, not whispering. "That sure does sound like the bear I made up, don't it? Told you it was coming this way. Last I saw, it was down at the creek, and that ain't more than a mile east."

With his accent, he pronounced "creek" like "crick." She liked the sound of it. Just not the context.

Okay, this bear was probably no longer hypothetical.

"How close is the bear now?" she whispered. "I heard that growl."

"No need to be scared," he said, as if he sensed her fear might paralyze her. He was so large and strong, the role of protector seemed to come naturally to him. "Sounds carry pretty far in the woods, all right? You can hear a bird singing from miles away. It's closer than that, but it won't come near us, not right now."

He reached his hand out to her, to help her get out of the tent. The cowboy seemed impossibly tall, towering over her. Megan looked up at him, her eyes wide.

What am I going to do?

Another sound—this one louder. Rustling in the bushes, another growl of something big.

"That sounded close," she whispered.

"You're safe with me," he urged. "That bear won't wanna tangle with me. It can smell and hear us—it doesn't wanna die, either."

Go with the man she'd just hit? *Or risk meeting the bear?*

"Now," he ordered, his voice deep and powerful.

With the keys still in her hand, she pushed out of her tent, purposefully ignoring the stranger's big hand, proffered to her.

Immediately, he took hold of her hand anyway, as if afraid she'd run in the wrong direction. Panic tightened the breath in her throat until she looked up at his face and saw no menace there. There was a look of concern in his (*beautiful*) green eyes, and she let the strength of his grip comfort her for a moment, her breath normalizing. It was if he really wanted to help her, and didn't even care that she'd punched him in the face only a moment before.

His skin against hers tingled with awareness where their palms met.

"Come with me," he said.

She was used to being ordered around, yet it still bred resentment. It felt a bit different with You-Betcha-Man, perhaps because he truly had her best interests at heart, instead of just wanting to dominate her. Maybe.

No. She was useless at determining whether a man was good or not. Hadn't she proven that to herself again and again? It didn't matter if there was something about his commanding tone she respected (or even liked).

Megan pulled her hand out from his. Somehow she had gone from being alone and independent for the first time in her life, to having a man ordering her around again, in short order.

She hadn't even made it on her own a full twenty-four hours.

"Hey," the man said, and gestured with his head for her to keep up. "If the bear hears us, he'll stay away. Bears don't wanna mess with people. But they *do* want food. I bet your campsite smells pretty good to the animals right now."

She glanced back through the trees at the mess, scanning the bushes to find the source of the growling. The trash bag she'd thought would keep her campsite clean had been torn to bits, and food wrappers, her leftovers, and empty cans of pasta and meat were strewn everywhere.

"Fine," she said. "I don't want to meet a bear either."

They moved briskly, walking through the zigzagging trail, passing trees, wildflowers, and beautiful scenery that—in another situation—she'd have stopped to admire. Everything here was Instagram-worthy. Not like that mattered anymore. She'd had to delete all of her social media accounts to keep her ex from contacting her.

At a sharp turn in the trail, the cowboy put his heavy hand on her shoulder. She startled under his touch.

"Please don't," she whispered, even though his hand on her felt...comforting, almost. He was kind, but still a stranger and she didn't know what he was up to.

"I told you I'm not gonna hurt you," he said, but he kept his large, warm hand firmly on her shoulder. "Don't want you to break an ankle, is all."

"Okay."

Was it okay, though? Megan tried to compare the nervous butterfly feeling she had right now, the feeling that made her tremble when this stranger touched her or spoke to her, to the sick feeling of dread she'd get when Todd did the same.

It was different. This man was not her ex, or at least, he wasn't tripping the same alarms. Even if he was telling her what to do and sort of…manhandling her.

"Okay," she repeated softly.

It seemed as if he could walk this trail blind, as if he'd followed it so many times he knew it by feel alone.

"Where are we going?" she asked, needing two steps to keep up with just one of his long strides. His hand on her body forced her to move faster, to stay with him. "Where can we go that's safe from a bear?"

"Well, we're putting distance between us, and we're also headed toward my pickup truck. We get to the truck, and drive, and then we're fine." He gestured for her to keep up. "The bear will almost for sure go into your campsite, so we need to let her do that, and then go back tomorrow for your stuff after she's moved on."

"Oh! I left everything in there. I need my phone," Megan said. "And my purse. My ID! I have to go back and get them." The rest of her cash was in that purse too.

"Not happening."

The cowboy kept walking, and his hand on her shoulder had gone from comforting to constraining in that moment. Her muscles tensed.

"I won't start my new life in Idaho as a charity case," she said, her voice as firm as his had been. "If there's any chance I might lose the only possessions I took with me, then I have to go back."

Would she even be able to access her mother's inheritance without proof of identity in a new town? Megan looked back at the path behind them, toward the campsite.

"Not on my watch," he said.

He dropped his hand from her shoulder to the back of her upper arm, as if quietly preparing to hold her against her will if she made a break for it. There was no pressure in the touch, but Megan knew from his superior size and muscle mass that he could grip her and pull her away from danger in an instant if he felt he needed to.

Yet the flutters in her stomach weren't from fear. Something about this man excited her senses, made her ultra-aware of his every movement, every point of contact between his body and her own.

"I told you I'd keep you safe," he said, his voice hushed and gravelly. "You need the help."

"I need my purse. And I'm going back." She shoved his hand off of her, and he let it fall.

From the strength of him, she knew he wouldn't have let go if he hadn't agreed to. Megan gripped her keys in her fist. If he tried to stop her, would she fight him, again? Even knowing he would undoubtedly win?

With a quick movement, he grabbed the keys from her fist. "I warned ya."

"Hey!" she gasped. "Wait—please don't throw them into the woods. I need my car keys."

He paused. "Fair 'nough."

Megan grumbled under her breath in response. He kept on walking—this time without his hand on her for guidance—jingling her keys. She followed him, even though the thought of being stranded without any money, identification, or communication was almost as scary as the threat of a bear. More so, since she hadn't ever really thought about what it meant to have a bear hanging out nearby.

"Ma'am, I can tell you're new here, and you don't get it. That's a brown bear that's making its way toward the campsite you want to go to. They're bigger and meaner than black bears, all right? I saw it with my own two eyes."

"But I haven't," she said. Now that they were away from the camp, uncertainty blurred the edges of the situation. What if those growling sounds were a product of fear and her imagination, and not a bear at all? "You are a stranger—and you could be...*tricking* me to go with you, for all I know."

"This is Bear Creek Saddle," he drawled. *Baayer Crick Saddle*, sounded like. "It wasn't named that for no good reason."

Touché.

"A person'd have to be from Mars to not know this is bear country," he continued. "And I hate to break it to ya, but *I'm* not the stranger here. You are." He grinned at her. "Maybe I should be scared of you. You do pack a mean punch."

"Ha ha," she deadpanned.

"Just saying, now's probably not the best time to be acting all cynical," he advised.

"Where I'm from—"

"Mars?" he suggested.

"New York," she said, ignoring his jab. "And in New York, that's not being cynical, it's called being safe."

Without another word, Megan turned on her heel and ran as fast as she could along the twisty trail, trying her best to make sure she didn't go off the trail at the wrong spot.

This wasn't a suicide mission, right? The rustling they'd heard hadn't actually been in the campsite, it was farther out in the woods.

Same with the growl. Sounds carried a long way in the woods, isn't that what the cowboy had told her? So she had time to get her stuff.

She had no choice but to get her phone, ID, and money. Other than a duffel bag of clothing, her backpack and her purse, she'd left most of her belongings in New York. This was important—without her own things, her own money, how could she be independent at all?

Did she want him to follow her back to the campsite? Yes. Wait—no. That would be scary. If he chased her...

There was no way she'd be able to outrun him. With his long, athletic strides, he'd catch up to her no matter what. And then what would happen, once he had her?

Megan gave her head a little shake. Back to reality. He wasn't chasing her. If he had been, she'd already be caught. Strangely, the thought didn't frighten her. He seemed like the sort of guy she could count on, even if she didn't even know his name.

Stop. All this unwarranted attraction was just the product of high stress, endorphins and hormones flying everywhere. Was it unwarranted, though? Goodness, the man dripped testosterone with every move he made, every word from his lips. She couldn't blame herself for being attracted to a cowboy on a mission.

As long as that mission didn't interfere with hers.

She veered off the trail to get to the clearing, approaching cautiously.

The campsite was still a mess, but there was no bear. Was it in the shadows, waiting to pounce? *No, thank God.* Even if the bear were only a short distance away, at least it wasn't there.

She ran past the trash and ducked into the tent. Megan put on the backpack she'd been using as an overnight bag, and grabbed her little purse and cell phone.

Did she have time to take down the tent? *No. No way.* It had taken her almost half an hour to put it up for the first time, and she'd never broken down a tent before. But where would she stay without it?

Branches broke somewhere out there. A loud cracking noise. She jumped, and a nearby bird took flight. Better to get in her car. She hefted her backpack and stepped out of the tent, leaving the campsite as quickly as possible.

Please don't let me run into the bear. Keep the bear far, far away.

The cowboy met her at the trail, his eyes flashing, his posture… intimidating. As if the big bad cowboy couldn't believe she'd put herself (and him) in danger for something as superficial as a cell phone and a purse.

At least now she could be one-hundred-percent sure he hadn't been trying to trick her all along. That meant his intentions might even be as good as he said they were. As good as she'd hoped they were.

"Next time you run off, I ain't following to save you, pretty girl or not," he said, shaking his head. "We're heading the wrong way. You don't want to head *toward* a bear. Someone told me that once."

Did he just say she was a pretty girl?

"I didn't make you follow," she said. "I told you what *I* was going to do. You can do whatever you want."

She pushed past him, her hand connecting with rock-hard muscle. He didn't budge—it was like pushing against a mountain. Still, she ran ahead, glancing back to see where he was.

Megan gasped as the man took one big stride, falling briskly in line with her.

"Hey—you don't need to be scared of me." His voice softened. "I'm on your side, okay?"

"Why? You don't even know me. And I punched you in the nose."

"This is my neck of the woods, and you're in it," he said, ticking the points off on his calloused fingers. "I can't blame you for defending yourself. That, and you don't have a clue what you're doing out here."

The way he said it, as if it were simple fact, and nothing against her personally, took the sting out of the words. Some strands of brown hair fell against his forehead, and some peeked out from under his hat in the back.

"I do so know what I'm doing," she said. "Sort of."

For now, though, she'd walk with him. She'd rather have this big cowboy with a gun next to her if that bear found its way to their path, than try to make a go of it on her own.

"You really did a number on me," he said. He didn't sound angry though, for some reason.

"Good. I just wish the pepper spray had worked. My hand still hurts from punching you."

"Yeah," he muttered, and handed the keychain back to her. "You coulda punched me with the keys." He nodded, as if thinking it through. "Yup. Next time, if a man enters your tent, you poke him in the eyes with the keys straight away. Don't just threaten or he'll take 'em from you, like I did before."

Megan raised her eyebrows at him.

"You didn't know I was one a' the good guys," he explained. "You're lucky. I could've been—"

"Todd…" she whispered, her voice cracking a bit.

"I was gonna say 'someone with bad intentions,'" he finished.

"Is your nose okay?" She reached up to his face, suddenly feeling the urge to fix what she'd done to the man who may have saved her from getting mauled. "It doesn't look too bad. I'm glad I didn't blind you. That would have been awful."

"But if I was going to hurt you instead of try to help you, you'd have my full permission—not that you need it—to defend yourself. Welcome to Idaho."

Ha. Welcome to Idaho. Yeah. She hid her smile by lowering her head.

Finally, they arrived at her car. *Hallelujah.* It felt like seeing home after being away. She slid into the driver's seat with a sigh of relief (*safe!*) and looked up at him through the window.

But he was already opening the passenger door. "I need to hitch a ride. My pickup's just down a ways."

He had to fold his long, muscular body practically in half to fit into her old two-door Mitsubishi Eclipse.

"Just a ride, okay?" she asked. The last thing she wanted to do was lead him on, make him think she kind of liked him (even if it was true). Megan couldn't handle being hurt by a man again…and she knew nothing about this man who had broken into her tent and was now attached to her hip. "Nothing else."

"Ma'am," he said, staring straight down into her eyes. "We need to set something straight, you an' I."

Megan swallowed hard, and started the engine, anything to not look at him.

"We started on the wrong foot," he said, "'cause ya thought I'd followed you. That I was breaking into your tent to hurt you. I'm a 'scary mountain-man-rapist cowboy,' right?"

"I'm sorry," she apologized, not knowing why she needed to, just that maybe it would stop the conversation.

"Don't need to be sorry. But I'm pretty sure I heard you scream that right before you punched me in the face." He frowned, as if her words had hurt him more than the punch. "That's not me. That's just what you're afraid I am. But you're wrong."

The words "I'm sorry" almost escaped her lips again, but instead she put the car in drive and gave it some gas.

The car wouldn't drive.

"You've got to be kidding me," she groaned.

"All right," the cowboy said, as if he wasn't surprised a bit. "If her engine starts but she won't drive…" he paused, and furrowed his brow in concentration. "Could be your transmission, or the CV joint. I can check 'er out and see what's wrong," he offered, "if you want. For now, we're safe in the car, anyways."

"That's good," she said. "Being safe is good."

She tapped her fingers on the steering wheel, trying not to stare at the handsome cowboy in her passenger seat, and revved the engine again.

"Don't flood the engine," he said.

"Don't tell me what to do," she shot back, with more force than she intended.

"Your car, your rules." He took his big tan hat off and set it in his lap.

His brown hair was deliciously tousled. He looked like he would've been a blond child. Even the stubble on his jaw had some blond hairs scattered through the brown ones…

Focus. She turned the key in the ignition again and tried to drive. Nada.

She paused to let her agitation seep out of her voice before she spoke. "You said you have your pickup truck somewhere?"

"Sure do. We'll have to hoof it." He set his hat back on his head, as if ready to jump out of the car that second.

"Wait! What about the bear?"

"We're practically on the main road," he said. "I don't think the bear's coming down this way. I think she was just waiting for us to leave your campsite so she could roam around there. She'd rather snack than mess with us. We should be fine to walk."

Megan breathed a sigh of relief, and they got out of her car. She touched the hood forlornly. What a pity, to leave her baby alone in the woods.

"Do you need a moment?" he asked, and grinned. His straight white teeth gleamed in the sunlight.

Wow... so shiny.

She gazed at his smile, momentarily awestruck, before reality set back in. "Hey... can I get a ride with you, please?"

"My truck, my rules," he said. "Got it?"

"Fine," she muttered.

"I wouldn't just leave you alone out here, anyway," he said, putting his hat back on. "What kinda man do you think I am?"

"I don't know. I don't even know your name," she said. "Can we...start over? Pretend we just met again now, after the gas station?"

"Yes, ma'am," he said. "I appreciate that."

She stuck her hand out. "I'm Megan Moore; nice to meet you."

He tipped his hat and shook her hand. "Name's Zach Walker."

"Looks like someone bopped you one in the nose, huh?" she teased, giddy with the idea of starting over. "Bar fight?"

"Nah, just me being stupid. I'm lucky I didn't get myself shot. Frankly, I'm lucky to be alive."

Megan laughed. "Welcome to Idaho. Where not getting killed makes you a lucky guy."

They arrived at his pickup truck. It was a bit beat up and it had mud on the tires, but it was a ride.

Zach reached his arm out like he was going to grasp her shoulder, and she took a step back, stumbling a bit over a stone. But no—he was just reaching for the passenger door.

Huh. He was opening the door for her. How...chivalrous. When was the last time a man had done that for her?

A small, quiet voice inside her whispered: *he's a good guy—it's okay.*

She tamped down the thought. *Don't get comfortable.* She didn't need a man to open the door. That was the whole point of coming out here alone—to do things on her own, including opening doors. She could probably handle that at least.

She paused before stepping up into the truck. If her sister could see her now, Lindsay would be yelling at her for getting into a stranger's truck.

"I think I know the answer to this," she sighed, "but for my sister's sake, I have to ask, just to be sure: this isn't all an elaborate plan so you can murder me, right, Zach Walker?"

"Never killed a person before, don't plan on starting now." He paused. "You don't have to believe me, New-York-Girl...Megan. Keep your fistful of keys handy. Maybe you'll let me teach you how to shoot one of these days, if you stick around."

Okay. That was promising.

Lord, I'm trusting You...please keep me safe.

She got in the truck.

Chapter Two

MEGAN REACHED UP for her seatbelt, and glanced over at Zach in the driver seat. Now that she knew he hadn't been stalking her after they met at the gas station, she could relax a bit. But *only* a bit. He was still a man, and worse, a man she was attracted to. All that could lead to was trouble.

"Guess it's a good thing you came along when you did," she admitted. "I'd be trying to walk out of the mountain on foot right about now, otherwise."

"No problem," he said. He smiled at her in a way that made it clear there were no hard feelings. Maybe he didn't even think she was crazy. "So... can I drop ya somewhere?"

Where? There really wasn't anywhere to go... This was it. This was where she wanted to be.

"Now that I'm here at Bear Creek Saddle," she said, "I'd planned on... staying."

"There's a motel down 95, little bit south of here," Zach suggested. "It'll take us less than an hour to get to. I could take you there."

A motel outside of town involved going the wrong way—both geographically and psychologically.

"I drove north forever on 95 to get here," she said. "I kept going because I wanted to finally *get here*. And now I'm here."

Plus, she'd spent most of her traveling money already on motels and gasoline. If she went backward, and stayed at another motel south of town, that wasn't good. She *couldn't* go backward. She needed a Plan B.

"Don't kill me," she said, "but what if we went back to the campsite, and got my tent and all my stuff?"

Zach laughed. "I'm not gonna kill you. The bear didn't make any promises, though."

Right.

"And we can definitely get your stuff," he added. "We should just wait until that bear's moved on to other food sources. Tomorrow, hopefully." He must've caught her sorrowful expression. "Aw, chin up, it's not so bad—what's one more day out of a lifetime of days?"

Yeah. Except she really did not want to go to a motel, and she definitely didn't want to leave Bear Creek Saddle.

"I don't really know where to go, then," she said softly, almost to herself.

Zach started the engine, and the truck started right up. He pulled out onto the dirt road and drove slowly, hands at ten and two, staring straight ahead, even as he spoke to her.

"My buddies and I have a cattle ranch not far from here. We grow grass, and the grass grows the cows." Zach paused. "Do New Yorkers like cows?"

Megan smiled. "This New Yorker does. At least, I imagine I do."

"The ranch, then," he said. "Unless you have another idea."

"What are we going to do at the ranch?"

Zach caught her eye for a moment and shrugged. "My cabin is there."

No alarm bells rang. *Should they?* Logically, it wasn't smart to go to a stranger's cabin. But every cynical fiber of her being—usually on such high alert in New York—either implicitly trusted Zach, or had gone to sleep on the job. Had she left her street-smarts behind when she'd crossed into Idaho? Or was she letting how handsome and sweet he was cloud her perception?

He cleared his throat, as if the potential impropriety of his suggestion had just now occurred to him while she'd hesitated. "I mean, it's just a place to wait out the bear. If you want. I could take you to the church inst—"

"I guess I could come by for a bit, just to have a place to figure out my next step," she said, her cheeks burning. "Thank you for the offer."

"Home it is," he said. "Folks probably already know you're here—an outta-towner is news. You know how word spreads in a small-town…"

"Actually I don't," she said. "There's so many people in Manhattan, everyone becomes anonymous. Invisible. I think only a few people have even noticed I've left." She shrugged.

"It ain't like that here. If you meet one person in town, every word you discussed will be everyone's news soon enough."

"Oh? Does that mean you've already disclosed our own chance encounter at the gas station?"

"Well, there *were* some other folks who drove past. They asked me." He grinned. "We're always interested when someone new shows up." Zach glanced over at her. "And trust me—a pretty girl like you? Can't help but notice."

He thinks I'm pretty. The lazily snuck-in compliment shouldn't have made her so happy, but it did.

Ugh. Stop. Who cared what a man thought about how she looked?

I'm here for me. Not him or anyone.

"It might be hard for me to fit in," she admitted. "But I kind of hope to find myself here, in Idaho. I don't want to be an anonymous girl in the city anymore. I want to live a life that...means something."

"You're preaching to the choir," Zach said.

He pulled up in front of a long dirt driveway. Huge logs made an archway of sorts over the entrance to the drive. The beautiful wooden sign that hung off the top log said, simply: BEAR CREEK SADDLE RANCH.

"Wow," she said. "I imagine a lot of ranchers around here would want to call their ranch Bear Creek Saddle."

"Nah," he said. "Most people name their ranches after the family name, or after what they brand the cattle with, or something that's meaningful to them. It actually used to be called Melody Ranch, till Melody passed on and Bill sold the ranch to us." He jumped out of the truck and ran around to her side to open the door.

"Are your friends here too?" What was she about to walk into?

"Well, they're somewhere on the ranch, least I hope so. They know we need all hands on deck right now. It's me, Eric, Jay, and

Chris. It was too hard to decide how to rename it, so we just went with the simplest thing."

He flashed her a grin and took her hand so she could jump out onto the grass. She grasped his palm too eagerly to be cool, then stepped out of the big truck with as much grace as she could manage—and somehow ended up standing mere inches from him, completely inside his bubble of personal space. Zach didn't seem to mind. Did he feel the electricity between them, too?

Ignore the electricity. Pretend it's not there. Megan took a step back for etiquette's sake and bumped up against the truck.

Zach put his hat back on and looked down at her. The height difference was even more pronounced compared to being seated in the truck. "Personally, I thought Walker Ranch had a real nice ring to it."

Couldn't argue with that.

"Come on," he said, gesturing to the cabin with his head.

Zach put his arm out for her like a gentleman. Who knew those still existed? So this was what a man acting chivalrous looked like up close... A hundred times better than what she'd become accustomed to: apathetic guys who would sooner take a video of a woman tripping than offer her a hand.

He led her to his cabin. At any other time, in any other place— and specifically, with any other man—there was no way Megan would have risked going inside a stranger's cabin, surrounded by miles and miles of nothing but land and cows. And other ranchers, allegedly. A dog barked inside, and Megan tensed.

"Guard dog?" she asked.

"That's just Inky, you met her at the gas station. Don't worry 'bout it."

They entered the cabin, and the big black Labrador retriever bounded up to the front door, barking.

"Inky, sit," Zach ordered. "That's enough."

The dog immediately sat, its shaggy black tail wagging like crazy. Okay, that was good. She wasn't trying to jump on Megan or eat her face or anything, so that was nice.

Zach looked at her. "Are you scared of dogs? Stinky-Inky's nothing to be afraid of," he said. "She's not even really that stinky." He ran his hand across the dog's back, head to tail. "That's just what Paige calls her."

Megan held her hand out slowly as the name *Paige* crashed through her skull, competing for top mental priority with Inky. The dog's whole body wiggled with excitement.

"Paige is your wife?" she asked. "Or, um…girlfriend?"

Zach shook his head no, and crouched down to be closer to Inky.

She shouldn't be so relieved at that, but she was. Not that it mattered if he was single or not—he was so off-limits to Megan that she was walking a thin line by even thinking about him in a less-than-platonic way. Besides, maybe he was being smart and staying away from romantic relationships altogether, like her.

Good. That made things easier.

"Give me your hand," he said, his voice low, soft.

She bent down to their level without hesitation, simply because he seemed so…confident. So in control of himself, like he had it all together, and if maybe she hung out with him, she'd be able to get her life together, too.

He took her hand in his gently, and held it in front of his dog's nose, so Inky could sniff.

"There ya go," Zach said. "That's right…"

He said it in a soothing way, and Megan wasn't sure if he was talking to Inky, or to her. But it did make her feel calmed.

There ya go…

The dog apparently approved of her scent, because Megan was rewarded with a sloppy lick. She laughed and wiped her hand on her jeans. Maybe Inky wasn't so scary, after all. Megan wasn't accustomed to dogs. She'd never grown up with pets, and the one dog she knew personally growing up was the forever-barking Chihuahua across the hall.

"Hey, wait a minute," Zach said, dropping to his knee. He lifted the dog's back left paw and inspected the pad closely. "Lookin' good. You'll be hiking with me again soon, girl."

She liked the way he was so careful with Inky. He clearly loved that doggy. Now that she could experience their interactions, it was easy to see the charm she'd missed seeing in dogs before. "Is she okay?"

"Oh, yeah. Just a little scratch. Ain't bothering her now, seems like." Zach grinned, and hopped up. "Now that you and Inky are acquainted, lemme just get washed up and I'll give you the fifty-cent tour."

He splashed water on his face at the kitchen sink, rinsing away the last remnants of blood from when she'd punched his nose. With a bit of soap, he appeared to be trying to prewash the blood-drop stains off of his T-shirt.

"That'll do," Zach said, toweling off with a dishrag.

"I'm so sorry," she said. "I'll buy you a new T-shirt."

"Don't worry 'bout it," he said. Totally nonchalant, while she felt like the biggest idiot ever. "Make yourself at home."

Megan took her purse off her shoulder, avoiding staring at him as if she had blinders on, and looked around for a place to set it down. Stranger or not, it wasn't as if she had to worry about him stealing it, considering he hadn't even cared if she brought the purse with her in the first place.

The cabin had basically no available flat space for her to put her purse. Every counter, the table, even the chairs (except for one), had things piled on it. There might be a place for her bag on top of those papers on the chair, or by the stack of books on the desk, or…no. The purse stayed on her shoulder.

It was a beautiful little home, if simplistic and rustic. The dining room table was made of wood, perhaps from the same logs that were timbered from the land. Same with the counters—all polished wood. And the floors. It was like living inside of a tree—well, a tree inhabited by a squirrel stockpiling his acorns.

"You sure have a lot of stuff," she murmured, and immediately winced. *Rude.*

She hadn't meant to say that out loud. And it wasn't like she could start rearranging his things the moment she'd entered his house—who does that?

Zach looked around, as if seeing the mess for the first time through new eyes. "I wasn't expecting company today." He shrugged. "I just need to get a trash bag an' throw out all this junk."

Megan smiled brightly, as if she had no idea what he meant. Surely it wasn't because she'd accidentally given his house the neat-freak-once-over glance, right?

"You don't need to apologize," she said (not that he had, exactly). "It's not that bad."

"We gotta make space for you to sit down at least," he admitted, and laughed.

Okay, so maybe he was a messy person, but not a hoarder. Hoarders would have a harder time throwing out their stuff, if reality television had any reality left in it.

At least there was space on the floors. It was just the flat surfaces, like the counters, table, and coffee table that had junk all over them. Used coffee mugs. Books. Ammo... Some hay? A broken something or other... A perfectly good upside-down wooden stool. Even a bottle of organic spray cleaner, although she doubted he used it too often.

Zach caught her staring at his stuff and laughed. "Gimme a break."

Ack! "No, really, it's noth—"

"Well, it *is* haying season," he admitted, as if she knew what that meant. "But I want to make sure you're taken care of first."

He moved in close. Too close...?

His arm brushed past hers, as if to pull her toward him, but instead, he grabbed a phone from the pile of junk on the countertop nook in the kitchen. It served as another flat space, and possibly, his desk.

When his body was so close, she could smell him... the scent of grass, and forest, and... man. He smelled good.

"You don't wear cologne," she noted.

"Mosquitoes," he said. "And I definitely can't go leaving my scent all over my hunting trails. It would basically be like hanging up a sign saying, 'human was here and intends to eat you.'"

She nodded, taking it all in. Maybe—hopefully—he didn't realize that she didn't know...well, any of the stuff that seemed like common sense to him. It just wasn't common enough in New York to be "common sense." Everyone here in Idaho was bound to discover what a complete newbie she was—and how completely in over her head she was. She had no idea what she was doing.

Maybe if she stuck near Zach, she could learn through osmosis.

Zach raised an eyebrow. "Why, do I stink?" He smiled that easy smile of his. "I might."

Megan leaned in slightly closer to him, heat radiating off of his neck, and took a long breath of mountain air and woods. "You don't," she said. "I like how you smell."

The silence bloomed around them, tightening her world to just him and her, his scent and her senses. This was all his fault that she felt this way—the testosterone and pheromones rolling off the man were so thick she could've sworn she could taste it in the air between them.

He laughed, breaking the moment. "Feel free to use my phone," he said, as if everything was normal. Guess it was. "And you should call your family, tell 'em that you're here an' that you're all right."

"Yeah," she said. "My cell is dead. Thank you."

He walked her through the cabin, which didn't take long. His jeans hung low on his hips. He grabbed a T-shirt from a chair and sniffed it before setting it back down.

"This is the kitchen, there's the sink—we've got fresh water from the mountain. No fluoride or anything like that."

"Don't you *want* fluoride in your water?"

Zach looked at her like she was crazy and shook his head. Huh. She'd need to Google that…if she could get internet service up here. There were too many questions to ask him. He was going to think she was a moron soon.

And this kind cowboy, a man who was so strong and capable,

was the last person she wanted looking down on her. She'd had enough of that from Todd. But how could she make Zach think she knew anything about living off the land?

Seriously, he already saw her attempt at camping. There was no hope.

"Well, so over here is the dining area I guess," he said, moving quickly through the small space, as if he was either in a rush, or thought he was boring her. "Here's the living room—you can charge your phone on the floor down there—there's the fireplace. Don't make a fire without my help, though." He glanced at her. "I'm aging my wood for winter."

"Why would I need to make a fire?" It was summer, and warm out.

"You don't," he said. "I got a proper stove if you need to cook."

That way he looked at her…as if he were studying everything about her…it was unnerving.

"It's hot enough in here already," he added. "I've been meaning to install some ceiling fans."

Megan laughed to cover her nervousness. "You don't have to," she offered graciously.

"There's the bathroom," he said. "And over here is my room."

The grand finale. The master bedroom. Maybe now she'd find out if her instincts that he was safe were correct or not.

Feigning disinterest, she kept her feet planted in the hall, but glanced over his broad shoulder through the open door to his bedroom. A king-size mattress with a wooden bed frame dominated the small room. The bed wasn't made, of course. Dirty socks littered the floor.

"Sorry 'bout the mess," Zach said, as if he'd noticed her expression. "I just haven't had time lately to clean up, haying season and all." He shook his head and grabbed a clean shirt from one of the dressers. "Nah, that ain't true. Sometimes I got plenty of time."

Megan raised her eyebrow, but smiled to soften her response. "Oh yeah?"

"I like to put my feet up on the couch," Zach said, lowering his voice as if he were telling her a secret, "with Inky all cuddled up next to me, and read a book. Or I go sit by the creek, an' take it all in. There're a lot of things I'd rather be doing than laundry and cleaning house." He grinned. "And *that's* the truth."

"Of course," she said. She could see Zach as the type of guy who would blow off cleaning so he could go for a hike with his friends.

"Hang on a minute," he said, and shut the door closed right in front of her.

Okay.

A moment later he emerged with a clean shirt on, and pointed to the other room off the hall.

"And that's the guest room. I use it as a home office," he said, "but that's a pullout couch in there." He pointed to a plain, navy blue, canvas sofa against the wall. "I can help you pull the bed out, if you want to hang out in there and get some shut-eye or something, till we can get your car and tent back."

"Shut-eye?" Why would she want to lie down, now, in a stranger's home? "Umm…"

"You know, like what ya were doing when I found you, not passed out at all?"

Megan blushed. Right.

"I just don't think I should do that…it wouldn't be appropriate. I really appreciate you finding me and all… and the whole bear thing." She stopped, flustered. "My sister will kill me when she finds out I followed a strange man with a gun from the woods, back to his log cabin in the middle of nowhere."

"I ain't *that* strange, am I?" Zach grinned, and she couldn't help smiling back at his teasing.

Still—when she said the reasons she shouldn't be there out loud like that, it sounded awful. But Zach felt good, so…comfortable, somehow. What would Todd say if he knew she was alone with a man she'd just met?

He'd call her an idiot, possibly a whore, and say she deserved whatever she got.

"I'm so stupid," she muttered. Forget it. She needed to *stop* letting her ex into her head. "This is not a safe situation I put myself into."

He took a step backward, giving her a wide berth, as if she were a frightened animal he didn't want to spook. "Well it ain't like I kidnapped you—you're free to go, same as before. Call a cab if you don't want to ride with me. I won't be offended." Zach smiled a bit. "Well, not much, anyway."

It was weird. She *felt* safe. Her gut told her she was safe with Zach. She had none of those instinctual bad feelings she got around creepy dudes or bad situations.

But logic was a different matter. Her brain was telling her what her stomach wouldn't. It was not safe to be in a house alone with a guy in the middle of nowhere, even if he did seem to be a normal, friendly guy with a genuine "Good Samaritan" vibe.

"I'm going to get out of your hair and pick up the mail," he said.

"And I'll take Inky with me, so she doesn't bug you. Feel free to stay and call people, get a bite to eat from the fridge, whatever you want. Make yourself at home. My house is your house."

"But you're just going to get the mail," she said.

"Yeah," he laughed. "That involves driving a ways up to the road. I could walk, but I just did a whole bunch of that."

"I really don't mean to keep you from your day," she insisted. "Maybe I could just wait a while here, and go back and see if my tent's okay later? To see if the bear's gone."

"Absolutely." He pulled the latest model iPhone out of his pocket.

Huh. She hadn't been expecting that. Not with the beat-up old truck, worn jeans, and the decidedly non-tech demeanor.

"Yeah," he said, apparently noticing her surprise. "It's a good way to stay connected. The guys here all got them so we could FaceTime each other, when we needed to. Sometimes you go all day without running into each other, even though we're all working the same ranch."

He rubbed his arm distractedly, and Megan couldn't help but notice his muscle definition again. Funny how there wasn't any gym equipment in his place. How did he get so fit? Her ex (goodness, it felt good thinking of him as her *ex*) had a treadmill, a rowing machine, and free weights, and he *still* couldn't hold a candle to Zach's naturally-fit physique.

Not that she should even be noticing something like that.

"This thing's also good," he said, interrupting her thoughts, "if I need to look something up, or show someone what's going on, like Big Bad Bill."

Big Bad Bill? She cocked her head to demonstrate her confusion without interrupting him.

"He used to own this place," Zach explained, "back when it was Melody Ranch. He ain't so bad—never mind his name."

"Gotcha." She grinned.

"Bill knows everything, including the fact that he knows everything." Zach smirked, a little dimple indenting his right cheek. "We've actually had the vet give us treatment recommendations, just based on one of the guys showing her a live video of the cow."

"Wow," she said. "I guess even cowboys use technology."

"Of course." He laughed. "Wait'll you see some of the machines we've got—although, to be honest, most of ranching is done the same way it was done a hundred years ago. We're just quicker at it now. Takes less people to run things smoothly."

Why hadn't she done more reading up on all this before she'd run away? Had she really thought that loving a picture of the place, and *wanting* to live off the land would somehow…make that happen? She'd be done for if she didn't learn at least some of the knowledge Zach took for granted as common sense.

She gave him her number, and he texted her. Her phone was dead, but after it charged she'd have Zach Walker's cell phone number in it.

"So… when will you be back? I only ask," she said, "because I…" She couldn't think of a good reason. "Because I want to know," she finished lamely.

That seemed to be good enough for Zach. "I have to go get the mail, and I was going to check with a friend of mine to see if he has my new holster. Custom-made. He wants me to look at it 'fore he finishes it up."

"That's cool," she said. *He* sounded excited about the holster, at least. Then again, custom, handmade stuff was unique in an age of mass-production. "So, I guess I'll just... be here? At your house."

"Call me if there's any problems." Then he texted her another phone number. "That's my friend Eric's number," he said. "He's the closest cabin to here. If you can't reach me and there's an emergency, text him and tell 'im you're my friend and you're at my place."

His friend? Her first friend in Bear Creek Saddle was a super cool cowboy who lived on a real ranch. Now she just had to keep him as a friend, and not go ruining it for both of them by giving in to the temptation of having a man's romantic attention. Assuming he would be interested in the first place.

"Thank you," she said, smiling. "I appreciate that more than you know."

"You'll still be here when I get back, right? You gonna be okay by yourself?"

For the first time since she'd left New York, Megan felt confident saying, "Yes. I'll be just fine on my own."

Chapter Three

ZACH GRABBED HIS keys and glanced one more time at Megan before leaving his little log cabin, closing the door behind him. He couldn't seem to get enough of looking at her, drinking her in like lemonade on a hot day. Something about her tugged at him, pulled him in to her. But he wasn't the type to be a pup on a leash, so if he was gonna get tugged, he better start tugging back. But how, without scaring the girl off for good?

Nah, bad news. No sense in even flirting with a woman he couldn't settle with. It was time to find a real relationship, find a wife who knew her way around a ranch. Who knew, at the very least, her way around a campsite. Forget it—that girl was trouble in a pretty New York City package.

Next time his romantic tendencies did some heart-tugging, he'd have to stop himself. No city girls allowed, that was for sure. Even the cute ones.

Today had not gone the way he'd expected it at all. This was his first (and hopefully last) time getting mistaken for a bad guy. He touched the tender skin on his nose and shook his head. After she'd punched him he'd been about ready to call it quits and leave her to her own devices. And she was so ornery, too. Not exactly what he'd had in mind when he imagined himself playing knight in shining armor. A prickly princess.

Couldn't fault the girl for punching him, though. In fact, that was downright respectable. Smart thinking, for a girl alone in the woods to attack a stranger entering her tent.

Probably should've thought of that before barging in on her—most folks out in the woods packed heat. But Zach just wasn't used to being a *stranger*.

In a small town, people got to know each other better than some people knew their extended family. Frankly, a lot of them *were* extended family. And everyone knew that Zach would never hurt a woman. Obviously Megan, being new to town and all, couldn't have known that. It had been quite a surprise for him, though, to be greeted by a furious woman instead of a passed-out drunk (one who might've, theoretically, been grateful he was trying to save her).

What was with all those juice boxes?

It was almost as if Megan had been acting like a kid on a first adventure—camping out in a strange place all by herself, even though she had no idea what on earth she was doing. Seriously, how did she not realize that mountains and woods had actual wildlife in them? This wasn't a theme park with fake birds in landscaped trees. At the very least, she could've made sure her campsite wasn't covered in enough food and garbage to throw a brown-bear birthday party.

Guess bears weren't a real danger in New York City. It just

wasn't on her radar. Must be nice...*never mind.* He'd take bears over crowds any day.

Zach whistled for Inky to jump in the truck, watching her back left paw for limping. Nah, Inky was good. Dogs knew how to shake things off. If only he could be as good at shaking things off as dogs were...

Inky jumped right up onto the passenger seat as usual, and put her nose to the window, waiting for Zach to roll it down.

"Come on girl," he said, and gave her a quick scratch behind the ears. "Let's go get the mail."

They drove back down the long driveway, all the way out to the road that connected the various hard-packed dirt driveways running through that part of the ranch.

Their private road took them up to the main road, where Inky liked to stick her head out the window, and bark at the cows grazing on the far corner.

"Was that stupid of me, leaving her at the house all by her lonesome?" He glanced at Inky as if she could answer.

She responded by lifting her snout all the way up, looking at him upside down. Her long pink tongue fell out the side of her mouth and lolled happily.

"Yeah," he said, "guess you're right. She's probably safe. Even if she is a New Yorker."

Zach drove to the local post office and gathered the mail for all the guys, as well as the company mail. Sometimes they got catalogs filled with pictures of bulls for sale (those always went straight to Chris). Personally, Zach preferred the local newspaper he picked up at the post office. It was the kind of paper where you could see who got arrested for doing what, who had a sale at their shop, and who was selling their old tractor.

Despite the ribbing the guys gave Eric, his buddy was very proud of the time he won the annual Independence Day hot-dog-eating contest at the park and the newspaper put a big picture of him—still wearing a napkin tucked into his collar—on the front page of the *Bear Creek Saddle News*. Goes to show there wasn't a lot going on 'round here, considering what was considered front-page-newsworthy.

Zach took the paper and the mail out to the parking lot so he didn't have to leave Inky alone too long. He leaned against the side of the truck and took a peek at the headlines. Inky stuck her head out the window and licked his ear.

Megan might think their local paper was the most podunk thing ever. She probably read the *New York Times*. Or maybe not… After all, she'd left New York for a reason. She wouldn't have left if she thought it was the end-all be-all. But why come to the boondocks, of all places? You'd think a city girl would go to another city. Why didn't she move to… Los Angeles or something?

She was certainly pretty enough to make a go of it as a movie star. With that long, dark hair, and those intelligent blue-green eyes… It was a striking combination. At the gas station when he first saw her, it was all he could do to quit staring at her. Granted, he would've been interested in meeting any new visitor to Bear Creek Saddle, but it had been a long time since a girl like that had waltzed in and graced the likes of his town.

Then again, seeing the mess she'd made of her campsite and the empty bottle of what he assumed could only be booze, he had to admit the second impression wasn't as good as the first. But then she punched him and he had to renege on that bad impression bit.

She had street smarts, if not wilderness smarts.

He'd have to show her the ropes if she didn't want to get all tangled up in Idaho.

Zach shook his head and smiled to himself. *Nah, she's bad news, bad news.* Just like the stories in the *New York Times.*

Inky licked his face joyously when he got back into the driver seat—as if she hadn't just seen him two seconds ago leaning on the truck—and they drove back to the ranch. He was going to have to do his rounds, riding around to check on the herds and the irrigation systems, but what about his new houseguest?

Was New-York-Girl…Megan…going to need a place to sleep tonight?

He tamped down the quick, inappropriate thought that crossed his mind. *No, don't think that way. Forgive me, Lord.* She hadn't even wanted to lie down at his house, much less spend the night. She'd made it pretty clear she needed to feel safe, and Zach couldn't blame her.

He did have a perfectly usable, albeit tiny, guest cabin out back—at least it would be usable, once he took out all the equipment he'd been storing in it during the winter. The guest cabin was a storage shed half the year, which made it virtually unlivable unless he took some Herculean steps to get it prepared for a guest. It was the first log cabin Zach and the guys built, as "practice" before they got started on the bigger cabins they'd built to live in. Since the whole purpose was to get accustomed to the concept of laying logs, dovetailing the corners, and doing basic plumbing and insulation, the cabin came in at only 160 square feet. Just big enough for a twin mattress in the loft, and a couch, bathroom, and propane heater (vented out their first practice-chimney) below that. If

Megan really needed a place to stay, though, it would do the job.

And she'd have all the privacy a woman needs. *If* she wanted to stay.

Word spread like wildfire through small towns, so if she *did* want to stay on their ranch, they'd have to casually let the word out that she was in the cabin, not his guest room in the main house. Imagine how people would talk.

There was no way she could camp tonight, and she seemed pretty insistent about staying in Bear Creek Saddle. What was it about his town that made it so special? *He* knew what made it special. It was the most beautiful place in America, as far as Zach was concerned. His family lived in town. All of his friends. His *ranch* was here.

Bear Creek Saddle was his home, and it was everything good under the sun to him. But what, exactly, was it to Megan?

He'd have to find out.

Could she be on the run from the law? Maybe she'd committed a crime in New York, and drove until her car broke down, trying to keep a low profile, away from the Feds...man, anything was possible. It wasn't every day a beautiful city girl landed so far from home. There *had* to be a reason that made sense.

Zach pulled up to the property and stopped at the ranch's main office building. Calling it their office building was being a bit kind to it. In reality, the ramshackle old farmhouse had come with the land, and they just put it to use for work stuff. They'd stayed in the farmhouse when they first built their cabins and needed a place to crash after a long day of construction.

Now, it was where they kept their desks, fax machine, computers, and filing cabinets. Maybe he could give Megan a quick tour later. Was she into old farmhouses, or boring business stuff? There was always something that needed to be kept track of, and clients to deal with. Being a cowboy when he owned the ranch wasn't as simple as riding around, herding the cows, and throwing hay—not like when they were all ranch hands on the very same land, working from sunup to sundown and never once getting on a computer or picking up a pencil.

It had been a great time, back then, working with his best buds. It was still a great time. Just more...intensive. But Zach craved the responsibility, thrived under it. Without a family, he may as well pour himself into the land and the livestock.

Honestly, the day Zach and his friends bought the land from Bill and became the owners—a big promotion from hired hand, for sure—well, that had been a dream come true. Still was. They'd all been working that same ranch since they were fifteen years old. He and his friends knew it as well as they knew that muscle aches came with the work, if you did it right.

No pain, no gain.

Even though Bill Edwards was a third-generation rancher in his prime, he'd been all too ready to sell to them when he could. Bill didn't have a fourth generation to pass the land on to, or the will to keep working (what used to be called) Melody Ranch... not without Melody.

Melody. Gone too soon.

"Man," he sighed. Zach couldn't imagine what it must mean to lose a wife. Life could be so unexpectedly short... Thank God that Bill had gotten a second chance with his new wife, Allie.

Zach wanted what Bill and Allie had together. That connection. The love.

He brought his truck to a stop and put on the brake. Inky jumped onto his lap, squeezing between him and the steering wheel.

"I ain't gonna forget you," he told the dog.

Inky gave him a sloppy lick on his ear. Well—he was nowhere near on the right path to finding a soulmate. That lick was the most action he'd seen from a female in ages.

Zach wanted a wife, a family. It was going to happen for him soon, he could just feel it. He wouldn't let his life go by without making it happen. All he needed was the right girl...

The right girl would be pretty much the *opposite* type of girl from Megan Moore, but with the same sort of romantic spark. No denying the spark was an important element. With Megan...just standing near her was enough to know their relationship would sizzle.

He raised his eyebrows at Inky. Wishful thinking at its best. No sense letting himself be attracted to the wrong person. Far as he could tell, Megan was about an inch away from skedaddling back to New York, anyway. He'd be lucky to find her still at his cabin when he got back from running his errands.

"Come on, Inky," he said, and opened the door of the truck to jump out.

The small, ragged pebbles that made up the gravel drive in front of the old farmhouse office ground together underneath Zach's boots as he and Inky walked the well-worn track—where the gravel was pushed down and there was more dirt than rocks—up to the front porch.

Gratitude still filled him every time he clambered up the steps to the porch. He'd never have thought he and his guys would be so lucky as to own the land they loved so much. To be able to make a living doing what they knew how to do best.

A few years back, Zach, Eric, Chris, and Jay had been the closest thing that Bill had to family. The guys had sworn to take care of the land, and not let the business go down the drain. After Bill remarried with Allie Crawford, he seemed a million times happier working at the diner they owned together in town. When Melody Ranch changed hands and became Bear Creek Saddle Ranch, Zach and his friends were thrilled to keep the ranch going.

As for the office, well, since they were maintaining an organic cattle ranch, there were strict rules they had to follow in order to call themselves organic. And that all required documentation.

Fortunately he and the guys only had to stop in to the office for about an hour or so each day, to take care of stuff. The rest of the day involved doing what Zach loved best—riding around his ranch, helping the grass grow. Well, that, and milking the cows. In the springtime, during calving season, he got to help the mama cows bring baby calves into the world. Right now, with the grass long and ready to be harvested for winter, haying season was upon them.

It was going to be tough to get all the hay in before the first frost now that the kids they usually hired were busy helping their own folks. Zach needed more hired hands.

Megan has hands. Lovely, slender, delicate ones...

But here he was wasting precious haying time thinking about the girl back at his cabin. Seriously, he'd almost forgotten those lovely, delicate hands of hers could also pack a mean punch.

Zach pushed through the front door of the farmhouse office and set the mail down on the table in the front hall.

"Anyone here?" he called.

"Hey Zach," Chris called from the back room.

Inky barked her greeting in response, and followed Zach down a little hall to Chris's "office"—a small bedroom in the old farmhouse with his desk and computer in it, and a whole lot of antlers on the wall.

"What's doing?" Chris asked amiably.

Zach put the new bull catalog on his desk.

"Awesome, man." Chris grinned. "Thanks."

"No problem," Zach said. "By the way—I have a woman at my house. So if you see her, don't shoot her."

He was only half-joking. It was Chris, after all, who'd wanted to keep the original ranch owner's sign by the back fences that said TRESPASSERS WILL BE SHOT. SURVIVORS WILL BE SHOT AGAIN, but their buddy Jay had pulled it down and replaced it with a plain PRIVATE PROPERTY. NO HUNTING sign.

Chris put down the catalog and lifted his head. "Which cow kicked you this time?" he asked, gesturing toward Zach's face. Then, "Wait a minute—what woman? You mean Paige?"

Zach shook his head.

"*You* have a woman at your house?" Chris asked.

Zach frowned. "You don't have to seem so surprised by that."

"Just have never seen you bringing girls back here, that's all," Chris said. "Who is this woman? How'd you meet her?"

"It's not like that," Zach said. "I ran across her campsite this morning, and she punched me—"

Chris made a face like he was about to interrupt.

"It's all good," Zach said hurriedly. "Her car's broke down back there, so I gave her a lift to the ranch." He took a breath. "A brown bear was right on our tail. I had no choice."

Chris cocked his head and touched the rim of his hat, which

he'd left on, as if he came into the office for something quick and planned on going back out into the sun right away. "Well now. Popped ya in the nose? Looks a little swollen, man."

"She's from New York," Zach said, as if that explained everything. "You did hear me say I saw a bear, right?"

"Yeah, turns out bears live in the woods. Someone told me that once," Chris said, smirking. The "someone" they often joked about was always one of them—and in this case, it had been Zach. *Wise guy.*

Chris paused. "You left a New Yorker alone in your cabin? She's a stranger, Zach. Why not just drop her off at the inn?"

"She won't leave Bear Creek Saddle, man. I can't figure it out either."

"Sounds like you're getting yourself into trouble," Chris said.

"Nah, I won't," Zach said, laughing. Pot-calling-the-kettle-black, that was Chris all right. "I think she needs somewhere to stay tonight, though."

"She can't stay in the farmhouse, if that's what you're thinking," Chris said. "Too much sensitive stuff here, including all of our bank accounts."

Zach stopped laughing. "She's not a thief, Chris."

"Really? You just met her, what, a few hours ago? And she's already beat you up? So far, that ain't a good sign."

Zach sighed. He was actually proud of Megan for defending herself, even if it was against him.

"I met her yesterday, anyhow. At the gas station."

"Ohh," Chris said. "I heard something about that. Blue Eclipse."

"That's her. I could tell her she could spend the night in the practice-cabin, ya think?" Zach rubbed his chin. Rats, he'd forgotten to shave that morning. The stubble on his chin was sandpaper against his thumb. "I'd have to go in and get rid of the spiders, probably."

Chris laughed. "You can't put her in that tiny cabin, man. You're really out of touch with how to treat women."

What? Zach raised his eyebrow. Then again, Chris got all the girls, so he probably knew what he was talking about.

"What'd I do now?" Zach asked defensively.

"You're supposed to offer a lady your nice big bed, and you sleep in the little spider-cabin. Didn't your mama teach you manners?"

"So's that what you think? I should have her stay at my place?"

"I don't know, man. That's on you. But if it were me, and I found a chick in the woods who then ended up in my house an' told me she wouldn't go to a motel, I'd be careful," Chris said. "Pretty convenient how you found her, am I right?"

Zach grunted. "That's what she'd said."

"Or rather, how she found *you*, twice? Have you ever considered the possibility she knows what this ranch is worth?"

What? No. Wait—

But Zach could tell just by looking at Megan, and interacting with her, that she wasn't manipulating him.

"She has no idea what she's doing, Chris. I wouldn't feel right about lending her my tent to go somewhere else. That girl's lucky she didn't get attacked by that bear as it was."

"I see what this is. You found another little someone cute an' lost to take care of—just like Inky. Except this time, it's a New Yorker instead of a Lab."

"It ain't like that." But the barb hurt. Was Chris right? "We're gonna need as many hands as we can get to throw hay."

"Right," Chris said. "She gonna run the baler, too? She's a city girl, Zach. Don't get attached."

"I'm not attached." He waved his hand, brushing off the idea a little too forcefully. "I've been telling myself the same thing you just told me, anyhow." Zach shook his head and turned around to leave. He still had to go take a look at that custom holster.

"What's she look like, anyway, if I run into her?"

"Long dark hair, 'bout yay high—" Zach marked a spot right below his shoulder. "Name's Megan." Zach touched the doorway with his fingertips. "And she's beautiful."

Chris looked up at him again from the catalogue. "I had a feeling. Well, go on. Don't do anything I wouldn't do."

Zach laughed and called back as he walked down the hallway, "That's a short list."

The irony of his situation wasn't lost on him. He'd been praying for the right woman to be dropped at his feet where his dumb-self couldn't miss her. A woman to settle down with, to marry and start a family—he was ready for it. Needed it. Instead, God had handed him a beautiful woman who was the *exact opposite* of what he wanted—right down to being a big-city girl who didn't know a black bear from a brown bear from an Idaho potato.

Great joke on him, huh.

And for Zach to *want* this wrong woman with every fiber of his being...yup, the joke was on him for sure. Being attracted to Megan was about the stupidest thing he could do, and yet there he was, hoping like crazy she'd be waiting for him at his cabin when he walked back through the door.

* * *

Megan looked around the cabin. It hadn't taken too long to clean. The place had been so untidy, she'd had to handle it.

After throwing out anything that needed to be thrown out— old newspapers, trash, putting all the dirty dishes into the dishwasher and running it, that sort of thing—the cabin was already looking much better.

Figuring out where to put stuff had involved opening all of Zach's cabinets (the vacuum was in the back of the coat closet), but once she had—and vacuumed up all of the fur bunnies from Inky's shedding—she was in the groove and feeling productive.

Relaxing in a messy place was impossible.

When she'd gotten a good look at her own trashed campsite, she'd nearly had a heart attack. And that was *before* she'd realized the seriousness of a bear in the area.

Under the sink, she found bleach spray, and also used the organic vinegar spray from the counter—not together at once, of course. There was only one bathroom, so it didn't take too long to wipe everything down. In his bedroom, she carefully made the bed.

He'd lain on this bed before. *This is where he sleeps…* resting that beautiful head of his on that pillow there, his long muscular body stretched out, probably taking up the whole middle of the bed. What did Zach Walker sleep in? A T-shirt and shorts?

Megan smiled to herself and shook her head.

Still. She really shouldn't be thinking about her host like that. It wasn't right. And for all her previous sins, everything she'd already prayed to God for forgiveness for, she really needed to be more diligent about keeping herself on the right path.

For all she knew, he had a girlfriend. After all, why would a gorgeous, successful rancher *not* have a girlfriend? It wasn't Paige, she knew that at least. But that didn't mean there wasn't another girl (or more) he was attached to.

No… if he had a woman coming over to snuggle with in front of the fireplace, surely he wouldn't have left his dirty socks on the floor.

Snuggling in front of the fireplace… with Zach. The thought sent a tingle of excitement down Megan's spine. With her ex, Todd, whenever he put his arm around her she felt… suffocated. As if he'd been holding on to her to *keep her with him*, instead of whatever snuggling someone was supposed to make you feel.

Whatever it was supposed to be about.

What would cuddling up to Zach be like? He was so good-looking that she couldn't help but keep thinking of him like this. Still, it would probably be wise to turn off the fantasizing.

Especially since being with a man, in any way, shape, or form, was just about the *last* thing she needed right now.

With all the dirty clothes in the hamper, the laundry started, the dishwasher running, and everything wiped down and picked up, the cabin looked like a completely different place. Anything she wasn't sure where to put ended up in a neat little pile off to the side. But most of the stuff was pretty easy to figure out.

She wasn't sure what to do with the dozens of guitar picks she found scattered around, so she just held on to them until she figured she'd found them all, then piled them up and set them next to his guitar by the fireplace.

Maybe he would play her a song sometime… what kind of music would Zach be into?

Books went on the bookshelf (she stuck little pieces of paper as bookmarks into all the books that were left open facedown. Horrible thing to do to a book spine, but apparently he didn't know about that).

You sure have a lot of books, Zach Walker.

Books on ranching, books on survival skills—which she really needed to borrow—books on hiking, memoirs from military guys, and other adventurous sorts. Not one but two Bibles. A lot of Louis L'Amour's old westerns, too. Who would've guessed? A bookworm cowboy.

That just made her like him more. And yet so far, as nice as he'd been to her, it was pretty clear that Zach was amazed she'd made it to adulthood alive with her current survival skills being what they were. He wouldn't be inviting her to be his girlfriend anytime soon, so there was no reason to daydream about whether or not she'd want to.

Especially since she definitely wanted to.

Staahhp.

Megan opened the curtains to let in some light, and poured herself a drink of water from the tap. Mountain spring water, just like that. The same water they bottled and sold for six dollars at her overpriced gym in Manhattan.

This place is so amazing.

Out the large south-facing windows, the mountains stood tall in the background, and the lawn was covered in wildflowers, as well as evergreen trees in random places. He must've left some of the trees for shade when he and his friends timbered the area for clearing.

Maybe she could pick some of those wildflowers later—it'd be neat to press the flowers between the pages of a book, like her mother used to do. If only she had some picture frames, she could make really cool wall art out of them. Especially if the frames were special. Handmade, like Zach's new holster he was getting.

Megan sighed. *So many ideas, so little time.* Speaking of time…she'd better call her sister, before he came back. It was just…she dreaded doing it. Lindsay would never understand.

Her sister hadn't understood why Megan would want to leave Todd in the first place. Why she wouldn't agree to marry him. And she certainly didn't understand why Megan couldn't handle living in the city anymore, not for even a second longer.

But driving cross-country to north Idaho was the most wonderful thing Megan had ever done for herself. It had been the only time in her life that she did something because she knew she needed to, even if no one else understood or agreed. It didn't matter what they thought.

Sometimes, you have to take care of yourself.

And that's what Megan was doing. It was a good feeling. To be free for the first time. Independent for the very first time.

No one could *pay* her enough to get her to give that up. Much less *guilt* her into it, which was Lindsay's specialty.

Sighing, Megan dropped to her stomach and found her phone on the floor. What an annoying place for an outlet. Then again, Zach had probably done the wiring himself. She should be grateful she hadn't been electrocuted yet.

"You have got to be kidding me." She sighed.

She'd never plugged the stupid phone back in after she'd unplugged it to use the vacuum. The cell was going to die on her soon, and she couldn't exactly make her calls while it was charging, all scrunched up on the carpet like this. She plugged it back in.

Well, Zach had told her she could use his house phone. No more excuses not to call and get lectured by her big sister. *Fun.*

"Megan, is that you?" her sister asked the moment she picked up.

"What the—how did you know it was me? This isn't even my phone."

"Megan! My goodness, you've had me worried sick! And I didn't know it was you," Lindsay admitted. "I've been answering every number I don't recognize like that since you ran away."

And...here we go. "I called you two nights ago, from the road," Megan reminded her. "And I'm an adult—I didn't 'run away.' I simply moved out of state without informing you first."

"Did you practice that? Because that's just great, Megs. Seriously. Fine, you 'moved.' But you need to come back home now," Lindsay said. "Todd is so depressed. I can't believe you left him like that."

"I can't explain it all over again to you," Megan said, "And I don't need to explain myself to either of you, anyway."

"He's your fiancé—"

"He is *not* my fiancé," Megan interrupted. "Never call him that again."

Lindsay exhaled audibly into the phone. "I'm just... so worried about you."

"I appreciate you worrying for me," Megan said. It was true. Lindsay was her only family, and that did mean something—it meant a lot.

"Where are you now, Megs?"

"I made it to Idaho. It's even more beautiful than that picture... It's more beautiful than I ever could have dreamed."

"I meant, where are you staying? Whose phone are you using?"

Megan didn't want to tell her she was at a man's house. But *not* telling her made it seem like she had something to hide, which she didn't. Besides, Megan was a grown woman and didn't have to get permission from her big sister to do whatever she pleased. Even if what she pleased was getting to know Zach Walker.

"Well… I was camping—"

"Camping?!" Lindsay laughed in a way that made Megan know how scared she was for her, out on her own. "Who are you and what have you done with my sister?"

"I'm going to have to learn all these skills at some point," Megan said. "I want to *live here*. I want to be completely self-sufficient, and grow my own food and stuff."

"Oh, of course, that's right," Lindsay said—so brightly that only her sister would've known she was being sarcastic. "Good luck with that."

Megan didn't even blame her for not thinking it was possible. It had definitely been a foreign concept even for Megan, a lifestyle only congruous with the reality TV stars on the Alaska wilderness show or with the few who eschewed modern conveniences like electricity. But now that she'd seen what Zach and his friends were able to do, working with the land every day…it was inspiring.

"Did you know you can be off-grid, and still have electricity and running water and all that normal stuff?" Megan asked, looking around at the cozy, well-lit kitchen as she tucked the phone under her chin.

"Megs, seriously—are you still camping?" her sister asked, cutting into her reverie. "Oh no, are you lost? Where are you?"

"Right now, I'm at a new friend's house. He actually… saved

me from a bear."

Lindsay gasped. "A bear! Are you okay?" Then, "Wait. HE?"

Here we go. "His name is Zach Walker. He's a rancher. A very good, safe, cowboy."

"What makes you think he's very safe? He's a stranger." Lindsay dropped her voice, as if someone might overhear her, alone in her apartment. "You're going to get yourself *assaulted.*"

"Oh come on now, don't say things like that," Megan groaned. "I don't feel like going into a whole speech about how if someone assaults me it's not because I made it happen. You know better than to bait me like that, seriously."

Lindsay sighed. "Sorry, but you still know what I mean."

"I've got my pepper spray," Megan said, omitting the fact that it was only useful as a paperweight at the moment. "He even offered to teach me how to shoot a gun, so clearly he's not planning on trying something. If he were, he'd want me unarmed, I assume, right?"

"A gun? What kind of house are you in?"

"A house in Idaho," Megan said, which was an explanation in itself. "Log cabin, actually. It's lovely, and pretty much the exact opposite of New York. You should visit. Anyway I gotta go," she rushed. "I love you, Lindsay!"

And then Megan hung up as quickly as she could. She'd done her job. She'd called Lindsay, told her where she was, and where she was staying. Now if she ended up dead somewhere in a ditch after all (*God forbid*), Lindsay had Zach Walker's name. If her sister was worried, then she'd have to suck it up, because there wasn't really much else she could do about it.

Zach had been gone for over forty-five minutes… well, he had said he had some errands to do. After rushing around cleaning the house, and sleeping in the tent all night, Megan felt grimy and sticky with dried perspiration.

Would it be totally weird if she took a quick shower, borrowed a towel, and put on some fresh clothes? She did bring her bag, after all.

Surely, if Zach were here, and she asked him... he wouldn't say no.

Probably not smart to get undressed in a stranger's house, though. Ugh. Lindsay was getting into her head. Megan planned on taking a shower, not getting undressed. Well, both, but it wasn't the same. It was the intention that differentiated between getting ready for a shower, and getting naked. And it wasn't as if he was there at the house.

Before she could talk herself out of it, Megan grabbed her bag from the front door and brought it into the bathroom with her, along with a clean (though badly folded) towel from the linen closet. Shower time—it would have to be quick, though, so she'd be done by the time Zach got home.

The bathroom was really cute and still smelled of bleach (in a good way), which made her a little happier she'd given in to her urge to clean it. It also had log walls and a big mirror over the sink. The tub was one of those old-fashioned claw-foot tubs, but it had a proper shower curtain. For some reason, Zach had chosen a curtain with a bluish-purple berry-and-green-leaves motif.

Huckleberries, maybe.

A woman must've helped him buy that. Guys usually didn't think to purchase berry shower curtains and matching towels all on their own. Could've been a woman who visited him a lot, maybe.

Someone he liked enough to bring her out shopping with him for house-stuff. Probably…who had he mentioned? Paige.

Why am I jealous? That was ridiculous. She'd just met Zach. She had no claim on him.

Stripping off her dirty clothes, Megan stepped into the steaming shower with a sigh of relief. It felt incredible. She'd forgotten to get her shampoo out of her bag, stupidly, so she made use of Zach's generic no-brand shampoo and soap. It was all unscented.

That was no fun—she was used to getting out of the shower smelling like flowers and herbal whatnots. Not like… nothing. But smelling like nothing was a lot better than smelling bad. And goodness, being clean was amazing.

Once she was out of the shower, Megan picked up the clothes she'd been wearing to see if she could re-wear her comfy-jeans. Ugh… no.

"You have got to be kidding me," she muttered. Her new mantra.

The clothes reeked of campfire smoke. How could she not have noticed that when she was actually wearing them? She'd gone nose-blind. It was a wonder Zach even let her into his truck, smelling like that.

Oh no…had he been trying to tell her that *she* stank, when he had asked her if *he* smelled bad? Maybe. She had been getting awfully close to him. But men didn't usually think to phrase things that way. As for herself, when she got chilly the first words out of her mouth were usually "Are you cold?" Backwards talk.

Zach seemed too straightforward for that.

Fortunately, she had some clean leggings and a T-shirt in the bag. She threw them on, wiped the steam off the mirror with a towel, and brushed the tangles from her long, dark hair.

The first person I meet here, and I punch him and stink up his truck.
Nicely done.

Suddenly the enormity of the changes she'd made to Zach's house hit her like cold rain. She'd rifled through all of his things…thrown so many things out—what if he'd been saving them for some reason?

"Oh no," she whispered, her voice catching in her throat.

She stepped out of the bathroom and looked around again with fresh eyes. It looked like a completely different house than the one he'd entrusted to her when he left with Inky.

He was going to be furious. How could she take such liberties with a complete stranger's home? And to think she'd been imagining what it would be like to cuddle with him by the fireplace or listen to him playing his guitar.

No chance of that now. Why did she have to be such a freak about cleaning? Why couldn't she just relax in a messy place for a short time?

If she had done something like this to her ex, he would have gone crazy on her. Screamed at her. Thrown something. Maybe punched a hole in the wall, and made her pay for the repair the following week. He'd done it all before. And whenever he'd have to search for something later down the line, he would have glared at her and reminded her that *she* was at fault for throwing out the back issue of whatever magazine, or his favorite torn shoelace, or something.

What would Zach do? How would he react? What if he was like Todd?

She needed to get out of there before Zach came home and saw what she'd done.

"Where do I go?" she asked aloud.

Fear overtook her—the same fear that had made her flee Todd's apartment back in New York.

She forgot to pray.

She just ran.

Out the front door with her bag and purse. No way was Megan going to stick around and find out if Zach had a temper.

Wasn't worth it.

Chapter Four

ZACH OPENED THE door to the cabin and Inky bounded in. "Megan?" he called.

No answer.

But the house looked amazing. Looked better than it did even right after they'd built it.

The clutter was gone; everything was in its place. The wooden counters gleamed. In the middle of the living room, there was an ottoman at the foot of the couch that he hadn't used in such a long time he'd forgotten he had it.

"Whoa," he breathed, once he was able to close his mouth. She'd cleaned his house?

That was a huge job. And a huge favor for her to have done it.

"Thank you," he called out. "Thanks, Megan, I really mean it."

No answer.

Her cell phone was still on the floor, plugged in and charging. Man, that meant he couldn't even text her to find out where she'd gone.

Maybe she'd called for the tow truck while he was out?

There were blinking messages on his landline answering machine. He didn't even know why he kept the silly thing—everyone who knew him called his cell phone.

He pressed play, and a man's voice assaulted his eardrums.

"Megan," the man's voice said on the machine. "It's me. I can't believe you left me like this. I've been worried sick about you. I hope you're having fun on your little adventure, because fun's over. You need to come home, now. Not tomorrow, not next week. NOW."

Beep.

Another message, right after the first:

"Megan, I know you're at this number. Stop ignoring me like a spoiled brat and pick up the phone. NOW."

Beep.

And another:

"MEGAN. PICK UP the phone. Did you forget how?" The man's voice dripped with condescension. "Use your little hand, reach dowwwwn and piiiick uuuup the phone. Surely you can keep that concept in your stupid little brain? I have no idea how you'll even manage to function properly without me, seriously, Megan."

Beep.

One more:

"Megan, I'm sorry. No, actually I'm NOT, YOU should be sorry for what you did to me, you—" The man's running monologue devolved into a barrage of cussing.

Zach recoiled in disgust. The man sounded like a domineering jerk. Who was he to talk to Megan that way? She wasn't a child, and she wasn't stupid. What "home" was he talking about, anyway?

Zach texted his buddies: *"Let me know if you see Megan walking around—she left her cell phone here. Don't know where she's at."*

Maybe he could find her. He grabbed her cell phone and refilled Inky's water bowl before grabbing his hat and heading back out.

He got on the four-wheel ATV and rode around the ranch, keeping an eye out for Megan. Where did she go? Back to the woods? She didn't have her car, even. She had to be somewhere on his property.

Why would someone be so nice as to clean his house and then just run off like that? Maybe it was the messages on the answering machine. Could she have heard those calls from…whatever guy that was calling and yelling at her?

Man, if he'd heard that, he'd run too.

* * *

Megan sat in the hayloft of the barn and stared down at the horses in their stables below. Bales of hay covered the entire loft platform, save for a couple that were open, with hay spread out all over.

It was pretty comfy, once she spread her jacket over it. Less itchy that way.

What if Zach found her? What if he was super mad?

Lord, please soften his heart toward me tonight, she prayed silently. *Don't let him find me until he cools off. Please make him not angry. Please let him be the opposite of Todd.*

Without her tent or her car or even her phone, she was stuck where she was, hiding in the barn.

Was Todd right about her, all along? She wasn't doing so well out on her own. A choked laugh escaped her lips at the thought. Understatement of the year.

Help me figure it out, God.

Please.

* * *

It wasn't until the following morning when Zach went to water and groom the horses that he found her.

Still asleep, just like last time.

"Megan?" he whispered from the bottom of the ladder up to the hayloft. "Did you sleep out here all night?"

She mumbled something and then sat up quickly, a piece of hay sticking to her long hair.

Megan's face contorted with worry. "I'm sorry—I shouldn't have touched your stuff," she said quickly. "It's all my fault. I have this thing where I can't relax when I see something really out of place… And once I started cleaning, it's hard to stop. I'm really sorry. I completely understand if you want me to leave."

She looked so nervous, so small and…afraid? *That jerk on the phone.* He'd done a number on this girl, to put her in a state of fear whenever she wasn't sure how a man would react. All Zach wanted to do was comfort her, to promise her anything in order to make her feel okay again.

Why was he feeling so protective of her? He barely knew Megan. And yet, her situation hit him as hard as if it were happening to him.

"I'm not upset," he said. "I'm grateful, honestly. I just wish I hadn't spent the rest of yesterday only half-working because I kept looking for you. Couldn't find you for nothing."

"I'm sorry," Megan said. "Should I…come down?"

"Be careful," he said, and spotted her as she came down the ladder with her backpack on and her purse strap across her shoulder.

Zach pulled her toward him and wrapped her in his arms. It happened so naturally he didn't stop to think if it was the right thing to do, to hug her.

"Whatever the reason you cleaned my cabin," he said, "you saved me the trouble, so I'm glad. Very glad. It looks like new."

"You're really not mad at me?" She looked up at him with those big blue-green eyes wide, a hint of fear still etched across her face.

"'Course not," he said. "I ain't like that guy who called and left those messages, Megan. You can relax a little here, okay? I told you before—I don't hit women. Ever."

"What messages? What guy?" The fear was back in her voice.

"Some guy called the house and left a bunch of messages, sounded…kinda mean."

Megan blushed and disentangled herself from his arms. "No, no—you've got it all wrong. I know who called. He never abused me. He'd never hit me, it's not like that."

"Ahh," Zach said. "So he's one of those 'non-abusive' types that just makes you feel terrible about yourself and screams at you."

At that, Megan smirked. "Yeah… something like that."

"I'm no therapist," he said, "but you might want to reevaluate your definition of 'not abusive.' That guy sounds like *he's* the one who needs to be punched in the nose. I hope he loses my number."

She nodded, no longer smiling. "I don't know how he got it. I'm sorry."

"If you want," he said, "you can hand me the phone if he does call again. You don't even have to say a word. An' I'll just hang up on him."

Megan looked up toward the rafters, toward the big beam that ran down the center of the cabin's peaked ceiling, and sighed. "Thank you," she said quietly.

"You look like you need some coffee," he said. "Come on, I'll give you a lift back to my place."

"All I've done is mess things up...why are you being so nice to me?" Megan shook her head. "Never mind. Sorry."

She seemed so wary. As if she thought Zach wanted something—he could guess what—in return.

That false assumption might've hurt his feelings, if it hadn't made him hurt for *her* more. What could he do to make her feel safe near him?

* * *

Back at his house, Zach went to the coffee pot, hit once again with how shiny and clean everything was. He'd thought those water spots on the faucet were permanent. Who would've thought it could look as shiny as it did when he'd first installed it?

"So, you want coffee?" he asked, looking over his shoulder at her.

She'd taken another quick shower, and emerged in the same clothes she'd slept in, but with clean, damp hair.

Man, she was beautiful. But so... unsure of herself. Like she didn't know how to get comfortable in her own skin.

"No thank you," she said, even as she looked longingly at the coffee pot. "You've already done so much, I don't want to bother you with anything else. I just need to get my car and my tent. I imagine the bear's gone, don't you think? I can get my tent, and I promise the next time I camp, I will be sure to..." She paused.

"To what?" he asked, genuinely curious.

Megan crossed her arms and sighed. "I don't even know. All right…just go ahead and tell me how people in Idaho keep food safe from bears."

He didn't want her camping alone out there tonight. He barely condoned her sleeping in his barn last night, like a cat up in the hayloft. But he couldn't force her to stay safely on the ranch with him nearby if she didn't want to—which, after leaving a relationship like the one she had with the jerk on the answering machine, it wouldn't surprise him if she didn't.

Zach went over to the table with two coffee mugs. "Drink," he said, and gave her a half-smile, to soften the order.

"Oh…in that case…" She took the steaming cup from him. "Thanks."

"The maintained campsites have bear containers that everyone puts their food into overnight. But when you're just camping in the woods like you were, you can keep your food and trash in your car."

"Right," she said, as if she'd already known that. "We were safe in the car."

"Although it's actually not unheard of for a bear to go into a car," he said. "Better than them going into your tent with you in it, though."

"How does a bear know how to break into a car?" Her eyes widened with amazement. "Bears are a lot craftier than I'd given them credit for."

"They can smell a candy wrapper; it's crazy," Zach said. "Some people put their food into a bag, and hang it high up in a tree far away from where they're sleeping."

"Great!" Megan said. "I can do that, then, since my car seems to be out of commission. I feel terrible about turning your whole day upside down yesterday, Zach." She set her coffee mug on the table. "I don't want to overstay my welcome—I should probably get out of your hair."

"When you get in my hair, you'll know," he said. "I don't get to see too many folks from outta town. You're doing me a favor by keeping me company."

He was hours late getting started with ranch work, though. The guys all knew what was going on, but the cows sure didn't. Still, he didn't want to see her go. Zach had an overwhelming desire to keep her safe…fact was, he had an overwhelming desire to keep her, period.

Don't do it, man.

Didn't matter much if he wanted to keep Megan around, if she wasn't a girl he was meant to marry. Zach wanted a wife, not a fling. In fact, one of the deciding factors in finally breaking things off for good with Paige—no more long, midnight phone calls when one of them had a lapse in judgment—was something Big Bad Bill had told him, after he'd found Allie:

"If you're holding on tight to the wrong woman, your arms won't be free to grab hold of the right one." That's what Bill had said.

At first, Zach had thought Bill was talking only about having to let go of his late wife so he could be with Allie. But then he'd realized—being with Paige, a girl Zach didn't love, kept him from finding a woman he *could* fall in love with. He wasn't gonna date around while he was still with her. The only way forward was out.

If Zach wanted a wife (and he did), then he couldn't afford to have Megan hanging around—especially considering how attracted he was to her. Getting to know her was the very last thing he should be doing. But…she'd practically fallen out of the sky into his lap—how could he not take notice?

Well, she probably won't be here that long, anyway. A few more days of slow country living and she'd be clamoring to go back to bright lights of New York City. Sure as the sun rose each morning—Zach wouldn't even have time to get attached. So no harm, no foul.

"I could call you a tow truck," he suggested. "They could come and get your car. The bear's probably moved on by now, hopefully. It does make me nervous, though, how close it was."

He paused, and looked at her. Did she really want to go, or did she want to stay and was just trying to be polite? *Nah.* New Yorkers weren't known for their politeness. But the fact was—no matter how anxious he was to get to know Megan Moore better before she flew out of his life as quickly as she'd flown into it—there was still a bear issue to deal with.

"I've never seen a brown bear this close to our ranch before," he said finally, "and I'm worried that means the bear's aggressive. I'm not sure if I feel right about you off alone in the mountain tonight."

"Oh," she said. She looked down at her hands. "Todd said I could never do anything for myself. That I'm useless. He told me I'd be homeless on the street if it weren't for him. Sometimes I wonder… if this proves he was right all along."

Beneath the table, Zach could feel the vibration of the table as her leg bounced up and down on the ball of her foot. Burning off nervous energy.

"Is Todd the guy on the phone?"

"Yeah," she said. "My ex-boyfriend."

"He wasn't right about that stuff, Megan, he was a *jerk*." Zach wished he could have reached his fist through the answering machine and punched that ex of hers in the face for the way he'd treated Megan. He softened his tone. "You jus' got here—you still need to get settled, that's all. No big deal."

Here goes nothing. An invitation he couldn't resist extending, even if it ended up all wrong. "You can sleep out back in the practice cabin—I mean, *guest* cabin. You'll have your own four walls but I'm just a stone's throw away. Problem solved."

Megan stilled, a freeze-frame in which he didn't see her blink or even take in a breath. He held his breath along with her without realizing it. Her pink tongue touched the edge of her top teeth and stayed there as she stared at a space somewhere to her left.

Megan had even more reason than he did to question whether taking him up on his offer was a good idea. He couldn't blame her for hesitating.

"I just have to take some equipment out of it," he added, trying to flesh out the plan for her, "and then maybe you could do your cleaning magic thing to make it nice for yourself. Shouldn't take long, it's real small."

"You're doing too much for me," she said. "Why?"

"It's no problem," he added quietly. "I'll feel better if you take me up on it. Jus' want to know you're safe. That I'm near enough to help you if ya need it."

"Thank you," she whispered. She tucked her hair behind her ear. It wasn't damp anymore. "That's very kind of you." Her foot had stopped bouncing, and she reached her hand across the table toward him, rolling her palm face up in an open gesture. "I just... I hate feeling indebted. Can I pay you?"

Zach looked down at her small hand, so delicate. There was no way he was taking payment. He wanted to meet her halfway across the table, to touch that smooth palm of hers, to see how small her hand was inside of his own. He swallowed hard, resisting the urge to take her hand in his, even as her open body language seemed to allow it.

Don't take that girl's hand.

"Oh no." She blushed and shook her head slightly, her fingers closing over her palm. "Pay you with *money*, I mean."

Zach raised his eyebrows. "If I was going to charge you to stay here—which I'm not—it wouldn't be like that. You don't...owe me anything."

"Oh goodness." Her cheeks reddened. "I'm sorry, I...misinterpreted what may have been going through your mind. I don't want to lead you on, that's all. I mean—" Megan looked down at the table.

She took a breath and spoke so fast that in order to process it, he had to mentally replay what she'd said: "I'm-not-going-to-sleep-with-you-just-because-you're-nice-to-me."

Huh.

Her face was flushed. "And I just had to say that to put it out in the open, if you're inviting me to stay at your ranch, guest cabin or not. I'm sorry."

Well. What should he say to that? The air hung silently between them.

He hadn't offered her a place to stay hoping to get lucky. But he understood why she'd assume his mind might be headed in that direction. Hard as he tried to keep his thoughts pure, as a red-blooded man he had to admit there was still a small, primal part in him that wanted nothing more than to haul the woman over his shoulder and take her into his bedroom. Most bachelors would have to say the same, if they were being honest about it.

Not that he would act on it, for goodness' sake. It was just a tiny flicker of a thought, and even those he tamped down when he could. *It's better for a man to marry than burn with lust.* Man, he really needed to find himself a wife, and right fast.

So maybe Megan had picked up on that vibe. Zach better get a hold on himself. Not look at her that way ever again, so she could feel safe with him.

Still—it was a good thing she said something, because with a clear boundary he wouldn't have to wonder how *she* felt about the situation. Now he knew. All that worry about getting distracted by his attraction to her was for nothing, because she didn't want anything to do with him that way.

That makes things easier. At least it should.

"You've drawn your line, ma'am, and I'll respect it," he said. "I can be a gentleman—my mom raised me up right."

Had she seen the interest in his eyes when he looked at her? Or maybe she'd just wanted to introduce the elephant in the room so they could start tiptoeing around it instead of crashing into it.

He may've been too forward before, embracing her in the barn and getting into her boyfriend-business like that. She'd just looked so small and upset, comforting her seemed like the only right thing to do.

Now he'd near scared the girl right out of Idaho.

"I know you have no reason to trust me yet," he acknowledged. He strode over to the counter by the phone, where he'd dropped his bag earlier. "I picked you up a new pepper spray while I was out.

They didn't have one in purple, so I got you…pink." Zach shrugged and handed it to her.

Megan took it from him with trembling fingers. "You didn't have to do this for me. But I… I'm glad you did." She tucked it into her purse. "That was really nice of you. I don't know what to say."

"Maybe having that nearby will help you sleep better, stuck out in the middle of nowhere with a stranger, right?" He grinned. "You'll never have to use it. I'll be keeping my hands to myself, Megan Moore."

A smile finally broke out over her beautiful face, and she looked so much more relieved and relaxed than she did even a minute ago.

"Thank you, Zach. I hope I didn't come across as rude. That's such an awkward conversation to have, I know." Megan laughed nervously. "So… what now? I don't want to be a burden. I want to help, and earn my room and board. Just not… not like that."

She nodded toward the bedroom, and Zach laughed with her, shaking his head.

"You couldn't have come at a better time," he said. "We need all the hands we can get when it's time to make hay. Think you can throw hay like a man?"

"Even better," she said. "I can throw hay like a woman. At least I imagine I can, once you tell me what that even means."

Oh boy. "All right then." He laughed. "If you want to get started, maybe you could help me clear out the practice cabin—I mean, guest cabin—and then do what you need to make it comfy while I do my rounds on the ranch."

* * *

Megan followed Zach outside and followed him down a trail in the grass, which was mainly worn down from feet and tractor wheels, it seemed.

The "guest cabin" was at least an acre or two outside of what looked like Zach's backyard area for Inky—not nearly as close to his cabin as he'd made it sound. Then again, she had no idea how to guestimate acreage, so who knew? It was a four-minute walk, at least she knew that much.

"Here we go," Zach said as they came up on it.

He opened the door, which was latched shut but not locked. Did anyone lock their doors up here? Would there be a way for her to latch it shut from the inside?

Would that be rude?

Doesn't matter. She wasn't going to be able to shed her cynicism and fear as easily as she'd been able to drive herself physically out of New York. *Wherever you go, there you are.* Fear wasn't a coat she could take on and off.

That tiny voice inside her made her feel safe again, though. An internal whisper that said everything would be okay.

Thank you, she prayed. *Just keep an eye on me, Lord, okay?*

This whole trusting God thing was new to her. Entirely new. She wasn't even sure if she was doing it right. She'd kept God at arm's length for so long because He hadn't even been on her radar. She wasn't raised with religion. Her ex was a militant atheist who had made fun of her on the few occasions she'd raised some innocuous questions about morality.

Would Zach make fun of her, too?

His back was turned to her as he reached into the cabin shed and pulled out a lawn mower, setting it on the side of the structure.

"That's just for hedges and whatnot," he said, defensiveness in his voice.

As if she knew what a good mower looked like? Ha.

"Obviously we use tractors and ride-on mowers for most of the ranch," he added. "But I like something small I can use with my hands if I need to."

She nodded. "Can I help?"

He handed her a huge bag of potting soil. "Set this on the side, if you can. Watch your back, tighten your stomach muscles when you lift or your body'll pay for it later."

Megan took it from him and sagged a bit under the weight. Tighten the abs. Bend with the knees. *Don't let him see you weak.*

After that, he handed her one thing after another until it looked like they were having a garage sale of tools and gardening supplies outside the tiny guest cabin—which, clearly, was and had always been used as a storage shed.

Better than the hayloft, and much better than nothing at all.

She peered inside, unable to see much after being out in the bright sunlight.

Zach flipped on a light switch and the space lit up. It was actually really cute, and really disgusting at the same time. Cobwebs everywhere, which meant spiders everywhere. She shuddered involuntarily.

"The spiders here aren't like the ones in New York," he said. "They're not poisonous. Just bitty house spiders, that's all."

"I'm not worried," she said. Maybe if she said that confidently enough, God would make it true. "I'll just vacuum everything and spray it down."

"After what you did in my house," he said, making a low whistle of approval, "I have no doubt."

Megan pasted a smile on her face. Was she really going to sleep in there tonight?

She had to. She was out of options. No tent, no car. No motel unless she wanted to leave, and even then…no car. Which meant relying on Zach for even more favors.

"Why weren't there spiders in your house?" she asked him.

"They hate peppermint, and it's growing like a weed all around my cabin." He paused. "You know what? Just take some peppermint oil and put it in a spray bottle with water, and spray walls, any cracks, anywhere you saw a web. They'll skedaddle."

Okay. She could do this.

"Take whatever you need from my cabin to make it nice," Zach said. "Got extra sheets and quilts in the—well, you know…you already went through it all."

She blushed. Yes, she had.

He laughed. "It's all good."

Lord, help me.

* * *

By that evening, Megan had completely scoured and sterilized every part of the inside of the shed, and it now finally looked like a proper guest cabin. It had a toilet, sink, and shower stall, a twin bed now covered in fresh sheets and a blanket, a fan to combat the heat, and a chair. That was about it.

She was able to plug her phone in to charge, and she plugged a tiny nightlight in as well for when it got dark and she turned the lights out. She wouldn't want it to be *too* dark.

Any cooking would have to occur…where? Zach's house?

All her food was back at her campsite, probably eaten by the bear.

Zach was out somewhere on the ranch, so she texted him:

"IOU: a box of Toasted O's, two apples, and I borrowed a drinking glass. I will replace everything. Thank you!"

He texted back: *"Early to bed, late to rise?"*

Megan laughed despite herself. *"Just early to bed for right now. Exhausted. Will try to be early to rise."*

As she lay on the firm mattress, staring up at the peaked log ceiling in the tiny "practice cabin," Megan had to wonder…was this really the place God wanted her to be? She wanted to start fresh, and yet she was starting out by owing Zach Walker so much. Being indebted to a man was the wrong way to go about things.

"Help me figure this out," she whispered. "Please, Lord. I want to do Your will, but I need You to show me what that is as clearly as possible, because I feel really clueless right now."

Amen.

Chapter Five

ZACH WAITED UNTIL eight a.m. before he knocked on the guest cabin door to wake up Megan.

"Knock, knock," he called. "Rise 'n shine, sleepyhead!"

Something clattered to the wood floor inside the cabin, and he heard her gasp.

"I'm up, I'm up," she said. "Um…what time is it?"

He could tell she was trying to sound wide awake, and failing.

"Eight in the morning," he said. "I been up for three hours already, you missed all the milking."

She unlatched and opened the door to the small platform the cabin sat on. Her long hair was tangled, and she was wearing the same shirt and leggings she'd worn yesterday. But she still looked beautiful.

"Let's go make the rounds," he said. "Do you know how to ride?"

"Ride…" she repeated.

"You know," he said, and grinned at her. "A horse?"

She shook her head, and just when Zach could see that look start to come over her face again—that look she'd had when she talked about her ex-boyfriend and when she said she was useless—Zach grabbed her hand and pulled her out into the sunlight.

He was going to have to wipe those lies right outta her mind. Maybe by showing her exactly how useful an extra pair of hands could be on a ranch.

"How much time ya need?" he asked. "Being a girl, and all."

"Two minutes to brush my teeth," she said. "Wait here."

Zach grinned. Low maintenance. He hadn't been expecting that from a city girl. Even Paige took at least a half an hour to get out the door in the morning.

She reemerged with a radiant smile, minty breath, and brushed hair. "I don't know how to ride a horse, Zach. I'll just slow you d—"

"You can ride with me, then," he said. He pulled his hat down low on his head. "You'll sit in front, I'll be very gentlemanly while sitting behind you, and you'll get the fifty-cent tour of the ranch."

Megan grinned back at him. "That sounds incredible."

* * *

Megan followed Zach out to the stables behind his house, adjusting the old baseball cap he'd tossed to her to protect her face from the sun, and pulled her hair up into a makeshift ponytail.

Her third proper day in Bear Creek Saddle, and she was going to ride a horse around on a ranch! Talk about jumping into country life with both feet. Thank God she'd finally come out here. Far away from the city, far away from Todd.

She'd never felt so alive. So…*free.*

The hard-packed dirt road beneath her feet, and the freshly shorn grass around it, indicated that Zach put a lot more attention into his land than he did to his personal living quarters in terms of maintenance.

He walked next to her, his hand swinging so close to her own— it was all she could do to keep herself from holding it. That would be nice… holding his hand, walking to the stables.

What am I thinking? I barely know this guy. And she'd also just told him yesterday point-blank that they would not be having sex. Giving him mixed signals was a surefire way to ruin everything that was starting to go right for her.

"Are you sure it's cool if I stay in the guest cabin for the time being?" she asked. "I can figure something else out if you need me to. I bet you're regretting telling me I should make myself at home, huh?" Megan forced a little laugh, trying to play off her concern as a joke.

"When I say something," Zach replied, staring down at her from his impressive height, "I mean it. Stop acting all nervous around me. I don't bite, I swear." He winked, then flashed his gorgeous smile at her.

Oh wow, he winked! That was insanely cute. Megan wanted him to do it again.

"Thank you, Zach. I mean it." She glanced up at him and smiled back. "How's your nose? It looks really good today—not swollen at all anymore…"

"It's good as new…not that you didn't do a good job punching or anything."

He touched the front of his hat and nodded to her, a sweet gesture she'd never experienced before while living in Manhattan.

There just weren't many cowboys in Manhattan.

At the stables, Megan was greeted by his horse, who made a friendly sort of snuffling sound and nudged at Zach's hand when Zach reached up to touch him.

"He's beautiful," Megan said. "I was admiring this one from the hayloft last night. Does he have a name?"

"Chewbacca." He patted the horse, who then looked at her with interest.

Megan nodded. "It fits him! Perfect name. Do you call him Chewy for short?"

Zach took her hand in his, and she bit back a gasp of surprise that was twinged with delight. He held her hand with such care, it was as if a different man altogether had practically dragged her out of the woods the other day.

He knew his own strength and didn't want to use it against her. That was…nice. A welcome change.

Zach put his large hand over hers and guided her to reach up and let Chewbacca sniff her. "You bet I call him Chewy," he said, grinning. "Don't I, mister? You're a good horse. You sure are."

"He's your pet," she said, noticing the coddling voice he slipped into as he poured attention on his horse.

"Yeah, I do treat him like a pet, I know," he said, shrugging, as if he had been caught doing something wrong. "But he's a good worker horse, and he works real well with me on the ranch."

Chewy kept looking at her with those huge, brown eyes and impossibly long lashes.

"He loves it when you scratch his neck," Zach said. "Go ahead, he likes you."

"You're just saying that."

"Nah, it's true. See his ears? That's the easiest way to tell if Chewy wants attention. He points those ears forward at you like he wants to hear everything you have to say."

Huh. The horse *was* looking at her with very attentive ears. "Hi Chewbacca," she said.

Zach took her hand gently in his again, and brought her hand up to scratch the horse's neck.

"Wow," she whispered. Beneath her fingers, the horse's muscles flexed as he moved forward slightly. "I've never touched a horse before."

"You're pulling my leg," he said. "How is that possible?"

"Um…I grew up in Yonkers. Lots of apartment buildings and asphalt," she said, shrugging. "Moving to the city—I mean, Manhattan—that was an upgrade. But if you want to see more than a patch of grass you've really got to go to Central Park—or drive an hour or so upstate."

Not like north Idaho. Here, there was grass everywhere, dotted with cows grazing in the sun. So much better for her soul than seeing cars and strangers and concrete every time she turned her head.

"Don't they have cops on horseback in New York City?" Zach asked, not letting up.

"They do." How did he even know that? "But the cops are really protective of the horses. You're not allowed to touch them. I have no desire to make small talk with police anyway."

"Huh." Zach stretched his shoulder. "On the run from the law?"

Because being on the run from Todd wasn't enough? Seriously. But Zach had asked far too casually for it to be anything but a serious question.

"Sometimes people just move to another state, you know," she said, defensiveness creeping into her tone. "That happens. People do that."

Zach laughed. "They sure do. They just don't move to Bear Creek Saddle." He patted her on the back in a casual "we're cool, buddy" gesture. "I've got a ranch to show you, if you're still up for it."

"I can't wait!" Megan said. "Do we need... helmets or something?"

"Don't have any helmets. I've got some for the kids who practice riding here, but they wouldn't fit you." Zach cocked his head to the side and looked at her, a little smirk on his lips. "How about this... since you'll be sitting in front of me, if I see you start to fall—I'll just catch you, how 'bout that? I'll be your bodyguard."

"Really?" she asked.

"You betcha."

Well, that sealed the deal, then. Megan laughed. "Sounds like a plan."

If she could run off to northern Idaho and sleep in the woods, surely she could figure out how to sit on a horse while someone else took the reins, right?

There was a lot of stuff she needed to figure out if she was going to make it out here.

"Let's go," Zach said.

He stood close to her, spotting her as she attempted to mount a horse for the very first time in her life. She put her sneaker in the little foothold thingy on the saddle, but now what was she supposed to do?

"Need some help?" Zach asked. His large, calloused hands grazed her thigh, ready to give her a leg up.

Yes...

No. Wrong road—and too well-traveled. Just because she was hyper-responsive to his touch, didn't mean she was ready to lose her independence. And right now, relationships and loss of freedom were too inextricably linked for Megan to separate the two.

"I'm good," she said. "I can do it on my own."

Megan intended to do things on her own as much as she could, from now on. Forget Todd.

Whoa. For some reason, Megan had never realized just how high up horses were.

I can do this. I can do this. With a grunt, she pulled herself up onto Chewy's saddle, swinging her leg over without a hint of grace, or shame. Good.

"I did it!" Megan grinned down at Zach.

"You look good on a horse," he said, patting Chewy.

That gorgeous smile of his was so sincere, Megan almost forgot that he did this himself numerous times a day, and probably thought it was no big deal. Then he swung up and mounted the horse, sliding easily behind her on the saddle.

Their bodies were so close together... His muscular denim-clad legs pressed against her outer thighs. The unbidden sensation sent a tingle through her.

Stay cool. No tingling allowed.

His chest was only inches away from her back. If he leaned forward, he would press against her.

Zach reached his arms around her waist and grabbed hold of the reins in one hand. "Are you ready?"

"Ready as I'll ever be." Megan turned her head back to smile at him, knocking his cowboy hat askew with the rim of her baseball cap. She gasped in surprise at just how close their faces were. "Sorry!"

Zach tilted his hat back into place. Was he trying not to laugh at her? "Ma'am."

Heat crept into her cheeks and she turned back to the front. Being called "ma'am" had never made her feel good before Zach Walker had said it. But out of his mouth, it worked.

Zach squeezed his thighs around the horse, and she felt that on her legs too. *Focus on the landscape, not on the man.*

The horse walked forward, keeping at a relatively slow pace, and made his way down the grassy hill that led to the western portion of the ranch. Or maybe it was the eastern portion. Everything was so big and the mountains all looked alike, there was no way to visualize a map in her head and compare that to the scenery around her. She'd learn eventually...hopefully.

One thing she had to give Manhattan—it was laid out like a grid, and so easy to navigate even a child could do it. She had, in fact, as a child traveling in and around the city. What would it have been like to have been raised in the country, instead?

"This over here," Zach said, pointing with his free hand, "see that path that goes around the bend there? Got a really great creek running through the property."

Crick for creek. She loved his accent—so different from New York. Not as harsh-sounding. New Yorkers added extra sounds and syllables to words, and Idahoans deleted them at will.

"That's what irrigates our land," he continued, "and where we get our water from. It's fed by a mountain spring. Got some great fish in it, too, if you like fishing."

"That sounds amazing," Megan said. "I've never been fishing before."

"Never been fishing?" he asked, with the same tone of disbelief he'd had when she'd admitted she'd never touched a horse. "We gotta remedy that."

Zach held on to her around the waist a bit tighter. "Hup," he said (to the horse, presumably?). His muscular shoulders and chest pressed against her back as he shifted forward in the saddle.

It was a cozy place to be for her, on the horse with him. With Zach so close, she felt safe.

"That's nice of you," she said. "I *definitely* want to go fishing."

It was a skill she'd need to learn if she was really going to make it out here on her own. Even without cows or chickens or the whole set up they had at the ranch, if she could fish, she would always have dinner. That was important.

The horse picked up pace and Megan held tightly to the bump at the front of the saddle. "I want to buy land. I don't imagine I need much. I could fit some dairy cows, a horse and a garden in a big backyard, even. Maybe? Who should I talk to about that around here?"

"Land, huh?" Zach asked, speaking to the back of her head as they rode. "Don't take this the wrong way, New-York-Girl. I'm guessing you've never even had a vegetable garden before, much less raised livestock. If you really wanna be self-sufficient, you'll need to learn some new skills…an' then you'll know how much land ya need."

He made a good point—a backyard probably wasn't enough, even if it was big. Megan really didn't have the knowledge yet to make a smart land purchase. Did she need to buy a few acres? A few hundred acres? Who knew?

Zach knows. There was still so much to learn. If only she could borrow all of Zach's knowledge for a little while, just until she could figure out what on earth she was doing.

"You just got here," Zach said. "How do ya know you want to settle down and buy land, anyhow?"

Megan looked around her, at the vast blue sky bursting with cotton-ball clouds, to the panoramic backdrop of the mountains in the distance. Just ahead, wooded mountains covered in evergreen trees rose out of the land like icebergs—beautiful, but dangerous to those (like her) who didn't have the experience to handle them.

"I just know," she said. "This place feels right to me."

"Why my town—why Bear Creek Saddle?" He leaned in to speak, right behind her ear. "Do you have any family here? Or friends?"

You're it, Zach Walker.

"No," she said, so softly her voice was carried away on the wind. "No," she repeated, stronger. "No family or friends here. Not yet. But I saw a picture, and I knew this was meant to be my home. It's almost as if... I think God wants me to be here." She paused. "That must sound crazy to you."

"Nah," he said, his breath warm on the back of her ear. "Not crazy."

The green grass, the structure they passed with hay stacked up to the metal roof, and the cows grazing, their heads and faces nuzzled into the green grass... it was just so peaceful. So beautiful and picturesque.

She glanced back over her shoulder at him once more, but this time she was prepared for how close their faces would be.

Zach's gaze had been on the path in front of them, but now he looked at her from under the rim of his hat.

"Hi there," he said, and grinned as Chewbacca slowed to a halt. "I think Chewy wants a moment with the clover. Wasn't planning on stopping just yet, but sometimes horses know best."

"It's so incredible here," Megan said softly. "I wonder, does living here your whole life make all of this mundane? Or can you still see the beauty all around you?"

He nodded, ever so slightly. "I can see the beauty."

But he wasn't looking around him at the landscape. He was still looking into her eyes.

The rumble of an engine broke the silence.

"Hey there, Zach!" a young man yelled from a bright green John Deere tractor. He turned the vehicle off, and Chewbacca neighed.

Megan sat up straight, and looked toward the voice, her cheeks flaming hot. *Oh my goodness.*

Zach nudged the horse forward, so they were right up next to the tractor.

"How's it going, man?" Zach asked, as if they hadn't been…almost having a moment. "Eric, this is Megan."

"Glad you finally found her," Eric said with a grin, and nodded in her direction.

"Yup. Now I'm trying to keep her around for haying season."

Eric cocked his head at Zach, some unspoken communication going on between them. "Wait a minute," Eric said to Zach with amusement. "New-York-Girl from the gas station? And the woods, with the bear?"

Wait, did that mean Zach had told his friends about her…*from their first conversation?* Word really did spread fast in a small town. She turned and raised an eyebrow at him.

Zach scoffed. "Thanks, man."

Eric ignored Zach's ribbing and tipped his hat to Megan—she didn't see any wedding ring glint in the sun.

"Eric," he said in greeting. "Nice to meet you, ma'am."

Megan smiled warmly at the cowboy and waved, since they were still too far apart to shake hands. Zach's friend was a strapping young fellow too. Goodness, it must be something in that mountain spring water they drank. Were all the cowboys on this ranch handsome bachelors? She might have to get her sister up here…

"I'll stay on to help you with the hay," she said, the words coming out of her mouth before she had time to think herself out of it.

"Yeah?" Zach asked, his face breaking out into a huge grin. "You can bunk at the practice cabin all season—room and board in exchange for your help. It's physical labor, I won't lie." He laughed. "You'll be begging me for one of my world-famous backrubs, I guarantee it—"

Zach froze mid-sentence. "Sorry," he murmured.

"Why does he keep calling the guest cabin the 'practice cabin'?" she asked Eric, pushing aside the thought of Zach rubbing her sore muscles by the fireplace after long hours throwing hay (whatever that entailed).

"'Cause it was just for practice back then," Eric explained. "First little cabin we all built together to get the hang of it, and it ain't that bad if I do say so myself." He grinned at her. "If the roof leaks, blame Zach—"

"Yeah right!" Zach interrupted with wide eyes. "I *fixed* those holes the moment it rained—" He turned to her with a concerned expression—as if she might think he wasn't a good roofer or something—but she just laughed.

"That roof seems pretty solid now," she told Eric with a smile. "I slept under it last night, and I stayed dry."

Megan turned her attention back to Zach and the situation at hand. If she was really going to stay, she was going to need to gain some skills that weren't yet in her repertoire. It was doubtful the cows would be interested in her showing them how quickly she could type.

"I can do physical labor," she told him. "But I need more than just room and board in your practice cabin. I need you to teach me how to live off the land—how to be completely self-sufficient and independent. Just like you. What do you think?"

Zach rubbed his jaw thoughtfully, exchanging a meaningful glance with his friend. Eric smiled and shrugged, as if to say, "Why not?"

Zach got serious as he tilted his head to the side and looked at Megan. "We'll be working where some things can be dangerous for rookies. I don't have time for any city-girl nonsense if you want me to be your teacher. You'll have to listen to what I tell you to do, for your own safety."

Megan nodded. "I can do that."

Zach stuck out his big, strong hand to Megan, and she shook it, her fingers enveloped in his calloused palm.

He tipped his hat to her. "Then you got yourself a deal. Welcome to Bear Creek Saddle Ranch."

Chapter Six

MEGAN FINISHED WASHING the dishes from lunch while Zach was at the grocery store. She'd offered him some money—she owed him some stuff she'd borrowed from his pantry—but he'd waved her off.

"Room and board, remember?" he'd reminded her as he climbed into his truck.

In the kitchen, the phone rang abruptly, interrupting her train of thought.

What was the etiquette regarding answering a phone in someone else's house? If it was someone's personal cell phone, she'd let it go to voicemail. But maybe she was supposed to answer it, in case one of the other ranchers was calling for something urgent? None of them had her cell number yet. She ran out to the kitchen and grabbed the old-fashioned telephone. *Old-fashioned* meaning it was plugged into the wall and had a cord.

"Hello?" she asked tentatively on the third ring. "Walker residence," she added.

"Walker residence?" a man's voice repeated in disgust.

It was Todd.

Oh no.

Her breath hitched, her airway tightening.

NO. Not here, not now. Any words she wanted to say caught on her tongue and stayed entangled in her throat.

How did he even have this number? She slammed down the phone as if it would bite her ear off.

Megan's knees turned to jelly, and she slumped into the chair by the small kitchen counter Zach used as a desk. This was her fresh start. It wasn't right for her ex to invade it with an unwanted phone call. After all those messages he'd left on Zach's machine, and no response from her, Todd should've gotten the message loud and clear—*stay away*.

But of course he didn't. Because he couldn't hear her. Nothing she ever said to him got through to him without being twisted by his own paranoid, rageful worldview.

Ring. Ring. Ring.

The shrill sound jostled her nerves and she could feel tiny hairs on the back of her neck bristle, like they do on a frightened cat.

Todd would just keep calling and calling until she answered, switching phones if he had to so she couldn't block his number. She knew from experience…that's why she'd ultimately had to change her cell phone number. And she didn't want him leaving even more awful messages for Zach to hear.

The machine picked up.

Todd started to leave yet another message—

Don't, please, Todd…

She picked up the phone, clicked off the answering machine so it wouldn't record them, and didn't say anything.

Todd spoke first. "Hello?"

A frustrated sigh escaped her lips, despite her intent on keeping silent.

"Honey, it's me," he said.

This was how he operated...angry and insistent until she gave in, then sweet, apologetic, or charming.

Don't let him fool you.

"I know something's wrong, sweetie," Todd said softly into the phone. "But we can't work it out unless you talk to me. I'm here for you."

Megan sighed. There was nothing they'd be able to work out. Her ex didn't even understand the concept of letting her have space, much less the concept that she might not want to be with him anymore.

"Todd, I need some time alone. That's why I changed my cell phone number and didn't give you the new one. I'm not trying to be mean—"

"But you *are* being mean," Todd interrupted.

Just like he always did. He didn't care what she had to say.

"I can't believe you'd just leave me like this," he continued, "right when we got engaged. How do you think I felt when I came home and saw all of your belongings were gone? I tried to call you and got a message saying, 'this number is not in service.' How is that not *mean*? You ripped my heart out, Meg."

She sobered. "That must have been... awful for you," Megan said, and meant it. She couldn't imagine how it would feel if the person she loved had done to her what she'd done to Todd. "I wasn't trying to be cruel, and I'm sorry for that. But we shouldn't have been living together in the first place, Todd. It wasn't right. I-I've *changed* and I've tried to tell you but…"

Even if she didn't want to be mean, there was no nice way to break up with someone who didn't want to break up. There would always be hurt feelings, feelings of rejection—there was no way around it. She hadn't done a good job of being straightforward with Todd about it. Maybe that was a life-skill she could learn from Zach Walker.

Standing up to Todd in person was near-impossible for her—he always knew how to twist her words and manipulate and turn things around. But maybe, now, with twenty-five hundred miles between them, she could finally make Todd understand her.

"I'm sorry you feel blindsided by me leaving you," Megan said carefully. "I tried to tell you I wanted to move out, I tried to explain that we can't get married, but it's like you…don't even hear it."

Megan gripped the cord attaching the phone to the receiver on the desk. How odd that any phone still had a thick, curling cord.

"You need to come home, sweetie," Todd said. "I love you so much. I'll do anything for you. Come home to me."

Home. Home was safe, it was what she knew. There were no bears at home, no new challenges involving pitching tents and starting campfires. There were no cowboys that made her unexpectedly tingle, no guns or big barking dogs. She could forget this madness about starting over and just sink back into the familiar. Todd would probably even pay for her plane ticket home…

Megan sighed.

Todd jumped on the chance that her sigh was a good sign. "You know *I'm* the only one who loves you and wants to take care of you."

Wait. No—her ex was not the only one who loved her and wanted to take care of her. God loved her, even though she didn't deserve it. And He would take care of her. He took care of the sparrows, didn't He? It had taken her twenty-three years to recognize it. At least she could put that knowledge to good use today.

"Come home to me, where you belong," Todd continued, as if he could tell by her thoughtful silence that his argument might be getting to her. "You can't afford living on your own. Think about it, sweetie—you can't do anything on your own. How will you make it without my help?"

She sighed. And… *thank You for the reality check*—for reminding her what a piece of work her ex was.

"I can be independent. I don't need you to be okay." She almost sounded like she believed it. She'd believed it last night… How quickly his words cut her down to the bone.

Todd chuckled. "Sweetie, you haven't been independent your entire life. You can't support yourself, not even when you had that stupid job."

"You always threw a fit when I'd talk about getting a better, full-time job, telling me I wasn't making our relationship the priority," she reminded him. "I never had a *chance* to support myself."

"If it weren't for me, you'd be living on the streets," he said. "I'm the one who pays the rent, who gives you spending money. What makes you think an employer would want you? All you had to do was be a good fiancée, and you can't even get that right."

"I won't marry you," she murmured. He wouldn't be able to understand that, though.

"*With* me, you'll have a husband, children, and you'll go to law school. You'll be a successful lawyer with a life most women would kill for."

"I don't believe that anymore," she said.

Even if he put her through law school, he'd never let her become a success. He'd get her pregnant and if she stayed home with the baby, he'd hold it over her head for the rest of her life as he paid down her student loans and handed her a small "allowance" to keep her on a tight leash.

That was another reason to be grateful she wasn't with him. He'd told her she was horrible with money so often that she'd started to believe it. Her small paycheck had gone straight into *his* bank account—which she didn't have access to—so he could handle her part of the bills and rent.

Thank God he'd never gotten a hold of her mother's inheritance money once she'd become old enough to access the trust. But that was only because she'd never told him her inheritance was anything more than some jewelry and old letters. It was a lie by omission, and it had haunted her conscience. A big secret to keep, one that had almost come out more than once since she'd turned twenty-one. She hadn't yet touched the money herself, either, for fear of messing it up just like Todd warned her happened whenever she touched money. A "financial moron," he'd called her.

But maybe that wasn't even true…she'd read about something called "gaslighting," when a person lies to their partner so often and so thoroughly that she started to second guess her own abilities— even her own sanity. The article had immediately made her think of Todd.

Oh Lord, I can't do this.

The idea of hanging up on him dangled on the edge of her

imagination, but now that he held her entrenched in an argument, it seemed as insane as driving off a cliff. If he told her something, she listened. That's the way it had always been. All she could do was sink back into her seat and listen to the same baloney she'd been fed for the past four years.

Her pulse raced as if she were in a fistfight, or running for her life. Todd couldn't hurt her here, not over the phone, but her body didn't know that. And besides, he *could* hurt her. It was happening right now. He knew all the emotional buttons to push to make her double over.

"You better listen to me, Meg," Todd said. He may as well have been sitting beside her instead of across the country. "You know I'm right."

You can do this. Megan pressed her palm, trembling with agitation, against the worn wood surface of the counter. The texture of the wood spoke to her senses, grabbing her thoughts out of the tornado surrounding her, pinning them down. Down to smooth grooves. To varnish. To grain.

"Without me… you're nothing." His voice was cold. "You know that."

"I used to know that," Megan whispered. She blinked away the tears filling her eyes. "I'm trying to *un*-know that."

"You're going to 'un-know' the truth?" His voice dropped, gravelly with swallowed rage. "Who is this Walker, when you said, 'Walker residence'?" He was no longer trying to seduce her or manipulate her, like before. Now he was just angry. "You're hiding something. You little whore…*are you cheating on me?*"

"No!" she cried. Her throat tightened, and the room got a little smaller around her. "This is totally platonic."

Even as the words tumbled out of her lips, they didn't feel true—despite her newfound celibacy and Zach's gentlemanly restraint. Still… how could she be cheating on a man she was no longer in a relationship with, anyway? She shouldn't be defending herself against Todd anymore. How did he still hold so much power over her, when it was supposed to be finished?

"Liar," Todd said, as if he could read her emotion all the way from New York. "*I know you*, Megs. Know you better than anyone. Maybe I should come find you…and talk with this Walker fellow. If he knew who you really are, he'd *never want your dirty*—"

* * *

Zach opened the front door and saw his houseguest sitting at his desk. The phone was cradled to her head, her face as pale as if someone had been slowly bleeding her out.

"Are you okay?" he whispered.

Megan looked up at him and attempted a half-smile, as if to reassure him, her ear still pressed to the headset. She held up her hand, as if to say, "Hang on."

"Please," she said into the phone, her voice soft and urgent. "I don't know how you got this phone number, but it's not *my* phone number. Please don't call here again… No, I'm not going to give you my new cell phone number. It's over. We're done."

The voice on the other end of the line was loud enough Zach could hear it from across the room: something about how the man—Todd? —thought she just needed some space for a while.

"Not just awhile…I need space from *you*— permanently. It's over between us. Don't call me again. Well—I won't answer. I'm… I'm sorry."

She pulled the phone away from her ear abruptly, a look of

shock and misery on her face. Zach could hear the man's voice shouting obscenities through the headset. Without a word, Zach strode over to her and grabbed the phone from her hands.

She jumped out of his way in surprise, her body shaking, her blue-green eyes wide with unshed tears.

"This is Zach Walker," he said firmly, interrupting the man's tirade. "This is my house, and no one yells at my guests. Do not call here again." He slammed down the phone.

"I am so sorry," Megan gasped. "I never gave him your number, I swear. He must've charmed my sister into giving it to him." She trembled, holding her arms across her chest, as if to comfort herself.

"Are you okay?"

Megan shrugged and shook her head as if trying to clear it. "I'm okay. Thank you."

Zach winced. "That was him, right? Your ex? Tell me I didn't just yell at your father."

"Ha. No—that was Todd, all right. He just *thinks* he's my father." She exhaled heavily. "Same guy from the voicemail messages. I...I really am quite sorry."

"There's nothing to apologize for," Zach said. It wasn't her fault her ex was despicable.

Megan stood from the chair. "Okay," she said. She shook her head again, as if forcing the experience out of her mind by flinging it out physically. "Let's just forget that even happened. Maybe I can help you do something, like get some chores done?"

Zach sat down for the first time since he'd entered and heard Megan getting berated on the phone.

"Sure thing," he said. "I'm gonna grab a quick bite and then work in the vegetable garden a bit. I like doing it later in the day, after the sun has a chance to cool off. You wanted to learn how to grow food, right?"

But she wasn't paying him any attention. Her gaze was unfocused, her breath shaky, as if the situation had winded her.

"Do you want to talk about it?" he asked.

She shook her head forcefully. "I think I'll just—if you don't need me right now, maybe I'll just…"

"You betcha," he said, a little too fast. Maybe she needed some alone-time to process the official breaking up with her boyfriend. Either way, he didn't want to make her have to find an excuse to do it.

"Oh, who am I kidding…I'll just end up hiding under the covers." Megan laughed, as if she were joking, or trying to make him think she was. "I'm sorry—my thoughts are a bit scattered at the moment. What did you say you wanted to do?"

"Tend to the vegetable garden and get some fresh air?"

The tightness at the edge of her lips relaxed, and she clapped her hands resolutely. "Let's do it. That'll be better for me than moping, anyway."

Zach grinned. "I agree. But if you need to take some time…I understand."

"Nope. Gardening it is. I want to know this stuff—it's why I'm here."

"Sounds like you're a bit more excited about this than you are about early-morning milking."

"Tomorrow morning, I'll be up," she promised.

"Nah, you can sleep in tomorrow," he offered. "Tomorrow's Sunday. I still gotta milk the cows and feed and water all the livestock, but we do our best to take the day off as much as we can."

"That's cool," she said.

"You want to come to church with us tomorrow? You can ride with me."

Her eyes brightened.

"Sure! I've...never been to church before," she admitted. "I've been really interested in God and everything lately—I have a Bible. I've been reading blog posts and stuff. It was a big part of the reason I wanted to move."

He couldn't imagine a person never having stepped foot in a church. It had been his home away from home since he was a kid and his mama took him. He'd stopped going for a while when he was a teenager, but God drew him back.

"I think you'll like it," he said. "I hope you do. And it's a good place to get to know folks in town."

"I can't wait," she said. "Do you think we can get my car back here, though? I need my clothing. I don't know if I can wait for the tow truck guy—Joe, I mean—to come back from...wherever you said he was this week."

"Missoula. No worries. Tell you what," he said. "We can go up this evening before it gets dark and I'll hook your car up to my truck, and tow 'er back. Luggage and all."

"Thank you so much." She seemed genuinely grateful.

"It's a date, then."

"Umm..." Her face looked pink.

Man. He shouldn't have said that—not with her getting over an abusive relationship. The last thing she needed was to think he was trying to ask her on a date.

She nodded briskly and was already out of the room before he could change his words.

* * *

It was 5:30 that evening, and Megan kept eyeing her cell phone, waiting for a text from Zach to let her know when they'd be heading up to get her car.

A date, he'd said. Not really though, right? They were just going to tow her car. Alone together…in the beautiful woods…at sunset.

For a brief moment, the thought of *what should I wear* crossed her mind—but no, she had nothing to change into anyway. She'd washed her cargo pants, so that was good. Not exactly form-fitting or anything, but pretty appropriate for a trek in the woods.

Her phone buzzed.

"I just gotta change out of these muddy boots and we can go get your car," Zach's text read.

"I don't mind muddy boots, LOL," she texted in reply.

"You'd mind these—manure stinks to high heaven."

Right. She'd forgotten about that. It was true—there was definitely the odor of cow in the air. Kind of hard to miss on a cattle farm. She must've gotten used to it. Thank goodness she was getting her luggage tonight, because she wanted to have something nice to wear to church in the morning. Her first time going to church… What would it be like? Would folks be able to tell she wasn't a proper Christian?

I am a Christian. True—she didn't know much; she hadn't grown up with it, and she hadn't been to church. But she was thirsty for knowledge, and hopefully church would be the right place to get it. But even just reading the Bible all by herself had been more helpful than she ever would have imagined. It was as if every question she had, there was an answer just waiting for her within God's Word.

Lord, please be with me tonight. Help me not say anything stupid.

She ran a brush through her hair and closed up the little guest cabin.

"You all set?"

She heard his deep voice before she saw him, and it startled her so much she jumped.

"Oh! Hi Zach!"

"Didn't mean to scare ya," he said, concern creasing his brow. "It won't get dark for another couple hours, so we should be fine to go now to get your car, if you're still up for it."

"Absolutely." She squared her shoulders and smiled, hoping it would remove that look of concern in his eyes. "I'm fine," she added. "I just wasn't expecting you to meet me here. I thought we'd meet at your truck."

"Now what kind of gentleman would I be if I didn't pick you up at your abode?" Zach grinned and winked at her. *That wink!* It was really cute.

He held out his arm and she took it, walking side by side with him across the gravel. He opened his pickup truck's door for her and gave her a hand as she hopped inside. He waited until she was all buckled in before closing the door and coming around to the driver's seat.

"The bear will be gone, right?" she asked.

"I expect so," he said. "But we'll keep our eyes and ears open, and look for tracks and fresh scat, to be safe."

Tracking an animal. That would be a good skill to know.

"How can you tell bear scat from other wild animal scat?" She laughed nervously—had she ever asked a grosser question? But he seemed thrilled to answer.

"I'll show you," he said. "Different animals' poop looks

different. And you can tell whether it's new or old too. Pretty interesting stuff, if you don't mind the fact that you're staring at scat." He smiled, but kept his eyes on the trail ahead.

As they drove up the winding road deeper into the mountain, the meadows and ranch seemed impossibly far away, and once again she was alone in the middle of nowhere with Zach Walker.

But she didn't feel afraid…there was something about him that made her feel safe.

"There it is!" Megan called, pointing to her blue Eclipse.

Please don't be destroyed by a bear.

Zach parked, putting on the emergency brake, and came around to get her. She could see him checking the ground and looking around as he walked, his head on a swivel. He opened the passenger door for her and offered his hand.

"I'm thinking the bear moved on," he said.

"Thank God," she said. "How's my car? Did the bear manage to…umm…break in?"

They walked over to her car, and while there was a big dent on the side that hadn't been there before, that was about it.

"It looks like the bear didn't put too much effort into getting into your car," he said in amazement. "That's lucky."

"I'm surprised it didn't smell my herbal shampoo and things," she said.

"Maybe she did, but got scared off, or had to chase after one of her cubs. You never know."

He went to the back of his pickup truck and pulled out a big chain. "Just give me a minute, and I'll get 'er hooked up to my truck."

He got back into his pickup truck and did a tight U-turn to back his truck up to the front of her Eclipse.

What if he were to just take off and leave her there?

No. He would never do that. Why would he? More importantly, why would that thought even cross her mind?

Todd. She just was not ready to have romantic thoughts—or even quasi-dates—with anyone until she let her fear go.

There wasn't much she could do to help Zach get her car attached to his truck, but she watched with interest.

"That should do it," he said, wiping his hands, gray with metal dust from the chain, onto his jeans. "Perfect timing, too."

He gestured with his head toward the west, where the sky was pink, the clouds lit up from below with golden rays from the setting sun.

"It's beautiful," she said.

"Pink sky at night, sailors delight," Zach recited, "pink sky in the morn, sailors be warned." He shrugged. "Guess that means we'll have another beautiful day tomorrow."

"I can't wait," she said. "For a beautiful day again, I mean…and for church."

"Have you really never been?"

"It's not that I don't like God. I've actually been… getting really interested in it all. When you said you are a Christian, I thought…" She sighed and trailed off. "Never mind, it's stupid."

"What?" He asked. "I won't think it's stupid, I swear."

"I thought maybe it was a sign from God that I was on the right track, by moving here."

He smiled. "You must not run into a lot of Christians in your social circle in New York," he said. "We're actually kinda common up here."

"You're right," she said. "I was being silly. Just a coincidence."

"Look at that," he said, staring off at the sunset. "I go to church on Sundays, but I can see God here, too."

"I know what you mean." She did. How amazing God's creation was. So beautiful. So expansive.

"I'm worried I'll stand out like a sore thumb at church," she said, and covered her mouth. She hadn't meant to say that out loud. Why share all of her insecurities with him? Wasn't she trying to be an independent woman?

"Don't worry about none of that," he said, shaking his head. "You may stand out, but that's just 'cause folks can't help but notice a pretty girl."

Hopefully the setting sun would hide her heated face. Was he just saying that to be nice?

Zach cleared his throat. "Sorry. I mean…and you stand out because you're from New York, and because it's a small town. But none of that matters. You'll get to know folks here the longer you're here, and they'll get to know you."

She smiled up at him. The sounds of the insects in the woods buzzed around them, and off in the distance, the first bats of the evening began their flight. "I'm looking forward to that."

"I mean, I wouldn't suggest punching them in the nose when you first meet them, or anything like that…"

She laughed, her cheeks pinking up again. "I'll try to remember that."

"Yeah, that's a good one," he said. "If you want to make a good first impression, don't punch someone in the nose straightaway. Someone tol—"

"Told me that once." She finished the sentence with him, and he chuckled.

"Ya heard that one, huh." He took his cowboy hat off and ran his hand through his light brown strands.

The five-o'clock shadow of scruff on his face was even thicker now that it was later in the evening, and she had an urge to reach out and touch his cheek. She kept her hand at her side.

"Well, I guess we should get your car back to the ranch," he said, regret tingeing his words. "It's a pity to miss the rest of the sunset, but those mountain roads are harder to travel in the dark, especially when you're trailing something."

"I understand," she said quickly. Had he seen the way she'd nearly reached for him? Had he seen the look in her eyes?

Lord, why have you put Zach in my life?

Zach set his hat back on his head and took her hand in his. "Let's go."

She walked with him readily, and he laughed.

"What?" Did she have a bug in her hair or something?

"Jus' remembering how hard it was to get you to come out of the woods with me the last time. You're much more easygoing now."

Easygoing? If he only knew how much his very presence made her stomach flutter with butterflies.

She had no business being interested in Zach in any romantic way. So why did her hand in his feel so...right?

Chapter Seven

MEGAN STEPPED PAST Zach, who held the door open for her and for several people after her, into the warm church. Overhead fans riffled her hair but didn't generate enough of a breeze to move the thin cotton of her knee-length dress.

"Welcome!" a middle-aged woman said to her with a warm smile. "You must be Megan Moore, the girl from New York City who's stayin' at the Bear Creek Saddle Ranch."

Wow. News does spread fast in a small town. Megan glanced over at Zach, who shrugged at her.

"She's making good use of the guest cabin, Ginger," he said.

Ginger's smile widened. "I'm glad someone besides the lawn mower is finally getting good use out of your practice cabin, Zachary."

"It's nice to meet you," Megan said, sticking out her hand.

Ginger shook it enthusiastically, covering Megan's hand with her other. "You can't find a better man than the boys at that ranch," she said. "I've known Zach since he was an itty-bitty boy."

He let the large wooden door close after another person walked in, putting his hand on Megan's lower back, guiding her to one of the long wooden pews.

Zach whispered in Megan's ear. "I'm glad Ginger knows that you're staying in the guest cabin. Everyone in town will know by lunch."

"And that's a good thing?"

"You certainly don't want people thinking you're bunking under the same roof as me."

She blushed. Of course. What would Zach think of her if he'd known she used to live with Todd? That she'd done so many things in her past she wished she could wipe away?

Would it matter to him that she'd prayed for a fresh start, for forgiveness for anything she'd done wrong? Or would he just look at her and see a woman with a reputation that didn't fit into his perfect little town and perfect church?

"You sit here with the guys," he said, gesturing with his head toward Eric, Chris, and Jay. "I'll be right back in a few minutes."

"Where're you going?" she asked, but he had already wandered off toward the front of the church.

She turned to Eric quizzically. "Why did he leave so fast? Did I do something wrong?"

Eric laughed. "Of course not. But shhh, you don't want to miss this."

Chris took his cowboy hat off and set it on his knee. "Let's see if he remembers all the words this time." He chuckled.

A hush fell over the church.

Zach was in the front of the church, on the...platform? Stage? What did you call it if it was in the church? Was it a stage? Maybe a dais or something like that, something she couldn't even pronounce properly in her head because she'd only ever read the word in a book.

He had his guitar.

She knew that guitar hadn't just been for decoration—not with all those guitar picks she'd found strewn across his house. But he'd never played for her.

Zach strummed a chord on his guitar. "Please stand with me an' help me sing out some praise this morning."

Everyone stood as he started singing a popular Christian country song she'd heard on the radio. At the chorus, anyone who wasn't already singing started to join in. Wasn't there supposed to be a choir and hymns or something? But no, this church was a bit different in how they worshipped—and it was kinda fun.

Zach grinned as he closed out the first song and said, "Give the Lord a clap of praise," which got everyone clapping, and he went into the next song. She didn't know the words, but she found herself swaying and humming along, watching Zach singing and strumming his guitar with a dexterity she hadn't known he possessed.

"He… he's *good*," she whispered in Eric's ear.

"Don't tell him that, he'll get a big head," Eric joked.

But she knew that Zach would never get a big head about that. He had such an amazing voice, he sounded just like the people on the radio. She could picture him singing in front of a sold-out stadium. And yet he was content to stay in a small town where the only people to hear his amazing God-given talents all lived within the same radius of the church.

After a couple more songs, a man stepped up to the podium.

The pastor. She'd seen him talking with folks before church.

"Thank you, Mr. Walker," the pastor said.

Zach flipped his hat from his knee onto his head and climbed down the stairs at the front of the stage. After setting his guitar in the front, he strode down the aisle on the side of the church and quietly slipped in beside her on the pew.

She turned to him in awe. "I had no idea you could do that."

"I had to pretend you weren't out here, or I woulda scared myself right out of leading worship," he said softly. "But it ain't hard when I'm singing for God." He grinned at her and winked. Zach took his hat off again, setting it on his knee as Chris had done.

The pastor began his sermon, talking about God's grace and forgiveness, interspersing with Bible quotes throughout. She tried to keep up in her own Bible, but couldn't find the chapters fast enough. Zach's Bible was well-worn, with pages dog-eared, and he seemed to know exactly where to turn.

In the seat one space next to her, Chris had a smartphone out and was following along on a Bible app. She held her book in her hands, hoping the words would filter in through her skin and her ears, because she couldn't keep up visually at this point. Maybe she'd get an app on her phone, too. There was something about holding God's words in her hands, being able to touch the thin pages with tiny text that made up the huge volume.

After the sermon, everyone stood and started talking. The small room became loud and hot, yet filled with a sense of joyousness that reminded her of a family reunion.

A young woman approached, holding hands with a very tall man in a black cowboy hat. His face was stern but his eyes seemed kind, and he smiled at his wife as she introduced them both.

"I'm Allie, this is my husband, Bill."

"Hi," Megan said, sticking out her hand. The guys gathered around Bill, patting his back and peppering him with questions.

Allie laughed. "You'd think they wouldn't still be asking Bill for advice on the ranch, but I guess you can't break an old habit."

"Oh," said Megan, "is this the Bill that owned the ranch before he sold it to Zach and the guys?"

"Yup—the one and only Big Bad Bill. Live and in the flesh. You should come down and see us at Freddy's Diner sometime soon."

"I'd love to," she said. She used to eat out in Manhattan all the time, to the point that she'd actually get tired of eating out. But here, she'd become so accustomed to eating in Zach's kitchen that she forgot the diner was really the only entertainment in town.

"I'm from the East Coast, too," Allie said. "Miami. But I really love it here. Did you know that the amount of people living just in Miami-Dade County alone is way higher than the population in the *entire state* of Idaho?"

"Wow," Megan said. "That makes sense. Same with Manhattan. I wasn't really thinking about it before, but when I was driving through Idaho it was really clear there were so few people and so much land."

"Beautiful land," Allie added.

"Absolutely." Megan smiled at the other woman. Maybe they would become friends. Both coming from far away to find something small, quiet, and beautiful here in Idaho. And yet Allie had found something truly big—love. Her husband.

Megan didn't want a husband. She didn't need one. Ol' Spinster Megan, that would be her.

Zach came back around and gave Allie a kiss on the cheek.

"Are you coming to the Sadie Hawkins party at our diner on Friday?" Allie asked him.

Zach shrugged. "I wanted to, but I'd need a gal to ask me, your rules." He looked over his shoulder at Megan quickly before turning back to Allie.

Wait... what?

As if his words triggered a cue, a beautiful blonde woman bounded down the aisle, squeezing past people until she reached Zach, her eyes shining. She laughed, maybe a little too loud.

"You're so silly, Zachary. You know I've asked you."

"Good morning, Paige," Zach said politely. He had completely ignored what she just said.

So this was the Paige who was not his wife, and not his girlfriend...

"Paige, have you met Megan? She moved here from New York and is helping us out on the ranch for haying season."

Only then did Paige look over at Megan, her smile still stretched over her face, not faltering.

"I've heard all about you," Paige said. "So you're staying at Bear Creek Saddle Ranch with Zach?"

Before Megan had time to respond, Paige pushed on.

"I hope you're very comfortable there," Paige said. She said it with a smile, but her tone chilled Megan to the bone.

"Personally," the blonde woman said, "*I* wouldn't be so comfortable attending church on Sunday morning if nearly everyone in town had seen my... *sports car*"—the way she said it sounded like a dirty word—"in Zach Walker's driveway. Overnight."

Megan looked at Zach in disbelief.

"She's staying in the practice cabin," Zach interrupted. He looked calm and collected but Megan could tell from the fire in his eyes that he was furious.

"Sure." Paige's eyes narrowed. "Except no one ever stays in that cabin. It's a glorified shed."

"I cleaned it out and it is quite comfortable," Megan said. "And bless your heart for inquiring after my comfort! Zach is a wonderful host."

"And a gentleman," he growled at Paige. "As you well know by now."

Allie, who had started this conversation by asking Zach about the Sadie Hawkins party, looked increasingly uncomfortable. "Well, I think Bill and I have to —"

"I understand," Zach said. "You know what? We gotta go too, right, Megan?" He put his hand on the small of her back and led her away from Paige.

"What on earth is wrong with that girl?" Zach muttered. "We dated in high school for goodness' sake. It ain't like she owns me."

"If she thinks that we're sleeping together, the whole town probably does too," Megan whispered.

"Ginger will get the word out about the truth," Zach said. "Besides, everyone's liable to know Paige is biased in this regard. She's always been jealous of any girl who even looks at me. I need to have a talk with her."

Yikes. She did not want to be anywhere near him when he was doing that.

"Speaking of," he said, pulling her aside as they walked over to his truck, "I know Paige was rude. Terribly rude. But I don't like what you said back to her, anyways."

Her stomach flipped. "What? I just said—"

"I know what you said, I was there. But don't say, 'bless your heart' all sweet-like when what you really mean is something entirely opposite. It ain't right, 'least that's how I see it."

"So now you think you can tell me what to say and not say?" She balked. Even though she knew he was right. Responding to Paige like that had felt entirely disingenuous.

"I ain't telling you what to do," Zach said. "Just suggesting you think about it for yourself. I know for me, I'd rather someone be upfront with me. You would've been completely in the right if you'd told her that her accusation hurt your feelings and that you hoped she'd let you correct the record."

He was right. And if she'd been truthful with Paige during that awkward interaction, Megan wouldn't have walked away feeling so gross.

"I'll think about it," Megan said. "Maybe I'll talk to her another day and set things on a better path. I left too much drama in New York just to create more here in Idaho."

"She don't represent us," Zach said. "Nor this church. Don't let the one person who tried to shame you make you come away from here with a bad feeling."

He was right. Everyone had been really nice. But maybe Paige was the only one who was speaking her mind.

But was she really going to avoid the only church in town, just because there were people in it who didn't like her? No. She wasn't going to let Paige keep her from learning more about God's Word—and she certainly wasn't going to let Paige's insecurities rub off on her.

"Hey Chris," she called over her shoulder to him. "Can you

send me a link to that Bible app?"

She'd be better prepared for next week—for both the sermon, and for Paige.

* * *

Megan sifted the rich, moist soil through her fingers and patted some on top of the pumpkin seeds they were planting.

"When you buy land," Zach was saying, "dig into the ground and see what your dirt looks like. Make sure you can grow things on your land."

"I will," she said, the corner of her mouth lifting into a smile.

She couldn't wait. If only she could do it right now. But she had no clue about homesteading, and this time with Zach was her education. Her university degree wouldn't help her grow her own groceries.

But was that all her time with Zach meant to her? Education?

The afternoon sunlight glinted against his skin. Some of the tiny, rough hairs in the scruff on his cheek shined like flecks of gold. Such a handsome, rugged young man.

Her breath caught in her chest when he turned to her, catching her staring openly at him.

Zach smiled and she blushed, quickly turning her face back to the soil.

"Now just water it a bit," he said, as if he either hadn't really noticed her watching him, or didn't care.

He stood, stretching his arms above his head, and swiveled a bit to loosen his back muscles. "Here ya go." He handed her a handheld sprayer attached to an irrigation hose. "Don't swamp the dirt. You want to feed thirsty plants, not drown them."

Right.

"Do you water them every day?" she asked, and turned on the hose. The water was freezing, and she squeaked in surprise as some splashed her hands.

"We've got irrigation systems set up for the grass and alfalfa crops, but for my own vegetable garden, I do it by hand. Don't need to, I could just snake a hose with holes in it around the garden an' have it go on automatically with a timer—"

"That's a great idea!" she interrupted.

"Yeah, I mean—it's great if you're going away for the weekend or something, but when I water by hand I keep a better eye on my plants. See who's doing well and who needs some help. If you get some sorta mold or disease on a plant, it'll spread to the whole garden if you don't take care of it right quick."

She nodded, absorbing the information as readily as the soil absorbed the water.

"So…" he said, adjusting his hat down a bit, "ya haven't said much about church. What did you think?" He paused. "You don't have to talk 'bout it if you don't want to."

What *did* she think?

It had been different than what she'd expected, but not in a bad way. She hadn't really known what exactly to expect. No one was speaking in tongues or handling snakes or fainting in the aisles.

And it certainly wasn't like the televangelists she'd seen on TV.

"Do you think everyone there thought we were…you know…" she asked. For some reason she couldn't say the words. *Sleeping together.*

"Nah," Zach said quickly. "People keep themselves to themselves. Ain't none of their business anyways. But the truth has a way of coming out, so don't worry about it."

The truth would come out. What would happen when he learned the truth about her past with Todd? That while she had amended her ways since finding Jesus, she hadn't been nearly as proper in the past?

An image of herself lying in Todd's bed alone, after he'd finished with her, flashed before her mind's eye. She'd been miserable. She wasn't going to let momentary lust, or the desire to keep a man's attention, keep her from making the same mistake again. The next man she made love with—

Could she even call what she and Todd had done "making love"?

—well, that man would have to be her husband.

Lord, forgive me, she prayed. Same prayer she'd been saying over and over since she became a Christian.

"I didn't mean to say that," Zach said, interrupting her thoughts.

"Say what?"

"To say, 'don't worry about it,' like it was no big deal to you," he explained. "I know how important a reputation is, 'specially when you're new in town. But I meant…Ginger will let folks know our sleeping arrangement, if anyone brings it up, that is. Most importantly, God knows the truth of it."

"You're right," Megan said.

Zach took the hose from her, shutting off the flow of water. "You're drowning 'em."

"Sorry."

He chuckled and shook his head. "My fault, talking your ear off."

"I like it."

"Me too." He stepped in toward her, his thumb grazing her face gently. "It's a freckle…I thought it was a bit of dirt."

"My freckles look like dirt to you?" she laughed.

"Maybe I just wanted to see you up close."

"Hmmm," she teased, lifting her face up to look at him just as closely. "I think you really do have actual dirt on your face." Megan wiped a fleck from his cheek, her fingers tingling from the sandpaper hairs.

Their lips were so close…she glanced from his green eyes to his lips. Would he close that gap between them, and kiss her?

"I like your freckles," he murmured.

"Just sun damage, really…"

"Maybe you should get a hat." Zach took his cowboy hat off and set it on her head. "Looks good on you, city-girl."

He pulled her closer to him and tilted the hat back. Her heart raced in anticipation of his kiss.

But—she shouldn't be doing this. "Wait," she said.

He pulled back immediately, dropping his arms from her waist.

How could she even consider getting intimate—even if they would stop at just a kiss—after everything she'd just escaped in New York City? There was no way she could bring herself to trust a man again so soon with her body, much less her heart.

This wasn't the time for her to get into a relationship. She had come to Idaho to be an independent woman.

"I'm sorry," she whispered. Megan took the cowboy hat off and handed it back to Zach. "It's not personal."

Except it was. There was something about Zach, specifically, that she was way too attracted to—something about him as a man that called to her. That made her want to forget all of her resolutions on the long car ride cross-country to set out all on her own.

"You don't have to apologize," he said. "I'm the one should be saying sorry. I'm lucky you didn't punch me in the nose again."

Megan laughed, and he grinned.

She could feel another person's presence before she saw her approaching.

"Good morning Zach," Paige said calmly. "Good morning, Megan."

Zach turned his head to their visitor in surprise.

"Paige," he said, "Didn't even hear ya coming up."

"You were…otherwise occupied," she said. "Not that it matters."

Her eyes were puffy and swollen, as if she'd been crying.

"Are you okay?" Megan asked, wiping the dirt from her hands onto her jeans. Surely Paige had seen the two of them flirting with each other…and nearly kissing. "Is everything all right?"

Paige started to nod, but then shook her head. Her eyes welled with tears. "I wanted to apologize for yesterday," she said. Her voice was nearly a whisper. "It wasn't my place to be so rude and judgy."

Megan looked over at Zach. His jaw was practically on the ground in the seeds. He adjusted his hat, tilting the brim down.

"That's mighty kind of you, Paige." He cleared his throat. "Just so you know, Megan really is staying in the guest cabin."

"I can show you," Megan jumped in, "if you want. I'm actually kind of proud of what I've done with the place."

"Okay," Paige said. "But I don't need to see it. I believe you… and even if you were staying with Zach, I suppose it's not my business anymore."

Megan smiled wistfully. She was right—Zach was no longer

Paige's boyfriend, but she knew that caring for someone was a habit that died hard. She couldn't blame Paige for having feelings for him. He was the best man she'd ever met, in fact. If she were Paige, she wouldn't give up on him so easily either.

So why was Megan pushing him away so hard now?

"Come on," Megan said, forcibly adding some cheer to her voice. "It looks quite nice and homey now," she added. "You'd never guess it used to be a shed."

Paige smiled and nodded, and they walked to the across the half an acre or so to get to the cabin.

"I see you put in air-conditioning!" Paige said, looking impressed at the box hanging out the tiny window.

"Yeah, that window unit easily cools the entire place, well— since it's just 160 square feet. I set it to low when I'm gone, and crank it up when I get in here." She was rambling in her nervousness. Would Paige notice?

Megan opened the door. But maybe it wasn't wise to show Paige that she kept it unlocked.

Don't be silly. Paige came here to apologize.

It wasn't as if Megan were still living in the city, and had been followed home by a stranger. How long would it take her to stop looking over her shoulder at every turn?

"Wow!" Paige's eyes widened as she saw the interior. "You did a really good job cleaning it."

"Yeah," Megan said, smiling. "I mean, thank you."

"You could be a professional," Paige added. "People would pay you good money to transform their spaces like this."

"You should see what I did with Zach's house," Megan said. "Not to brag."

"He actually let you clean that junk-pile-upon-junk-pile of his?"

"Um... I didn't exactly ask," Megan admitted. "But he was really nice about it and didn't get mad."

"He's a good guy." Paige's gaze appeared to be fixed on some point in the distance, lost in thought. "He's never going to marry me, is he..."

Oh no. "I don't know how to answer that," Megan said quietly.

"We were such a great couple, all through school—middle school... High school... Even when I left to get my bachelor's degree in Washington, whenever I came home, we would pick up just where we left off. But for the past few years... It's like..." Her thought drifted off.

"Like you're growing apart?" Megan prodded.

"No," Paige said. "I'd be perfect for him, and he knows it. He's perfect for me. But he's not drawn to me. He doesn't love me back, and I've been trying to hide that fact from myself for a while now."

"I'm so sorry..."

"It's not your fault," Paige interrupted. "You coming here just made it clear to me, that's all. I suppose I should thank you. Better for me to know it's over now, before I waste more years of my life trying to get him to settle down."

"You deserve someone who loves you back as much as you love him," Megan said firmly.

Paige walked over to the small wooden chair. "May I sit?"

Megan nodded and gestured with her head.

Paige sat heavily. "I bet if you painted the inside of this cabin a nice light color, maybe pale yellow," Paige said dreamily, "it would really open up the inside and make it seem larger. Maybe put some mirrors up."

"That's a good idea," Megan said. Though she wasn't planning on staying in the guest cabin that long. At some point, she'd be able to move to her own land, to her own cabin. And start her own life.

But she'd miss seeing Zach every day. Miss being just a "hop, skip, and a jump" away from his home, and him.

"You should be with him," Paige said. "If he wants you. I give my blessing."

"Thank you." Megan paused, unsure if she should tell Paige the truth. "I'm not in a position to start dating anyone, though."

"You have a husband?" she asked. "Boyfriend?"

"Ex-boyfriend," Megan said. "And that was enough of a bad experience for me to not want another boyfriend ever again."

Paige nodded. "Zach will probably just ask you to marry him, then, and skip right over the dating part. He's been wanting a wife and some little ones for a while now."

Wait—what?

"Don't look so scared." Paige laughed. "God knows I'd jump at the chance, if it were me."

If Zach was really looking to start a family...then why was he about to kiss her out in the vegetable garden?

What would she do if Zach was looking at her as a possible wife?

Run.

No, wait, a quiet voice whispered inside her. *Wait...and see.*

Chapter Eight

ZACH LOOKED OVER at Megan sitting in the passenger seat of his pickup truck. She looked beautiful—she always looked beautiful, but this evening she'd put on one of her sundresses and some sandals and her hair looked like a commercial for shampoo. It was cute that she had chosen to dress up a bit to meet his mom.

"Are you sure it's okay you're bringing me to dinner at your mom's house?" Megan asked.

"Sure I'm sure," he said. "Mom's been asking to meet you for two weeks now."

"I feel bad she's going through all the trouble of cooking."

"She loves to feed people."

That was an understatement. His mom always cooked way too much food, and he was always happy to take home leftovers. He'd stopped bringing Paige over for Sunday dinners at his mom's house ages ago, and his mom still asked about her. He had a feeling Paige was visiting his mom still, which he couldn't blame her for... After all, she'd grown up knowing his mother really well. And just because

Zach wasn't with her anymore, didn't mean he had a right to take away her friendship with his mother. But…it did make for some awkward dinner conversations.

Especially now that he was ready to settle down and get married.

What would his mom think of Megan? She was the exact opposite of Paige. But even though Paige seemed perfect for him on paper, Megan was perfect for him in real life. He wanted to be with her all the time. He couldn't stop thinking about her. His first thought when he woke up was wondering if Megan was also awake. And when he said his morning prayers, lately he'd been praying for her heart to soften toward him.

If it was God's will, of course. *Is it Your will?*

His mom greeted them on the porch as he drove up, idling onto the gravel drive. As Megan started to take off her seatbelt and open the truck door, Zach had to run to get around to the other side fast enough to help her out. She never seemed to want to wait for him to get the door for her.

But he loved offering her a hand. She took his hand with a smile and looked up to the gray, weathered boards of the porch on the house he grew up in.

"Mrs. Walker," Megan said warmly, "I'm so glad to finally get a chance to spend some time with you."

"And here I was, about to say the same thing!" his mom said with a smile.

"I love your birdfeeder," Megan added, gesturing to the old birdfeeder hanging from a tree branch in front of the house, half filled with seeds. "What a great idea!"

"It's nice to feed birds," Zach agreed. "But the downside is getting bird poop on your car if you park near it."

His mom laughed and swatted him. "It's worth it for their pretty little bird songs, and you know it. Now come on in, come on in—I've got food in the oven and I bet you're starving."

"I'm always starving, mom," he said, and wrapped his arm around her shoulder, kissing the top of her head. She'd used the same hairspray for as long as he could remember, and the scent of it reminded him of home. That and the smell of meatloaf cooking in the oven, of course.

Megan followed them in, her gaze dancing around the place with apparent interest. "Is this where you grew up, Zach?"

"Born an' raised."

His mom bustled into the kitchen and donned oven mitts— red-and-white ones that looked like roosters. "You two go sit down and get comfortable," she said, "and I'll bring dinner out."

Megan set her purse down and ignored his mom's command, knocking on the doorframe (though there was no door) into the kitchen. "Is there anything I can do to help?" Megan asked. "Let me set the table."

"Oh, that's already done," his mom said. "Maybe you could bring in this pitcher of lemonade to the table. I just made it fresh myself."

Zach took the large pitcher from Megan as she came into the dining room, condensation glistening on the outside of it. Before setting it down, he poured himself a large glass and gestured toward her cup.

"Please," she said.

Zach poured a glass for his mom, who came in with a big plate of pot roast and set it on the center of the table

"Hang on, I gotta get the potatoes an' veggies."

Zach's mouth watered. Nothing could beat his mom's cooking, and he was ready to dig into that pot roast. As soon as his mom sat down, he put his hand out for her to grasp so they could get started.

"Zach, honey," his mom said, "why don't you say grace."

"Lord, thank You for this food. Please bless it to our bodies. Thank You for our family and friends and the opportunity for Megan and my mom to get to know each other. I pray she loves her as much as I do." Zach held his breath in shock. Had he just said that out loud? Maybe Megan would think he meant he loved his mom, and hoped Megan loved her as much… He cleared his throat. "We thank You, Lord, and we pray in Jesus' name, amen."

"Amen," they said in unison.

Zach's mom dished him out a big serving first, then served Megan, and last of all herself, as usual. Whenever he tried serving her first, she'd prompt him to serve a guest or take as much as he wanted first—it was just her way. Back when he was a little kid, sometimes she wouldn't even sit down for the whole meal until the very end. Before his dad left.

Zach was never going to be anything like his father. He would never leave his family, leave his child and wife all on their own. He had to do it right. He had to break that chain and raise his kids—his future kids—the way he himself wished he'd been raised.

"This is delicious," Megan exclaimed. "What's your secret?"

"I just use a slow cooker," his mom said, giggling as if she'd been caught doing something lazy. "In the morning, you put the meat in, throw in the potatoes an' cover the whole thing with a bottle of barbecue sauce, and eight hours later you got yourself a mighty fine meal."

"That's amazing. Thank you so much for cooking for us," Megan said.

His mom smiled. She looked happy. But would Megan ever replace Paige in his mom's mind? As far as his mom was concerned, he and Paige were meant to be together.

"So," his mom said. "Tell me all about New York City. Is it like on TV?"

Megan's smile fell from her face. His mom probably didn't realize just how bad her situation in New York City had been… or the many bad memories the place held for her.

"Mom—she didn't come all the way to Idaho to talk about New York," he interrupted.

"It's okay, Zach," Megan said. "There're a lot of amazing things about New York City, lots of culture, museums, skyscrapers. Lots of people from all over the world, all gathered in one place. It has more people than the whole state of Idaho."

"Wow," his mom said. "Sounds crowded."

"It is," Megan agreed. "Some people love that, but…it just wasn't for me."

"How did you pick Idaho?" his mom asked. "No one picks Idaho."

At that, Megan smirked. "You know, my sister asked me the same thing," Megan said, and a smile returned.

Seemed as if she liked talking about Idaho.

Megan took a bite of potatoes, then pressed her finger against her lips, as if to remind herself to finish chewing before she spoke. "I saw a picture—a photo—of the mountains and plains right here in Bear Creek Saddle, believe it or not. It was just so beautiful, and open. It seemed like a really great place to escape to."

Megan looked down at her lap.

Zach caught that word—*escape*. Had his mom noticed?

"What were you escaping from?" his mom asked. She said the words casually, as he often did himself when he knew it might be an important question and didn't want to influence the answer one way or the other.

Megan shook her head. "Just…New York." She sat for a second, her fork halfway between her plate and her mouth, before setting the fork down again. "Actually, to be honest, Mrs. Walker, I had to make sure I left my ex-boyfriend very far behind. It was the only way I was going to start over."

"I see," his mother murmured.

Mom looked at him briefly across the table. Zach nodded nearly imperceptibly. It was her way of asking him if he knew what Megan was talking about.

If only Megan could understand that not all relationships would be like the one she had with Todd. That he, Zach Walker, would never try to control her every move, keep her on a tight leash, debase her, or yell at her the way her ex did. He would *never*.

But even if Zach could help her, moving past her relationship with her ex was something she needed God's help for. It wasn't something that Zach could do for her, even though he wished he could. He wished he could take her hand and that all thoughts of her history with Todd could vanish from her mind and no longer cause her any pain.

Would she ever be ready for a relationship again? And if she was, would she even want that relationship to be with Zach?

***

After dinner, Zach and Megan stood at the sink, washing dishes, despite his mother's protests that she would take care of it later.

"Your mother is lovely," Megan said. "I can see how you've grown up to be such a good guy."

"Thanks," Zach said. "I give her a lot of credit. God knows my dad had nothing to do with it." He couldn't keep the scowl off his face.

"And your mom never found anyone else?"

Zach started to answer—no, his mother never had found another man... But the faraway look on Megan's face as she dried a spoon gave him pause.

Was she thinking about her own situation?

"You know," Zach said softly, "my mom loved my dad, but he wasn't good for her. When he left, it really hurt her. I don't think she's ever gotten over that. She's been alone the past twenty years, and may even be alone for the rest of her life, because she's still waiting on my father to come to his senses and come back. But that ain't gonna happen."

"She seems happy enough," Megan said.

"I guess so. She's got God, and she's got me. I think that helps, having a kid."

"It would be hard to retire with no children or grandchildren," Megan whispered.

He could barely hear her over the rush of water from the faucet, but he was afraid if he turned it off it would break the spell. He handed her a clean dish to dry, and she took it from him with a shaky hand.

"I figure I'll just be Ol' Spinster Megan," she said, and she forced a laugh. "But maybe that's not as appealing as it sounds."

"I really want to get married someday," Zach said. "Actually, not someday. Soon. I want to have kids of my own. Ain't no reason I shouldn't settle down, especially now that I've got the ranch going so well."

"I can think of a reason you shouldn't settle down now," Megan said, turning to him. "You haven't found someone to marry yet."

He hadn't?

Yes, I have found someone. You.

But he couldn't tell her that. She wouldn't believe him. It'd only been less than a month since she'd arrived. That wasn't enough time to decide if she was his soulmate, right?

"I don't think you necessarily have to be head over heels in love, or have known someone forever, to know there's a real spark and that you want to be with them." Zach tore his glance away from her and scrubbed a spot on the plate the meat was on. "I think sometimes you just know that you want to marry somebody, and I've never had that feeling before. Until…" He handed her the dish to dry. "Until you."

"What are you talking about?"

"I really like you, Megan. I care about you. We have some sorta chemistry together I've never felt with any other girl. I've been praying for a wife, and God put you here." He paused, taking a breath. "I think maybe we should get married."

The dish dropped from her hand, shattering as the ceramic hit the tile floor.

Megan jumped back with a gasp. "I'm so sorry!"

"What was that?" his mom called from the living room.

"Just the dish, Mom—don't come in here, I don't want you to get cut. I'll take care of it."

"Broom's hangin' in the pantry door," she yelled back. "Unless it's leaning against it."

But Zach already had the broom in hand. He swept the broken pieces of yellow painted ceramic onto one of the tiles, his ears hot. What was he thinking, asking her to marry him like that? He hadn't even tried to butter her up first, to soften the blow of such an outrageous request.

"I'm sorry," Megan said again.

"Don't worry about it," Zach said, "I've dropped a million dishes. Mom just buys new ones whenever she sees a yard sale. That's why none of the dishes match."

"I didn't mean about the dishes," Megan said. "I mean—I *am* sorry about the dish, of course—"

"Don't worry about it," Zach interrupted. "I understand. Of course I understand. You just got out of a terrible relationship—"

"I like you," Megan said suddenly. "And I know what you mean about chemistry."

She took the dishrag from his hand and dried her own, then threw it over her shoulder and took the broom from him. She swept rapidly as she spoke, her words coming in a staccato rhythm, so fast that he couldn't tell if it was because she'd memorized her speech or if it was just everything she'd been thinking suddenly coming out superfast.

"Here's how it is," Megan was saying. "I need to be independent. That's why I came to Idaho. Had to get away from Todd, from the relationship, from him. From men. Not all men, of course. You're a good guy. I really like you. I think I've said that before, but it bears saying again. I like you. But I don't intend to marry—not just you, *anyone*. Does that make me a bad person? I just don't want to get married. At least, I thought I didn't. But then when you say things like that, when you say you want to marry me—it's all so crazy. And I have to wonder, *is* it so crazy? If I find a guy who's kind, attractive, and isn't going to abuse me, is it so wrong to just want to get married and be safe and happy?"

She slowed down and leaned on the broom, finally looking at him. "I've never been as happy as I've been since I met you," she whispered. "Becoming closer to God has a lot to do with it, I know that. And maybe that's the entire reason I'm so happy. But you're a part of it, I can feel it. It's just..."

Zach didn't speak for fear of interrupting her train of thought.

"I don't know. I have to pray on it."

Zach nodded. His hand went up to where his hat normally sat— he wasn't wearing it, so he just dropped his arm again. "I get it. Of course. I didn't mean to rush you or nothing, make you make a decision you'd regret. But if you do actually intend to think on it... You have my word that I would never hurt you, Megan. And I wouldn't let anyone else hurt you either. You'd still be your own woman, just as I'd still be my own man. But we would work as a team, together."

His mother walked into the kitchen, surveying the intense scene.

"I'm so sorry, Mrs. Walker," Megan said. "I'll replace the plate for you as soon as I can."

His mom shrugged and smiled. "You should tell that to Eric." She laughed. "I don't know how many plates that boy has broken. And I know Chris and Jay have broken their fair share in their time, too."

"Most of those dishes happened when we were going through puberty," Zach interjected. "Eric shot up three inches overnight one day and had no idea where his arms and fingers ended anymore." He laughed, willing the tension in the air to dissipate like steam from a kettle. "Same happened to me one summer."

His mom shook her head, smiling. "Well, I clearly interrupted *something*. Hopefully it wasn't all about the plate, because a broken plate should never cause that much drama." Mom stopped in the doorway and turned her head back to look at Megan again. "I just wanted to let you know I had such a lovely time tonight, and Megan—you're welcome back any time."

Zach looked over toward Megan. Her eyes welled up with tears, but she blinked them back.

"That's so kind of you, Mrs. Walker. Thank you."

As his mom walked out of the kitchen, Zach wrapped his arm around Megan, wanting to offer comfort for whatever was causing those tears in her eyes. She curled in to his chest, pressed her forehead against his shirt, and took a long, shaky breath.

When she looked up at him, her tears were gone.

"She reminds me of my mother a little…I still miss her," she said. "Thank you. You're really good at hugging."

She didn't get it. It wasn't just that he was a good hugger. It was that he wanted to hug *her*, specifically. And not for reasons of the flesh, either… as nice as it was to feel her body pressed against his. He wanted to comfort her, to be her rock, her shoulder to cry on.

He wanted to be there for her. He wanted to be there for her in a way that his father was not there for his mother.

There had to be a reason God had put her into his life. Even if she wouldn't marry him, wouldn't start a family with him, Zach intended to stick around Megan Moore for as long as she'd let him.

* * *

Megan pulled her hair out of her face and looked out at the rolling green pasture dotted with cows. They were enjoying grazing in the afternoon sun. She still needed to check on the three rows of corn she was helping Zach grow in his yard, and make sure the chickens were all set for the evening.

Zach rode his horse along the east fence, his beige cowboy hat shielding his face from her. She smiled at the sight of him. *He looks so good on that horse...* His broad shoulders and well-worn T-shirt looked better than any man in a business suit would ever look to her.

As if he could feel her watching him, he glanced up and waved. She waved back, and he rode up to her.

"How's it going?" he asked, the golden sunlight behind him silhouetting his frame.

She reached up and gently touched the spot between Chewy's eyes that the horse seemed to love having rubbed. The horse nuzzled against her hand, pushing into it.

"I'm almost done for the day," she said. "How about you?"

Zach dismounted, then patted Chewy on his flank. "You know everyone in town's gonna be at the diner for the Harvest celebration party tonight," he said casually.

Too casually? He had a way of doing that sometimes.

"I heard something about that," Megan said. Was he trying to ask her out? Why do it so last-minute?

"I really wanted to go to show my support...I'll probably just show up either way..." he said.

"Sounds fun. Did you... want to go alone? Or are you telling me because you want company?"

Zach grinned broadly. "Are you asking me on a date, Miss

Megan Moore? Because if you are, then I will absolutely take you up on it. Allie made me promise I wouldn't break her Sadie Hawkins rule. The girls are supposed to ask the guy, something like that."

Oh, that grin of his. She'd walked right into his plan. Megan laughed. "Okay, I guess I just asked you out. But I'm asking you to go to a diner with me for a party, not to get married, got it?"

Zach nodded. "I'll take what I can get." He took Chewy's reins and started walking him back to the stables. "Pick you up in an hour?" he asked over his shoulder.

"Sounds good." She had to hurry if she wanted to finish her chores and get a shower in before the party. Before… their date.

Was she crazy, to agree to a date with a man who had literally just told her he wanted to marry her, even though they weren't in love? Wasn't that just leading him on?

Or worse… perhaps she was leading *herself* on. Because the fact remained that she really liked Zach. Not only was she attracted to his good looks, but also she couldn't help but be attracted to his kindness and generosity of spirit.

The butterflies in her stomach at the thought of going to a party with Zach shouldn't have surprised her, but they did. How could she let herself start falling for a guy when she still had the bad taste of Todd's memory to deal with?

Todd wasn't the one. But what if Zach is?

She didn't pause to examine the fleeting thought. She had chickens to attend to, and a date to prepare for.

As she hiked over to the chicken coop, her mind raced.

If this is Your will, Lord, please show me. Please make it clear to me, because I don't know which way is up or which way is down anymore. I need

Your guidance... Help me figure out my own feelings. I don't want to rebound into a relationship.

Her mind calmed, the butterflies rested. A new thought occurred to her:

I also don't want to actively avoid a specific relationship if that's what God has in store for me.

Well, that was progress at least. She hadn't even realized herself that she no longer wanted to actively avoid a relationship with Zach, not until she prayed about it.

Thank you, God. Just please... Please don't let him break my heart.

* * *

Freddy's Diner—named after Big Bad Bill's late uncle, according to Zach—was hopping. Little white Christmas lights were strung all around the outside of the diner, and along the post-and-rail fence surrounding the gravel parking lot—never mind that it was nowhere near Christmastime yet. But it looked beautiful in the dark night.

Megan took Zach's proffered arm as they entered, and everyone they passed waved and said hello, or clapped him on the back. Folks looked friendly enough, that was for sure. She wasn't getting the stink-eye as she'd feared she might—Ginger must've spread the word that she wasn't staying in Zach's house the way Paige had assumed.

Zach looked really good—he definitely cleaned up well. His muddy, stinky work boots were replaced with clean, fancy-type boots that were definitely more for show than for anything useful on the ranch. He'd told her he kept at least one pair of boots free of manure all the time, just in case.

With the warmth of his sturdy hand on the small of her back, Zach guided her toward a booth near the platform and small dance floor in the back of the diner.

"Do you want to sit just the two of us," Zach asked, "or do you want to sit with the other guys?"

"Whatever you want," she said. Though really, Megan wanted to do both—she definitely wanted to be just with him, because then they could spend more time getting to know each other. But she also was worried she'd get pulled up into something she wasn't ready for—

Like marriage?

Don't be silly. She tamped the thought down.

It wasn't as if sitting alone at the diner together in the middle of a crowded party was going to lead to them eloping.

Eric and Chris were standing by a booth and caught their eye, waving her and Zach over to them. *Well, that solves that.*

Maybe this was God answering her prayer by showing her clearly that she needed to keep it friendly.

"You guys make a very cute couple," Eric said.

"Subtle." Zach laughed.

Eric shrugged and grinned. "What? I call it how I see it."

Okay… So now what was God trying to tell her?

Lord, please be really *specific with me. I'm not good at interpreting subtleties.* She smiled at her own internal prayer and shook her head.

Allie, who owned Freddy's Diner with her husband, Bill, waved at them from across the diner and made her way toward them. It was taking her forever, though, because everyone was stopping her to say how much they were enjoying themselves. Everyone was eating, and there were a ton of people eating fries, celebrating their new deep fryer.

"Free fries for every couple," Allie said, handing the two of them a basket of golden, crispy fries glinting with salt.

Megan's mouth watered. The food smelled divine.

"Zach, you're going to play for us, right?" Allie asked hopefully.

Zach glanced at Megan. "I was kinda hoping to spend some time with Megan—" he started to say.

"I would love to hear you play here," Megan interrupted. She'd heard him play his guitar at church, and it was amazing. She'd be interested to see how he sang when he was letting his hair down a bit, so to speak.

"Well, I did bring my guitar in the truck, just in case you happened to ask," Zach admitted, causing the guys to erupt into raucous laughter.

"Of course you did." Chris laughed. "What happened to our shy Zachary?"

Zach shrugged and grinned at Megan. "The lady gets what the lady wants."

Megan smiled up at him. She could get used to that.

Fifteen minutes later, Allie stepped up onto the platform with Bill.

"Thank you so much for coming out tonight," Allie was saying. Bill looked so tall next to her, his black hat pushed down low on his head, his arm around her waist. He didn't seem to talk much— looked like Allie was the talker. That was good. Every couple needed to balance each other out, right?

Does Zach balance me out? Did she balance out Zach?

City girl and country boy. *Maybe opposites do attract.*

After announcements about bingo night and kids eating free on

Tuesdays or something, Allie gestured to her husband, and handed him the mic.

"And now we'd like to welcome our favorite—and only—local country star, a man I've known and respected since he came to work on my ranch when he was a boy. Put your hands together for our own Zach Walker, folks."

Everyone cheered and clapped as Zach took the stage, his wooden guitar in hand. The tips of his ears were pink, something Megan had come to recognize as a sign that he was feeling self-conscious. It was super cute. If she hadn't seen the pink on the tips of his ears, she wouldn't have been able to tell, though.

He tipped his hat at everyone and grinned. "Mighty kind of y'all."

He put the guitar strap around his neck, strummed a few chords, and got right into it—singing an old favorite, "Hallelujah."

His voice was incredible. People around her were singing along, pretty easy to do when the chorus was just one word, really—but Zach's voice still rang out, clear as a bell on the microphone.

The words of the song made her wonder.... What did the song mean, when it talked about some woman sitting someone down in the kitchen and shaving their hair? Was it about the prodigal son returning home, and needing to get back down to basics? Was it a kidnapping scenario? She'd never actually thought about the lyrics before, but seeing Zach sing them, it made her wonder.

"Hallelujah... Hallelujah ..." Megan sang along as the chorus resumed, smiling up at him. When he hit the final chord, he looked at her directly and winked.

Zach Walker, that wink of yours... She liked it. Maybe she liked it a little too much.

Zach launched into some more upbeat country songs, and people moved their feet to the rhythm.

"There's a dance floor, folks," he said with a smile. "Go ahead and use it, that's what it's there for."

Eric stepped onto the varnished square of wooden planks by the platform and waved her, Chris, and Jay over to get the crowd going. They weren't really dancing, per se, more like clapping and moving exuberantly to Zach's cover songs…but it sure was fun.

This is the life. Nothing could ruin the freedom she felt in Idaho.

A shiver ran down her spine and she shook her head as if to fling the bad thought away—

She hadn't heard from Todd in weeks.

And that wasn't like him. He never gave up so easily.

Don't think about him. Forget it. Focus on the good.

What was he up to?

Lord, keep me safe from him.

Chapter Nine

ZACH WIPED THE sweat off his brow with the back of his hand, and took a sip of water from the plastic jug he kept in the shade of the barn.

"How is it only 10 a.m.?" he asked in amazement. "I was sure it was near lunchtime."

Eric jumped down from the bales of hay they'd been stacking and grabbed a hay bale from the back of the trailer. He carried it with ease—and Zach knew from experience those things weighed eighty pounds easy. Eric lifted it like it was an empty box; the result of years of hard work on the ranch.

"Ain't time for lunch," Eric said brusquely, and bucked the hay bale up into the stack. "Sun's not even overhead yet." Without waiting for a response from Zach, Eric looked back into the stacks, and turned the bale so it neatly stacked against the others.

Since when was Eric not hungry?

"Don't work yourself to death," Zach said with a laugh.

"If you pulled your weight this morning I wouldn't have to," he shot back.

Zach gritted his teeth and willed himself to be slow to anger. This wasn't Eric's usual style. Something had to be bugging him.

Zach hefted a bale of hay and threw it right next to Eric, who quickly finessed it into place.

"She's good at the raking and riding the baler," Zach said. Because this had to be about Megan, right? That's the only thing that was different. "But she's a tiny thing and can't throw hay like you or me. Ain't her fault. Most work she's ever done before involved typing, maybe cleaning."

Eric sighed. "This ain't about the girl. She's doing good."

Oh.

"Okay, brother—what did I do to ya then? You've been spitting bullets all day."

Eric jumped down from the haystack and grabbed the plastic water jug for himself, taking a deep swig. They shared germs, didn't matter.

"It's not you, either, Zach." Eric looked over at him with a grim smile, as if he were trying to smile like normal, and failing.

"Is your mama all right?" Zach held his breath waiting for the response. Eric's mom had been in remission from breast cancer for going on six years now—what if that had changed?

Eric shook his head. "She's good, thank God. Just got some bad news of my own, that's all."

Zach looked at his best friend—a sturdy, healthy young man. Built like a horse and worked even harder than one. He didn't look sickly. Definitely didn't appear injured. "What's going on?"

"I heard back from my doctor," Eric said slowly. "Turns out..." He exhaled heavily. "It's crazy to even say this, man—but...I can't have kids."

What?

"Wait…" Zach said. He felt like he was interrupting, but Eric had stopped talking. So he spoke into the heavy silence. "What do you mean?"

"Long story short, one of those injuries I got playing football left behind scar tissue. I had no idea anything was wrong 'cause everything's… in working order." Eric cleared his throat. "Everything looked normal, seems *normal*. I thought everything was fine. That was over ten years ago, for goodness' sake!"

He slammed his hand onto the wooden slat behind him as he spoke, his frustration shaking dust from the beam.

Zach took his hat off so he could inspect it, instead of staring at his friend. "But it…it ain't fine after all?"

"Far as I know, from what the doc says… it don't matter if everything *seems* fine. Not when scar tissue blocks my swimmers so I can't make a baby."

"Wait… so nothing comes out when you—"

"I *just said* that wasn't the case!" Eric interrupted him, raising his voice. "I thought everything was A-okay. You need a microscope to know this kind of thing. I don't have a doggone microscope, all right? I just found out."

"Oh man, Eric." Zach cleared his throat. "I'm so sorry, man."

Eric looked up at him, his face a mask of disbelief. "Who would even want to marry me now? I love kids. I always wanted a kid of my own. A couple of 'em, if we could. And any woman I'd marry, would be the type of girl who wants to be a mom, too."

"What do you mean?"

"I mean when I get married someday… how am I going to find

a woman that doesn't want to have kids, or is okay with not having a child with me, but is still the type of woman I want to marry?" Eric sighed. "Always thought I'd be a dad someday. My future was just ripped out from under me, an' I don't even know why."

Zach hadn't even realized how important having a family was to his friend…as important as it was to Zach himself. Eric had had the good fortune of having a healthy relationship with his father— of having a father, period. Unlike Zach. It made sense…having a father he looked up to, respected…that had to be a big part of what Eric thought of, when he thought of being a man—being a dad. And now he couldn't be that person he'd always thought he'd be.

If Zach couldn't have kids, he'd be devastated… He wouldn't be able to right the wrong his own father had committed when he'd abandoned him and his mother, if Zach wasn't able to have children and stick with them. It would be life-altering and terrible. He could only imagine what Eric was going through right now, or what deep-seated needs wouldn't be met for Eric if he couldn't raise a family.

"Man…" Zach shook his head, his thoughts too tangled to express. He looked at his friend, hoping the despair he felt for him wouldn't show on his face.

What could he say? There was no solution, nothing he could offer to help fix the problem. This was no leaky roof he could patch for his friend.

Lord…give me the words.

Zach took a breath.

"God's got this," he said. "Because… God already knew this was gonna happen, and somehow…He's already got a plan for you that takes this whole thing into account."

Eric swallowed hard and nodded.

"The Big Guy's got it worked out—you know it."

"Thanks, man." Eric closed his eyes briefly, the tightness in his jaw relaxing a bit.

"If you ever want to talk about it or anything…" Zach drifted off. He wasn't accustomed to having such an intimate, painful discussion with his stoic friend.

"Yeah, I know. Thank you." Eric glanced up at the hay bales they'd stacked that morning. "Maybe it *is* lunchtime after all."

Zach grinned and clapped him on the back. "That's what I'm talking about."

* * *

Even after they were done for the day, the conversation he'd had with Eric kept replaying in his mind.

Man, he felt so bad for Eric. Zach didn't know what he would do if he couldn't have kids. Being a dad was one of his goals in life. He knew how important it was for a child to have a good father, because he'd suffered the absence of one. He couldn't wait to get married and start a family.

Would it be right to marry a woman who didn't love him, if she were willing, and all? Couldn't she grow to love him? Surely, once they had a child together, that love would grow. But what if it didn't? There was no reason for Megan to take that chance.

And really, if he just wanted to have an instant family, he could marry Paige tomorrow. She already loved him, and he cared for her, though not in the way she wanted him to. On paper they made a great match, and they'd probably have some really cute kids, too. Little blond babies, if they were anything like Paige—and he'd been a blond kid himself.

But instead of a blond baby, he envisioned a baby with Megan's sparkling blue-green eyes, and a head full of dark brown hair. He could see Megan in his mind's eye, gazing with unconditional love at their child, and looking up at Zach with a smile.

That was what he wanted. No doubt.

But this wasn't one of those cases where he could just decide on a goal and then make it happen. Love was a two-way street.

Zach picked up his guitar and absently strummed a few chords. What could he do to win Megan's heart?

His fingers slid down the neck of the guitar, dancing over the frets, and he slipped into a comfortable love song he'd heard playing on the radio last night in his truck.

"What can I do..." he half murmured, half sang as he strummed.

He tried some new chords, a different melody. Lyrics ran through his mind, and he sang quietly to himself as he played a tune he made up as he went.

You're my New York girl, running to Idaho
Ready to stand on your own
You've got strength running deep
You got Jesus. You got me.
You can stand on your own—
But you're never alone.

* * *

Megan waited for the train in the distance to stop honking before putting her earbuds in. The railroad tracks that went through the mountain were used by freight cars mainly, trains that came down from Canada and delivered supplies to the northern states. There was a railroad crossing in town where a street intersected the train tracks, and every time the train went through, it sounded its bellowing horn at least three or four times.

The gorgeous late-afternoon sun and mild breeze would pair well with some Hillsong. She clicked one of their albums from her playlist on her phone, and put on her gardening gloves. Megan was getting pretty good at this whole gardening thing…well, at least she was getting more accustomed to touching dirt, and not overwatering the plants. It would take her years to learn all of the things Zach already knew when it came to growing her own groceries.

What was that sound?

She took off her gardening gloves so she could press pause. Maybe she had heard an animal crying or something…?

In the split second it took to realize it wasn't an animal on the ranch, the hairs on the back of her neck stood up. She pulled out her earbuds and stood, turning around to face the man walking across the yard toward her.

"Todd?!"

How did he find her, after she'd run so far away? Had her sister given her up so easily? Maybe Todd had charmed her again…or worse, threatened her.

Todd flashed a smile at her, as if nothing were amiss. "It's so good to see you again, Meg." He took a step closer, as if he wanted to hug her.

Megan took a step back, wincing as she heard the sound of one of her plants crunching beneath her feet. "What are you doing here?" she asked. "I didn't invite you."

"I came in person to apologize," he said, his handsome face contorted into what Todd probably thought would pass for sincerity. "I'm so sorry for everything. I want you back, and I'm willing to do *whatever it takes* to get you back."

This was what he always did. He was like a snake charmer, and she had been the defanged snake with its mouth sewn shut, once powerful, but now under complete control.

Not any longer.

"I appreciate the apology," she said evenly. "But I am *not* going back with you. Our relationship is over."

There was a crack in Todd's superficial façade as anger flashed through his eyes. But just as quickly, the angry look was gone, and he put on a sorrowful face.

"Can't you just give me a chance, Meg?" He wiped at his eye as if he were tearing up, but she saw no tears. "I've missed you so much since you left. My apartment is not home without you in it."

How could she have fallen for his act for so long, before? Now his lack of true love and caring for her was so obvious. No matter what he said, his heart was still the same. Cold and empty. He wanted power and dominance over her, not a loving relationship.

"Todd, I'm sorry you flew all the way out here just for me to turn you down. But if you would have listened to me when we spoke on the phone, you wouldn't have made that mistake."

She carefully sidestepped out of the vegetables, and to her dismay, Todd moved with her, shadowing her movements.

"I had to see you face-to-face," he said.

"I'm a different person now," Megan said. "I know this must sound crazy to you, but I've changed from who I used be. God changed me. I really think He led me here for a reason. Manhattan is amazing, but it's not where I belong. I don't belong with you, either."

"You're right, Meg." His voice dripped with condescension. "That does sound crazy. At least you can still recognize that. That's a start."

She sighed. "Gimme a break, Todd. You can live your life how you want—just let me live mine."

"Wow—they've thoroughly brainwashed you up here! Or have you been drinking a lot of that unfluoridated well-water?" He rolled his eyes. "Come on, you have a bachelor's degree in science—you don't really believe all that church nonsense, do you?"

She crossed her arms. "It's not nonsense. And I started looking into it before I even left New York, just so you know. They have churches in Manhattan—maybe you should check it out for yourself. Maybe you wouldn't think it was such nonsense if you gave it half a chance."

A strange look passed over his face. She knew that expression...he was formulating a plan of sorts. If he were a cartoon, a lightbulb in a thought bubble would appear over his head whenever that look crossed his face.

"I see..." Todd said, the elite condescension stripped from his words. "You wanted to be with someone who shares your beliefs, is that it?" He smiled at her. "Megan—I'd be willing to go to church with you. Maybe you're right; I really never gave it a chance."

But something about the way he said it... He wasn't being sincere. A small voice inside of her whispered:

Don't believe him.

Megan swallowed hard. "I think that's a great idea," she said carefully. "But you should go for yourself, not for me. I'm going to be staying here."

"There's nothing I can do to change your mind, is there." He stated it as a fact.

It was a fact. He wasn't going to change her mind. She was no longer the same person; she could no longer be charmed by him, or fooled by him. No longer would he be able to devastate her one moment, apologize the next, and expect her to just pick up the pieces and move forward with him. It was done.

"Todd, I appreciate that you felt you needed to see me in person to apologize. I accept your apology. But I think you need to go home, back to New York." She gritted her teeth, fighting the urge to raise her voice.

Todd took a step toward her, and she stumbled backward.

"Stop moving away from me," he commanded. "Can't I give my ex-fiancée a kiss goodbye at least? After the way you left me, without so much as a Dear John letter?"

"You're being manipulative, and I don't like it. Just go, please."

"Manipulative?!" He laughed uproariously, as if she'd said the funniest thing in the world. But it was far from funny. "You're the one manipulating everyone here."

Zach seemed to come from out of nowhere, riding up on his horse. "What's going on?" He looked at Todd, his eyes narrowing. "And you are?"

"I'm Todd, Megan's fiancé."

Megan shook her head angrily. She was *never* his fiancée; she certainly wasn't now.

"Ex-boyfriend," she mumbled at the dirt. But Zach already knew that, right?

Todd smiled at Zach, clearly trying to win him over. "You have a beautiful ranch here, Mr. Walker. You are Zach Walker, right?"

"That's me." Zach dismounted from Chewbacca and held his reins. The horse chuffed. "Megan didn't say she was expecting visitors."

"I wasn't," Megan said pointedly. "I don't even know how you found me," she said to Todd.

"Your sister's a romantic at heart." Todd shrugged. "I told her I wanted to see you in person, to ask for forgiveness, one-on-one." He smiled at Megan once more, his demeanor changed from even a few moments ago—now that he had an audience with Zach. "I wanted to propose again," Todd said.

"Don't," Megan whispered. "Just leave, and don't embarrass yourself any further."

"I think you mean…don't embarrass *you*."

Megan's face heated up. "Just go."

Todd ignored her and looked over at Zach. "She called me manipulative," Todd said, as if that were the craziest thing ever. "But she's manipulating everyone, and she knows it."

Zach looked over at her, and while she wanted to shrug as if she had no idea what Todd was talking about, she…she knew: it was going to all come out now. How she was a fraud. A sinner. That she wasn't the girl Zach thought she was.

"Todd," she pleaded, "stop this plan of yours. I know what you're trying to do. Just go…please? I'm happy here—please, just let me have this."

Todd's mask of normalcy fell from his face, and a look of grim delight took its place. He always did seem to take pleasure from her emotional pain.

He ran his hand through his thick, dark hair and smiled in a thin way that did not reach his eyes. "Why would I? You've already made it abundantly clear that you'll never marry me. Why should you get to be happy when I'm not?"

Zach huffed in frustration. "What's going on here? Megan— you want to talk with him or do you want him gone? Because if you do…" Zach looked at Todd sternly "…then he's trespassing."

Todd raised his hands near his head in false surrender. "I'm not trespassing! Hold your horses."

At that, Todd laughed at his own unintentional pun, since Chewbacca's reins were literally in Zach's hand.

"Ha," Zach deadpanned. "Now leave. You heard the lady—she wants you gone."

"Alright, I will—I can leave. You enjoy yourself with this one. She can be pretty wild in the bedroom, but I guess you already know that." Todd's laugh was a low-pitch witch's cackle. "How quickly did she give it up for you? At least tell me that."

Zach's eyes widened and Megan could feel his gaze on her. Her cheeks burned and she shook her head.

What could she say?

"It ain't your business," Zach replied, "but just so ya know— Megan is staying in a separate sleeping quarters from me. And I ain't gonna listen if you keep talking that way about her."

At that, Todd burst into laughter. "Ah, so that's the game she's playing! She's not really a virginal goody-two-shoes, you know that, right? She slept with me on our third date. We were living together for *months*," he said. "*Living in sin*, as you would say." He laughed again, that obnoxious fake-sounding cackle.

Megan wished the earth would swallow her up, but instead it stayed steady beneath her feet, grounding her.

Lord, give me the words to say. I know I keep asking for forgiveness for everything—but please, God—forgive me again, and help me now. I need You.

What must Zach be thinking about her right now? She dared to glance up at him.

So handsome, big and tall, but with an innocence that Megan unfortunately no longer had. And he was hurt by this news, she could tell. He looked like a lost puppy who'd been kicked.

"You're a liar," Zach said to Todd. His hands were balled into fists, as if he were prepared to fight for her honor.

"No," Megan said softly. "He's not lying. I did all those things. But that's not the woman I want to be—I vowed I'd be a different woman, with God's help. That's why when I came here, I was…"

"A virginal goody-two-shoes?" Todd interrupted.

"Trying to do right." She bit back the pain in her chest.

I need You, God.

Zach took Chewy's reins. "I need to get Chewy some water." He wasn't looking at her. "I'll take 'im back to the stables. Let me know if you need anything."

"Zach," Megan called as he walked off. "I'm sorry. I didn't mean to fool you into thinking…that I was someone I'm not."

But he was walking away, and didn't look back at her. She knew he heard her, by the stiffness in his spine. He looked over his shoulder at Todd.

"You better be off my property in five minutes, sir, or I'll have you arrested for trespassing."

With that, Zach walked off to the stables.

Todd smirked. "He doesn't know you like I do, Meg. Look at him, he couldn't even stand to see your face after I told him who you *really* are."

Megan looked up at the sky and blinked, trying to force back the tears welling in her eyes. Why did Todd have to come here and ruin everything?

But then again… The past was bound to come out at some point. Maybe Todd had done Zach a favor—by letting him know the truth about her, before he got in too deep.

"Just go," Megan said. A runaway tear slid down her cheek, and she swiped at it with the back of her hand.

"He's not going to marry you," Todd said, his voice stark and cold. "But I'm willing to. You should take what you can get."

"Is that what this was about?" Megan gasped. "You wanted to come here and destroy any chance of a relationship with someone else, so that I'd have to settle for you? It's not going to happen."

She turned on her heel, storming back toward her cabin. Their history together had taught her that nothing good happened after his voice got all icy and clinical like that. It wasn't his calm voice—it was his psychopath voice. The same voice he'd used right before he'd thrown his dinner plate across the dining room so many nights ago—where it had shattered and a small piece cut her ankle.

But now she had plenty of space to leave him—to get out of the path of the brewing storm. As soon as she got inside she intended to lock the door and stay until he was gone.

"Where do you think you're going, Meg?"

Todd grabbed her wrist.

"Stop it," she growled.

Megan tried to twist out of his iron grip and stumbled over her feet, falling to the ground.

No no no. This wasn't good—he had a crazy look in his eyes, and Zach may as well have been a million miles away instead of just at the stables.

"Get away from me!" she yelled.

But Todd just laughed. "I'm not the one that put you in the dirt, you did that all by yourself."

Pepper spray.

She had pepper spray!

Her fingers wrapped around it in the deep pocket of her shorts, and she pulled it out— aiming it right at Todd's eyes, but didn't press the trigger. Not yet. "You don't want me to use this."

Todd spat on the ground. It landed an inch away from her foot. She kept the pepper spray trained on him.

"I always knew one day you'd point that thing at me," Todd said. "That's why I disarmed the vile weapon the moment you got it." He cackled again, and a shiver ran down her spine. "I emptied the whole thing, so you could never spray it at *me*, you... Stupid. Little. Whore."

So that's why the pepper spray hadn't worked on Zach when she'd tried to keep him out of her tent!

"Zach bought me this one," she said, forcing her voice to remain calm. "This one will work. And I'm not warning you again."

Todd lurched forward to grab at her pepper spray.

It was just like Zach had said in the woods—don't tell an attacker what you're going to do, or they'll just use the knowledge to disarm you, the way he had taken her keys.

With that last lurch toward her as Todd attempted to pry the spray from her hands, Megan was done warning him. She pressed the trigger, turning her head to avoid getting spray in her own eyes.

Todd screamed, a high-pitched shrill she'd never heard him make before. She coughed—some pepper got in her lungs. She pulled her shirt up over her nose and mouth.

"You've blinded me, how could you do this you dirty little—"

"*Get out of here*," Megan interrupted. "And don't ever try to find me again."

Todd stumbled forward, as if trying to get away from her but not knowing how. His swollen, red eyes streamed tears as his eyes attempted to cleanse themselves automatically. He coughed and choked dramatically.

He was getting angrier and angrier—if that was even possible—alternating between screaming and cursing at her with pleading for her to help him.

"I will *fully destroy* you for this, Megan Moore," Todd screamed.

She turned and ran back to her cabin—running fast so he wouldn't be able to catch her. She dared a peek over her shoulder. He wasn't following her—his cussing still emanated from where she'd left him.

Megan grabbed her cell phone and called Zach as she unlocked her door. He answered immediately.

"Are you okay?" he asked, his words coming so fast she didn't have time to reply. "Did he leave? Lord have mercy, I should never've left you with him. I'm heading back to you now."

"I pepper-sprayed him," Megan said. "I don't know if he'll be able to drive out of here."

"I'll bring some milk and he can wash his face off, and then he can drive out of here good enough for me."

Megan hung up the phone and peered out the small window, but it didn't have a clear line of sight to where he'd been.

She texted Zach: "*I'm in my cabin, with the door locked. Be careful around Todd.*"

Zach texted back: *"I've got him. I'll help him wash up and get him GONE. And then"*

The first part of his message came to her, but the rest didn't. She held her breath as she watched the three dots in the gray message bubble that meant he was typing.

"..."

And then—what did he mean, exactly? Would it be *her* turn to be escorted off the property?

It seemed like he was typing a long time for the short text that finally showed up. Maybe he'd written something first, changed his mind and deleted it—leaving only:

"when Todd's gone, we really need to talk."

Megan's chest felt tight. *"Okay,"* she texted back. *"I'll be here."*

This was it. The end of her dream. The end of her relationship with Zach, even before it could truly begin. And while she wanted to blame Todd for all of it, she knew deep down that she couldn't.

She was just too different from Zach. They came from such different backgrounds. She'd lived for twenty-three years as an unbeliever, and not just an unbeliever, but one who fell in line with what all of the magazines and articles and TV shows told her was perfectly normal and cool. And in doing so, she'd hurt herself, and now... the man who she truly loved and wanted to be with.

Love. *Do I love Zach Walker?*

Yes.

Yes, she did love him.

At least she could tell him that one truth, before he told her goodbye.

* * *

Zach paced in his living room, transferring the guitar pick in his hand to his mouth and back again. No guitar—he just needed something to fidget with. He didn't know how he felt now. Maybe... duped. Betrayed.

It wasn't as though Megan had lied to him—it's not like she came to Idaho and proclaimed herself a "virginal goody-two-shoes" as Todd had so bluntly put it—but she had become that to Zach, somehow. Now his favorable impression of her seemed tarnished, which, although it wasn't fair to her or any other folks who'd changed their lives, still left a cloying sense of discomfort behind.

"Lord, forgive me," he muttered.

One of the things he'd learned from his time flipping through the Bible was that Jesus had told his followers that simply not committing adultery outright wasn't enough—that any man who even looked at a woman with lust had already committed adultery in his heart. And Zach was guilty of that for sure.

He tried to be as gentlemanly as he could on the outside, and he tried to keep his thoughts clean on the inside to match. But he was a red-blooded man...and Megan was a beautiful woman.

He wanted her. But not just for what she could give him physically—he wanted to have all of her. Her heart, her mind, her generosity of spirit. He had fallen in love with her.

Love.

So she was it, she was the one. After all these years, he'd found her.

Zach paused mid-pace to fully grasp the realization.

God must have a sense of humor to give him the exact opposite of what he'd originally thought he wanted. Megan wasn't a cowgirl, though she sure as rain was trying. When she'd first come to Bear Creek Saddle Ranch, it seemed she couldn't even tie her own shoes, much less be the independent, self-sufficient woman she wanted to be. Now, after only a few months of putting her mind to it, she was getting there. She really was.

Had Todd coming to town changed all that?

No. Zach wasn't going to let the vicious verbal attacks he'd heard from Todd, the disgusting things he'd said about Megan, affect the way Zach felt about her.

At least, he didn't *want* what Todd had said to affect him.

Lord, help me make that true.

It wasn't fair of Zach to expect her to show up from New York City, escaping an abusive situation and unaccustomed to country life, and yet still be his ideal version of a wife right off the bat. So what... she wouldn't be a virgin on their wedding night.

And he would be.

Was that what was really bothering him? Zach would be the inexperienced one on their wedding night. That could be awkward. Or would it be? That was, if she'd ever agree to marry him, which didn't look likely.

Zach sighed, and the guitar pick he'd placed between his lips fell to the ground.

He knelt to retrieve it, his fingers grazing the carpet as he paused in that position before standing.

I need to talk to Megan, and propose properly. On one knee. With a ring.

When he brought it up before, it was as if he was suggesting she fill a job application for the role of wife. But the fact was, if he'd wanted that, he could've had Paige fill the role in a heartbeat—she'd pretty much spelled it out for him, as had both of their mothers. After all, she'd be the perfect rancher's wife, and Paige already had a lot of affection for him. Paige wasn't rough around the edges, she didn't have a New York City accent (cute as it was, it certainly pegged Megan as a city-girl straight away)… Paige already knew all the tricks of how to grow vegetables and ride a horse well and how to gather eggs and feed chickens and buck hay bales onto the back of a pickup truck, and ride a tractor and help him with the cattle.

Megan was getting better at *all that*, though if there were a competition, Paige would win. Only problem was, the only category Paige wouldn't pass with flying colors was the only one that mattered…it all boiled down to one thing in the end. Chemistry. Love. That soul connection.

Something about Megan seemed right for him. Like they were a perfect fit, despite their differences. Maybe even because of their differences. Paige would make some other lucky cowboy a great wife… but it wasn't going to be Zach. She'd even be a virgin on her wedding night, seemed like.

Zach shook his head. *That doesn't matter anymore.* He was a sinner even when he tried not to be—how could he throw stones?

Megan was a Christian now, she'd made that clear. She hadn't slept with Zach. Yes, she'd made choices that ended up badly, but she'd gotten out. Started over. Her past shouldn't matter, because she was different now—she had changed for the better.

He wanted Megan, flaws and all. God knows he had enough flaws to go around as well.

How was she doing now, after seeing her past come back to haunt her? Would she be okay?

Zach had gone straight to his cabin after Todd was gone, because he'd needed to calm down, and think. To pray. He'd assumed Megan needed the same space that he did.… But maybe that wasn't the case. Maybe he'd just abandoned Megan right when she needed him most.

Oh no—he had to go talk to her and make sure she was okay.

Chapter Ten

ZACH FILLED UP Inky's water bowl and left his house, jogging over to the practice cabin. He knocked, and knocked again.

"Hang on," Megan called from inside.

He heard a deadbolt turn, and Megan cracked the door. She'd been crying. Her eyes were puffy, her nose red. She was still beautiful as always.

"I'm kind of a mess right now," she said.

"Need a hug?" It was all Zach could think of to offer.

She nodded, fresh tears rolling down her cheeks, and opened the door to step outside and into Zach's arms. He wrapped his arms around her, holding her tightly against his chest, and pressed his cheek against the top of her head, feeling the silky smoothness of her long dark hair.

"I can't believe Todd found me here," Megan said, her words muffled against his chest. She pulled back a bit and looked up at him. "I'm so sorry you had to deal with that drama."

"No," Zach said, "I'm sorry that *you* had to deal with that drama. Todd never should've come here."

"I'm going to need a new pepper spray," she said. "I think I used it all on him."

"Absolutely." Zach knew it wasn't right, but he couldn't help but smile at that. "You're good at defending yourself, Megan."

"Thank you," she said, the edge of her mouth turning up in a smile, brightening her tear-streaked face. "It was a pretty awful confrontation. And he said some awful things… I'm sorry you had to hear them."

"It doesn't change how I feel about you."

"I'm a different person than I was before. The girl Todd knew, the one he abused and manipulated, she's gone. Or maybe not gone… just… transformed."

God can transform anyone. It was really amazing to see it happen before his eyes during her stay at the ranch.

"Do you want to get a restraining order against your ex?" Zach asked. "I could call the sheriff."

"I'll think about it," Megan said. "But I think that Todd saw I'm not someone he can push around anymore. I don't think he'll be flying back out here anytime soon."

When they'd hugged, the connection was so clear. Could she see it too? Zach didn't have a ring yet, but he wouldn't let that stop him.

Zach dropped to one knee, holding her hands. "Megan, I love you. I love the woman you are, and the woman you're becoming. Would you marry me?"

She stared down at him, her eyes wide. Silence.

Please, God, let her say yes.

"I can't, Zach." She took a shaky breath. "I'm sorry. It's not that I don't care about you—I do. So much." Megan smiled wistfully. "I think I've fallen for you too, Zach, despite my best efforts not to. I really do."

Zach's heart soared at her confession. But she'd still turned him down. And he was still on his knee, wondering how it all had gone so wrong so fast. "Then...why? Why not marry me?"

"I need to prove to myself I can be on my own," Megan said, "without having a man take care of me. I need to know that I can do it. Being with you on the ranch and learning how to be self-sufficient has been awesome," she continued. She tugged on his hand, urging him to get back on his feet.

Zach adjusted his hat, pulling the brim down. "I'm sorry to hear that." He shook his head. "Not sorry that you had an amazing time at the ranch—sorry you won't marry me. I was sorta hoping."

"I'm sorry," she said again. "There's a huge part of me that wishes I could say yes. But I know if I do, I'll always wonder if I could take care of myself."

"I understand." Zach swallowed hard. He had to give her space after all.

"I think I should move out, Zach—rent a place on my own, and see how it goes. You've been an amazing host and friend and I don't want to overstay my welcome."

"If you're gonna move out because it's something you need to do, that's fine, I...I get it. You could never overstay your welcome with me, though. I just asked you to marry me, for goodness' sake." He chuckled softly. "That means I want you around as much as I can get you around."

"Thank you," she said. "You're right—not overstaying my welcome isn't why I need to jump from the nest. It's just...I won't ever get to practice spreading my wings if I never take that leap."

"Okay," he said. "You can borrow my pickup truck and the guys and I can help you move." He cleared his throat. "But... just so you know, you don't have to leave the guest cabin. You could stay here. If you don't want to work on the ranch, well—I mean, if it would make you more comfortable, you could even pay rent or something. You don't have to leave. Me asking you to marry me wasn't an all-or-nothing proposition. You don't have to marry me to stay. *We can keep going as we were.*"

He didn't want to be without her.

"I appreciate that, Zach. But I think I need some space to figure things out for myself."

Zach nodded. "Well, I'll let you be, then. Holler if you need me."

"Wait!" Megan called when he was only a few yards away from her.

He turned back to her. She ran up to him, and planted a sweet kiss on his cheek.

"Thank you," she whispered, "for everything."

Zach slid his hands around her slender waist and pulled her closer to him, looking down at her from under the brim of his hat.

"It's hard to let go of you, knowing I love you, and maybe you even love me."

"I know." Megan kissed him again, this time on his lips—a soft, feathery kiss that left him aching for more. "Give me time and space. It's what I need."

A knot formed in his stomach at her words. Once she left the ranch...would she ever be back?

Chapter Eleven

DURING THE PAST two months since she'd moved out of Bear Creek Saddle Ranch, Megan had developed a talent she'd never known she possessed. Unfortunately, it was not farming.

Megan walked slowly through the woods, her eyes on the ground. An interestingly shaped twig that had fallen from its branch caught her eye.

Perfect. She picked it up and added it to her basket, which was already halfway filled. She'd been making these walks more and more frequently, to collect more fallen twigs and brush. Ever since she learned that the interest on her mother's inheritance money paid a substantially smaller monthly stipend to live on than she'd hoped for, but it was something. She'd rather have her mom alive than any amount of money.

Thank God she'd finally gathered the courage to go talk to a financial advisor and actually do something with her money, which had mellowed uselessly in a savings account.

Todd had been wrong—she wasn't a mess when it came to

finances. She at least was able to talk to several advisors on the phone and online, and visit a couple places in town over an hour away to figure out the best course of action she felt comfortable with.

Ultimately, she decided something more stable that gave her a monthly interest payment was going to work better for her than something fancy and high risk (though higher-paying).

She didn't dare touch the actual capital of the inheritance money—she would need it when eventually she bought her own place. For now, the tiny one-bedroom, one-bathroom cottage she rented on a quarter acre served just fine. It had just enough land for her to dream big enough for a garden, though not livestock. She had spent hours already planning out her summer garden.

Now that it was autumn, with winter coming, she'd have to wait to start sprouting some seedlings inside. So much for growing her own groceries. The money she did get each month from the inheritance-interest covered her rent payment, which was relatively cheap (super cheap compared to New York!). And on Paige's advice, she picked up a couple of weekly housekeeping jobs in town. But the best part was…she'd discovered a skill she never knew she had—and it came about the very first week she'd moved into the cottage.

She'd been sitting at the kitchen table, alone, wishing Zach and the other ranchers were still there, helping her set up everything. She missed them. The fact was, she needed to be on her own— needed it so much she was willing to give up what was potentially her one chance for love with Zach.

There was no way a man like that would wait for her. And who knew how long it would take for her to feel ready? What did feeling "ready" even mean?

She wanted to be self-sufficient. Independent. She had to make that happen before she could hitch her wagon to someone else.

Ha. She was starting to sound like Zach, even in her own mind.

It was that picture of Bear Creek Saddle, the picture she'd printed out from the internet, that had encouraged her to drive all the way out West. She'd wanted to frame it and put it on the wall, but she had no frame, and no money to buy one. She did, however, have a hot-glue-gun and some twine, and nature had provided her with a variety of awesome twigs and sticks.

That evening almost two months ago, she'd made her very first rustic twig frame for her photo. On the advice of her sister, she took a photo of it and offered one like it for sale on a popular online marketplace. While she rejected Lindsay's advice to forget the whole thing and come back home to New York, she did appreciate the advice of selling something she made herself.

Megan had been shocked when the first order rolled in, followed by a second, a third, and soon…people were leaving glowing reviews. She charged for shipping and handling, so she wasn't out any money making these, and her customers were happy. Many of them lived in cities, where it was difficult to find rustic decorations for their "country homes" or "summer cabins." Must be nice, to need to decorate a second home.

When she'd found a big chunk of wood from a downed branch, she started cutting into it to make more material for her frames, when she'd realized it would work perfectly for a small birdfeeder, kind of like the one Zach's mom had outside her home. That was when she started adding handmade wooden birdfeeders to her online store.

Another twig caught Megan's eye, a thick one, and she picked it up fast—as if someone else might come along and take it first. She laughed.

Who would've thought that the way she'd find financial independence would be from selling her handmade crafts online?

She'd had this fantasy that she would move to Idaho, grow her own groceries, have a cow (or goat) for milk, and raise chickens that gave her eggs for protein. She'd build her own house with her bare hands and not really need any money at all because she would be completely self-sufficient.

True, there were people who lived off-grid, creating their own electricity using a combination of a windmill and propane tank; and she'd even seen water wheels that turned with the river current and created energy that went into a battery bank, which powered the homes. She hadn't seen too many solar panels, probably because they were expensive, and the people living off-grid were often doing it either for financial reasons or because the properties were so far from town, as opposed to just being eco-trendy.

But this cottage she rented was hooked up to power lines, a shared well, and the monthly utility bill was small. She was able to heat the house easily too, using the woodstove. She didn't really need the heat yet, but with winter coming, she would. It was a small enough place that it wouldn't be hard to keep warm, according to the owner.

So she was finally doing it. She was living on her own, like a proper adult, and although her job was unconventional, she was consistently making enough money to stay afloat.

Still, she missed Zach. She even missed Inky. Stinky Inky who wasn't even that stinky...

Maybe she should get her own dog. She kind of wanted a pet pig, too—but then she'd have to give up bacon because she'd probably end up loving the pig. That wouldn't do. Bacon was too good.

She missed the ranch. What did it really mean to be her own woman? She still needed to—and *wanted* to—rely on God. She was never truly on her own because of Him.

She was starting to build her credit score already. When she was living with Todd, her credit score was essentially nonexistent because he'd maintained such tight control over everything. It was his name on everything—every bill, their rent—and her parents' name on the student loan. Having no financial history was almost as bad as having bad credit. But now she had the rent to pay and some bills, and the man at the bank even spoke to her about how she might be able to get a farm loan for women farmers, for when she wanted to buy a property.

She loved that idea—but would it ever really be home without Zach?

Wherever Zach Walker is, that's home.

Why was she torturing herself? What would it take, how long would she have to be on her own and self-sustaining as an adult before she could believe she was good enough, or prepared enough, to be with someone else?

Her basket was full. It was getting heavy. She turned back and retraced her steps down the trail through the woods and back to the unpaved road. She looked both ways—there were no stoplights or stop signs, but also no cars except for the occasional one—and crossed over to the road that led to her cottage.

She had to call Zach. She missed him. He'd been giving her the space she had asked for—he hadn't texted, or called, or stopped by unannounced. And while she was grateful for that, there was more than a small part of her that wished he would.

That's silly. Zach was a good guy—and since she told him she wanted to be on her own, he'd respect that. He wasn't Todd; he wasn't a stalker. Zach wasn't trying to control her, or manipulate their relationship.

Thankfully, she hadn't heard from Todd at all either. Lindsay told her Todd had stopped contacting her as well. Good. And good riddance.

After washing her hands and rehydrating, Megan pulled out her phone and texted Zach for the first time since he'd helped her move in: *"Do you have the barn full with hay bales yet? Someone told me it snows a lot in the winter up here."*

She giggled to herself… that "someone," of course, was Zach.

He was typing back! The anticipation put butterflies in her stomach. Hadn't felt that in a while.

Megan checked the time on her phone—it was still light out, which meant he was probably still out on the ranch getting stuff done. There was a lot to do before winter—even after the first crop of grass had been grown, cut, raked, put through the baler, and thrown and stacked in the barn, Zach and the guys did it again with the second and third cutting to get as much hay as they could.

The cows all had to be checked on for their health and to make sure they were eating well. And moved to different pastures when they ate all the grass in one. The irrigation had to be checked every day to make sure water was getting to the grass, and of course his personal gardening needed to be attended to, and the dairy cows the ranchers kept for milk, and the chickens for their eggs. It was surprising Zach was able to respond to her right away, but thrilling as well.

Zach's text read: *"Hey Megan! Good to hear from you. You should come over and check out the barn—not only is it full, but we had to put a big tarp up and stack more hay outside. Cows and horses like to eat!"*

That had to be the longest text he'd ever sent her—plus, an offer to come over to the ranch. She wanted that so much.

But maybe Zach should see her place, see what she had done with it. She hadn't even told him she was selling picture frames and birdhouses online made out of twigs and branches. Wow, that sounded strange when she said that to herself. Who would've suspected that would be her secret talent? God knows she didn't have the upper-body strength to buck hay the way Zach and the guys did. But that was okay. She still found a way to make it on her own...with a latent talent.

She texted: *"I'd love to see that! Though maybe you should come here? You could advise me on my plans for next summer's veggie garden, and I think you really need to take a look at the land and the soil to tell me if it's gonna work or not.... I could make dinner?"*

Zach responded immediately: *"You betcha"*

You betcha. She chuckled to herself. It seemed like forever ago that she only knew him as "You-Betcha-Man."

"Tonight?" she texted.

Zach: *"I just need to shower so I don't stink. Can I come over in an hour?"*

"Absolutely." She added: *"If you have any tomatoes left from the garden, and maybe a zucchini or two, could you bring them with you? I've been pretty busy and never actually got started with planting."*

Zach: *"Too late in the season for that anyway, don't worry about it. I'll bring over a sack of veggies."*

Her hands trembled as she responded with a thumbs-up.

He was coming over. She hadn't seen him since he'd said goodbye after helping her move into the cottage.

What if she found out that he was with Paige now?

What if she found out that, after being without her, he'd had enough time to realize or to think about whether or not he really wanted her after all?

Lord, if it's Your will, please let him still love me. Because You know I still love him.

* * *

Zach pumped his fist in the air and pocketed his phone. "Let's get you back to the stables, Chewy—I've got a date!"

Chewbacca turned his big ol' horse head toward him with interest, as if he could sense Zach's enthusiasm.

"Don't worry, Chewy—it's with Megan. We know only Megan will do."

At that, the horse gently pressed his long snout against Zach's shoulder, as if to prod him to get going.

Zach mounted his horse, and it took every bit of restraint that he had to keep the horse at a walking pace to get to the stable. He wanted to gallop there, to get ready and show up at Megan's place as soon as he could. There was no reason to scare the chickens by rushing around like a madman, or to wear out his horse after a long day. He'd waited twenty-five years. What was a few more minutes?

When he pulled up an hour later to Megan's house, he nearly forgot the sack of veggies he'd plucked from the garden and put in the front seat of his pickup truck. He turned back toward his truck before he reached her front door, grabbed the sack, and re-approached the painted white door.

A small wooden birdhouse, seeds spilling out onto its tiny wraparound bird-porch, hung off a hook from the cottage's awning. Zach grinned at the memory of birdsong waking him in the mornings when he was a kid.

Before he could rap his knuckles against the wood, Megan opened the door.

"I saw you pull up," she said with a smile. "Come on in."

"Want me to take my shoes off? These are my clean ones, not my work boots, if that matters."

Megan shook her head, and smiled at him again, her blue-green eyes sparkling under thick black lashes.

"You look beautiful." He handed her the bag of vegetables. "That's probably what I should've started with."

"Thank you," she said, taking the vegetables, though it wasn't clear if she were thanking him for the veggies or the compliment. "How... How are you?"

He followed her into the kitchen, which really only meant taking a few steps, since the cottage was so small. Bigger than the practice cabin, but not by much. One room served as the living room, dining area, and kitchen. Off of that main area was the bathroom, and next to that, the small bedroom. That was it. It was nice though—really cozy. And she kept the place really clean, which always amazed Zach. He couldn't seem to keep his place tidy for the life of him.

His house had been a lot cleaner when Megan was around, though... It was as if magic cleaning fairies sorted stuff out when he was off taking care of the cattle.

Not that he wanted Megan for her housekeeping skills, but it was kind of nice.

"I like what you've done with the place," he said, and grabbed a zucchini off the counter. "We should wash these, I literally just grabbed them from the garden. Picked fresh."

"Awesome!" She seemed nervous. Or maybe that was him? "You want to cut those up, and stir-fry them? We can have that with rice and chicken."

They worked next to each other in silence for a moment; the only sounds were his knife hitting the cutting board and the oil sizzling as she prepared some chicken for the pan.

This was nice. Cooking together.

"So, how's it going with the whole independence mission?" Zach asked. He winced internally. "I didn't mean that in a condescending or sarcastic sorta way. I really want to know."

"Well… the things I wanted to do originally, like build a house myself, have egg-laying chickens, a dairy cow, and grow my own vegetables, everything that I wanted to do…" she trailed off.

"Hey, you'll get there," he said. "You're just starting. I still have to take you fishing, ya know. That will help fill your fridge. And if I bag an elk this season, you know I'll share meat with you."

"That would be awesome," she agreed, "though I'm not counting on feeding myself from fishing or hunting alone. I just don't have the skill set, yet, and I'm okay with…"

"I know it takes money to get started, too," he added.

"Well, about that… I found some things I'm good at, and I've been able to make enough money doing it, so it's worked out anyways. I mean… I still love all that stuff, I think it's cool. But I'm glad to know I'm not dependent on my own beginner skills as a neophyte farmer to survive after all."

"Wow, that's great." He raised his eyebrows with interest. "Did you get a job? Do you have to drive into the city?"

"I've been doing some housekeeping part-time at a couple of homes in town…Paige actually gave me that idea. Just a few hours a week."

The chicken sizzled in the pan, browning nicely. She turned down the heat to let it simmer and motioned him over to the wall behind the couch.

She had decorated it with really cool frames made out of sticks and twine, in all different shapes and sizes. Some of the twigs were scraped down to the wood, and others she'd left the bark on. It looked like a mix between rustic and professional, if that made sense.

"You made these frames?" He reached out and gently touched one, feeling the sturdy construction.

"And some birdhouses."

"Oh wow—I saw that birdhouse on my way in—I thought you'd bought it, it looks so good," he exclaimed. "You made all this stuff?

"What do you think?"

"I love them," he said honestly. "They look exactly like what a picture frame in a house in north Idaho should look like. Nothing's hanging on my walls at all… Could you make me a frame? I'd have to figure out what to put in it."

Megan appeared to be biting back her smile as she nodded.

Zach took his phone out and grinned at her. "Can we take a selfie together? Then I'd have something for the frame."

Megan smiled and scooted in closer to him. He wrapped his arm around her shoulder and held the phone out in front of them to take a picture. Still leaning into him, she put her hand out for him to pass her the phone so she could see how it turned out.

"Will you send me a hi-res copy of this?" She adjusted the photo's brightness and saved it before handing it back to him.

He wanted the moment of being close to her to linger, but she was already walking back to the kitchen, again only a few feet away.

"Dinner's ready."

She put the chicken and veggies into two mustard-colored ceramic bowls and set them on the small dining table. Zach grabbed the pitcher of water out of the refrigerator and two glasses, and they sat down.

"Would you like to say grace?" she asked.

He cleared his throat, took her hand, bowed his head, and closed his eyes. "Dear God, thank You for this food. Please bless it to our bodies. Thank You for this opportunity to see Megan again, and for giving her the gift of turning sticks into something people want to buy. That's really cool. And for her being so good at cleaning up, people pay her for it. Maybe You could gift me with some housekeeping skills, too." He cleared his throat… this grace was going off on a tangent, the way it often did when he was eating alone. "Thank You for everything, Lord. In Jesus' name we pray, amen."

"Amen." She was smiling.

He grinned at her and grabbed his fork. Dinner tasted great, but it was being in Megan's company that made it even better.

"I've really missed you, Megan." He paused. He didn't want to ruin anything. He didn't want to ruin this amazing night.

What if she just wanted to be friends?

No. He couldn't pretend that he didn't love her. She already knew the truth—and yet she still had made the choice to move forward without him. There was nothing he could do about that, but he wasn't going anywhere. He would wait for her.

And yet now, waiting for her to respond to his admission, his heartbeat increased as if he couldn't wait even a second longer.

She exhaled slowly and reached her hands across the table. He took her hand in his, her warm small hand nearly swallowed inside of his large one. It was like having an exquisite rare bird in his palm, so that he had to hold it reverently and carefully. Scared that if he made the wrong move, it would fly away.

"I've missed you too," she said finally. "I've missed you a lot."

"I'm real happy for you—living on your own, proving to yourself that you are able to do that. That's huge. I know how important that was for you."

"Thank you. It feels huge."

"I don't want to be... weird, or anything," he said. How could he say this so she took it the right way? "Just wanna let you know...you're always welcome back at the ranch. If you want, you could live in the practice-cabin rent-free, and you don't have to work on the ranch or anything—you could make your frames and birdhouses. Sell 'em online from the ranch. Still do your housekeeping business. You could save up your money that way, an' then buy some land like you wanted."

"That's a very generous offer, Zach."

She looked down at their hands, and Zach relaxed his own, giving her the opportunity to pull away if she wanted to. But she didn't. He smiled at her, but she didn't see it, because she was still looking at their hands intertwined.

"Turns out, with the small inheritance I got from after my mom's passing—I mean, I split it with Lindsay, of course—but it's enough that I could buy something now if I wanted to. And according to the bank, I'm eligible for some loans for women farmers. Since I'm a beginner I'd need a mentor to qualify—"

"I'll be your mentor," he interrupted.

"Thank you," she said. "But you know what? I'm okay. Right now, just knowing that I *could* do that feels like enough. And really, I'm not so great at ranching just yet."

"Don't say that, you're getting better at it—" Zach said. He didn't want her to be down on herself. "It takes time to learn something if you've never done it before."

"It's okay. I'm okay with that. God gives everyone different gifts, and like you said, He gave me the gift of making... I guess it's art, kinda. Would you call my frames 'art'?"

"You betcha, I would." He pushed his chair back and walked back over to the wall full of her frames. She hesitated at the table for a moment, then followed.

"I mean, I'm no art connoisseur or nothing," he said. "But people are buying your frames, so you got fans and everything. You could make all sorts of things out of wood that folks'd like, I bet."

Her face brightened. "I was thinking about that. Sometimes I see these really long branches and long sticks—and I think about maybe nailing some pieces together, even making something bigger, like a coat rack maybe. Or a place to hang your keys. A napkin holder... There are a lot of options. I have definitely been thinking about it." She smiled.

Man, he loved that smile. She was a new person compared to when she'd first arrived in Bear Creek Saddle. The anxiety that had plagued her before, the constant worry she expressed, had been replaced with a serenity he loved to see on her beautiful face.

"I'm real proud of you, Megan."

Her cheeks grew pink, and Zach grinned. "Didn't mean to make ya blush."

She laughed and looked up at him, and before he could overthink it, he leaned down and kissed her gently on her lips.

She accepted his kiss, even took a tiny step closer toward him. He wrapped his arms around her, and breathed in the scent of lavender in her hair.

"You ain't gonna run away, are you?"

* * *

Megan shook her head no. She wasn't going to run—not this time. Not ever again.

"I've missed you so much," Zach said again. "You and me... Can you feel it? We're meant to be together. Am I being crazy?"

"You're not crazy," she said softly. "I've missed you, Zach. And I feel like I've been missing out on a best friend, too. Every time something cool would happen—when I had my first sale online, I just wanted to tell you all about it. I've been pushing myself to stay away from you so I could try to make it on my own. And I guess, with God's help... I've done it."

"Yeah, you have."

As he held her close in his arms, every ounce of her being wanted him to kiss her again.

"I...I wrote you a song," he said. "I couldn't stop thinking about you, so I just...put it to music."

She craned her neck to look up at him without needing to pull away from his embrace. "Can you play it for me?"

"I don't have my guitar." He frowned. "I can hum a few bars

for you…and play the rest later, when I've got my guitar handy."

"Okay," she said. Had he really written a song about her? He really was thinking about her all this time when she'd been wondering.

Zach started to hum a soft, slow melody in her ear, and she swayed in his arms. She imagined him strumming his guitar, how the chords would sound like the sweet music he hummed.

Quietly, with her head against his chest, he started singing, holding her close, dancing with her.

"You're my New York girl," he half-whispered, half-sang, "running to Idaho… Ready to stand on your own. You've got strength running deep…You got Jesus. You got me."

He swayed with her, and she could feel the thrum of his voice in his chest against her cheek.

"You can stand on your own," he sang softly, "but you're never alone…"

She didn't want the song to ever end, but he was done singing, and he held her in his arms as they swayed in the silence, with only the sounds of the cicadas outside for music.

"Now that you're here," she whispered, "I don't know why I've tried so hard to keep you away."

"Hearing you say that…" He pulled her close to him and hugged her tightly. "Listen, Megan… You don't have to say yes if you don't want to, you know that—"

"Say yes to what?" She pulled back so she could look up at him, and he dropped his arms from her waist.

"I don't want to scare you off. Tonight's been so good. Seeing you again after all those weeks…man, I just keep repeating myself. I had to keep myself from texting you too. I kept fixing to drive over here. You should've seen how many zucchinis we had. Ended up donating a bunch to the church's kitchen, but I really wanted to bring them over here."

"I do have a certain…fondness for zucchini bread," she said.

"I know, I'm sorry. I was jus' trying to give you your space. So does this mean… does tonight mean that I don't have to stay away from you anymore?"

"You mean, like… could you, theoretically, bring over a bunch of zucchinis whenever you wanted to?"

"Something like that," he said.

"You betcha," she said, mimicking his accent, and grinned.

"Is that what I sound like?" Zach laughed. "How about if I don't have zucchinis, but I just wanted to come over an' hang out with you?"

"Yes."

"What if maybe you wanted to come over to the ranch, an' ride around with me?"

Megan paused, as if she had to think about it. "Could I drive the baler again?"

"I'd let you ride the *cows* if that would bring you back to the ranch."

She laughed. "I'll settle for Chewbacca and the baler."

"So…can I text you whenever I want?" he pressed. "If I'm thinking about you, or I see something you'd like? That's been happening this past while."

"Yes," she said, "I think about you so much. I kept wanting to text you, too."

"I like eating with you," he replied. "Do you think if I brought the food, I could come over an' we could fix up dinner again?"

"Yes. I'd like that."

"Can I come over tomorrow night an' do that? Or you come to my place."

"Your place—I miss Inky," she said.

"You won't get sick of me if you see me that much, will you?"

"No. definitely not," she said. "I mean, you might get sick of *me.*"

"No way," Zach said. "Can we eat together every night?"

She didn't even hesitate. "Yes."

Zach knelt down and looked up at her from one knee.

Lord, let this be what I think it is. She trembled, her breath hitching.

Give me another chance to say yes, Lord. Just one more time. I'm ready to say yes.

He pulled a small, three-stone diamond ring out of a zippered pocket on his pants.

Megan gasped. As much as she'd been hoping for it…it was still a wonderful surprise. The ring was gorgeous.

"I've been thinking about you," Zach said, gazing into her eyes, the heat from his own reaching her very soul. "I didn't know if I'd ever get a chance to give you this—it's got three diamonds on it, for the past, the present, and the future. I love you, Megan. I love that your past makes you who you are today. I love the woman you are today, and seeing how God's transformed you for the better." Zach swallowed. "That third stone is for the future. Our future. I'd like it to be together…if you'll have me."

Megan's eyes welled with unshed tears, and she smiled so hard her cheeks ached. *Yes. Thank You, God.*

She took a shaky breath and nodded.

"Megan, will you marry me?"

"Yes." She was certain. There was no more fear, no uncertainty. "Yes, forever *yes*."

He stood and slid the ring onto her trembling finger.

"It's beautiful, Zach. I love it...I love *you*."

The End

Sign up for <u>Shoshanna Gabriel's newsletter</u>
<u>http://shoshannagabriel.com/subscribe/</u>
to know when
the next BEAR CREEK SADDLE Series book releases!

Acknowledgements

FIRST AND FOREMOST, I would like to give the glory to God for making me a storyteller, for which I am forever grateful! Thank You for sending us Your Son.

Thank you to my readers. Without you, I would be writing into the abyss. And a special shout-out goes to the Shoshanna Street Team—thank you for your support, and for spreading the word!

Thank you to the inspirational Christian authors who have encouraged me to write the stories I feel called to write, and for my readers for joining me on this journey with my new name as Shoshanna Gabriel, and my new genre. I'm so excited about the Bear Creek Saddle Series.

Thank you to Karen Solem of SpencerHill Associates, for your support.

Thank you to my beta-readers, and an extra-special thank you to Bonnie Paulson.

Thank you to Therese Marie of ChristianProofreaders.com, for editing this book. Any errors or omissions are my own.

Thank you to my cover artist, Rob Sturtz, from SelfPubBookCovers.com for my cover. I co-founded SelfPubBookCovers.com with Rob to help fulfill my dream of having quality covers at an affordable price available to all indie authors, instantly. If you're a writer, too, you might want to check out the amazing artists we have on board!

Last on the list but not in my heart: thank you, Dear Husband, for being awesome and for being my soulmate, and to my children, for going to bed so sweetly every night, so Mommy can write while the household sleeps. I love you!

About Shoshanna Gabriel

SHOSHANNA GABRIEL WAS previously known as Shoshanna Evers, a *New York Times* and *USA Today* bestselling author who wrote over twenty-plus secular romance novels and novellas, and published with big New York publishers, small presses, and through indie-publishing. After much thought and prayer, she decided to **change her life and career path to be for God's glory**. Shoshanna Gabriel is currently writing Christian inspirational romance novels. For a detailed explanation of this big change, read her blog post "Saying Goodbye to Erotic Romance" (http://bit.ly/GoodbyeErotica).

While published as Shoshanna Evers, Amazon had listed her as one of the "Most Popular Authors in Romance," as well as one of the "Most Popular Authors in Contemporary Romance." Reviewers have said Shoshanna has "…**beautiful writing**, and a **truly imaginative** and wonderfully descriptive storyline" (Night Owl Reviews) with stories where "the plot is fresh and the pacing excellent, **the emotions…real and poignant**." (The Romance

Studio) She hopes to bring her gift of storytelling to her new inspirational books written under the Gabriel name.

Shoshanna used to work as a syndicated advice columnist in NY and a registered nurse, but now she's a full-time author and a homeschooling mom of a son and boy/girl twins. She is also **the co-founder of SelfPubBookCovers.com**, the world's largest selection of high quality, affordable book covers for indie authors, available instantly. She lives with her family and three big dogs in northern Idaho, and loves to connect with readers on social media.

*Faithfully Ever Afters…*ShoshannaGabriel.com

Want to know when my next book comes out?
Sign up for my newsletter to hear about new releases first, and read excerpts you won't find in the sample pages!
ShoshannaGabriel.com/subscribe

Visit ShoshannaGabriel.com for monthly giveaways of different inspirational romance novels!

Let's be BFFs!

@ShoshnnaGabriel (Twitter.com/ShoshnnaGabriel)
@ShoshannaEvers (Twitter.com/ShoshannaEvers)
Facebook (facebook.com/ShoshannaGabriel)

To my readers:

If you enjoyed this book, I'd love if you could **leave an honest review,** *because your opinion matters!*

Reviews are so important; thank you for taking the time—I really appreciate it!

Bonus Content!

HERE'S A SNEAK PREVIEW OF
THE RANCHER'S CONVENIENT PREGNANT BRIDE,
BOOK 3 IN THE BEAR CREEK SADDLE SERIES.

First, an overview:

The Rancher's Convenient Pregnant Bride:
Book 3 in the Bear Creek Saddle Series

ERIC HUNT, A HANDSOME young rancher in the small mountain town of Bear Creek Saddle, Idaho, learns he can't have children of his own. His desperate prayers to God for healing are answered with a crystal-clear vision: a beautiful woman with warm brown eyes—his future wife?—and she's holding a baby. *But how?*

Across the country, Lindsay Moore's glamorous Manhattan lifestyle is ripped out from under her when she falls victim to an investment scam, loses her job as an executive at the bank…and finds out she's pregnant by a man who wants nothing to do with her, or her baby.

When Lindsay's sister asks her to come out to Bear Creek Saddle Ranch to be her maid-of-honor and help plan her upcoming wedding, Lindsay has nowhere else to go. But she's completely out of place in the mountains, and without the sense of importance and identity her career and money used to give her, she feels lost. She's no longer sure of her value, and she never imagined she'd be in this predicament...single, broke, and raising her baby without a father.

Eric is the groom's best-man, and when the bride-to-be's beautiful sister Lindsay arrives, he offers her a job to help her out, and to get to know her better. He's heard a lot about her already, and since her sister has blue-green eyes, he'd assumed Lindsay would as well.

But she has warm brown eyes. Could Lindsay be the one from his vision?

They find themselves drawn to each other, despite all of their differences. And when Eric discovers Lindsay is pregnant, he knows God sent Lindsay to him for a reason.

Eric wants to marry her and be a father to her baby, even if they're not in love yet—she's beautiful inside and out, and he feels called by God to make the proposal. For Lindsay, it's a way out of the mess she's made of her life—an offer for a modern marriage of convenience that she just can't refuse.

But can a man and a woman with nothing in common, find common ground...and maybe even love...before their child is born?

KEEP READING FOR THE FIRST CHAPTER OF ERIC AND LINDSAY'S STORY...

The Rancher's Convenient Pregnant Bride

Book 3 in the Bear Creek Saddle Series
by Shoshanna Gabriel

Beginning of Book 3

"For you created my inmost being; you knit me together in my mother's womb. I praise you because I am fearfully and wonderfully made; your works are wonderful, I know that full well. My frame was not hidden from you when I was made in the secret place, when I was woven together in the depths of the earth. Your eyes saw my unformed body; all the days ordained for me were written in your book before one of them came to be." *Psalm 139:13-16 (NIV)*

L INDSAY MOORE PRESSED into the seatback of the yellow taxi cab and stared out the window at the pedestrians weaving their way down the over-crowded New York City sidewalks. At least the cab driver hadn't given her the side-eye when she'd told him her destination...not that she'd have blamed him, if he had.

Her sister didn't even know anything that had happened to her, since Megan had left Manhattan and moved all the way out to the small mountain town of Bear Creek Saddle, Idaho. She didn't know about how Lindsay had gotten scammed out of her half of their mother's inheritance. How she'd gotten fired. Then evicted. How she'd spent weeks couch-surfing, until her girlfriends were done with being charitable, and finally, done with her altogether.

Megan didn't know the very worst part of it all. The stupidest mistake Lindsay ever could have made...and now, here she was.

God, I need You. What do I do now?

Just...help a girl out. Please, help me now.

As if on cue, her phone rang—the upbeat country music she'd programmed to play whenever her sister called. The cheery guitar strums seemed out of place in the dreary cab interior.

Thank You.

Lindsay accepted the call, barely able to control her emotions. "Meg! How are you?"

"I just had this urge to call you," Megan said, her voice bright and clear as day, even though she was on the other side of the country. "And I thought, 'you know who's good at planning events?' You! What do you think? Will you help me?"

Lindsay laughed and blinked back the tears that threatened to escape her eyes. "I don't know anything about planning a wedding outside of Manhattan. I get shaky on the details if I stray too far from the Upper West Side, even."

"I'm positive you have tons of vacation days and sick days stored up that you never take. Come on out to Idaho. You can stay with me. Who better to plan my wedding than you?"

"You'll get sick of me, if I come out an entire month before your wedding. That's a long time."

Megan's voice sobered. "I miss you, and I'm excited for you to get to know Zach before we get married. There's plenty of room at the ranch for you."

"I don't have…" Lindsay paused. What could she say at a time like this? "…a dress yet."

"It's Idaho, not Mars. You can buy anything you need here. And it's not like Amazon doesn't ship here, if you can't find what you want. You don't even need to pack a toothbrush, much less your fancy-pants shampoo." Megan laughed into the phone, and Lindsay could just imagine her younger sister's big smile.

"Let me think on it, and I'll get back to you," Lindsay said. "Love you."

"Love you more."

Ending the call brought Lindsay back to reality—to the chilly, dark cab, to the steadily increasing cab fare, and the final destination she never, ever had wanted to go to in the first place.

"Wait—" she called to the driver through the plastic partition.

The driver slid the partition open. "What?"

She thought about the money Grant had given her this morning, nonchalantly handing over the bills as if they'd had George Washington's face on them instead of Benjamin Franklin's.

"I can't—I don't want to go to the women's clinic after all."

"You want to get out here?" The driver tapped the meter. "You still pay."

Lindsay took a deep breath. "Drive me to JFK, instead, please."

He groaned. "The airport, now? I'll have to turn around."

As if that minor inconvenience was going to change her mind now.

"Thank you," she said, and sank back in her seat once more, this time with a sigh of relief.

Her sister had no idea what a huge impact her invitation had. The timing couldn't be a coincidence. That *had* to be God.

If only she'd asked Him for help sooner—before she'd even gotten into this mess.

While Megan probably wasn't expecting Lindsay to show up on her doorstep so soon after their conversation, there was no way Lindsay could risk going back to Grant's place—where her few remaining personal items were—unless she'd "taken care of things." His words.

As if it were so easy. No big deal.

If she went back, he'd convince her all over again to do the one thing she did not want to do. At least at her sister's house, Lindsay could expect some love and support. There was no going back now. Only forward—to Idaho.

What was a born-and-bred Manhattan girl going to do in the mountains with a bunch of cow ranchers?

A small voice spoke inside of her: *You'll live... You both will.*

Lindsay laughed out loud, the sound breaking the silence in the cab. This was happening. It was really happening.

She gently placed her hand on her abdomen, even though there was nothing to see or feel just yet.

We're going to be okay, Little One.

* * *

Eric Hunt took in a deep breath of the clear mountain air, and looked toward the rising sun over the evergreen trees. The rays filtered through the woods, glinting off a small puddle of water on a rock near his boots. He tipped his brown Stetson lower over his eyes.

It was a good hat. He'd bought it—a better version of the old cowboy hat he'd had—the same week he'd become an official co-owner of the ranch he'd been working on as a wrangler, since he'd been a teenager.

'Cause now, he wouldn't be all hat, no cattle.

"Thanks for coming with me," Eric said to his brother, who walked next to him. "Barely see you anymore these days, feels like."

"Wait till you get married," his brother said with a laugh. "You won't want to be away from your wife for too long, either."

Ryan, his elder by three years, didn't know about the recent bad news Eric's doctor had given him. No one would marry Eric now that he couldn't have kids. At least no one that he'd be happy being married to, as far as he could tell.

He wanted to be with a woman who wanted to be a mom and raise a family—but from now on, he was only going to be able to date women who didn't want kids at all. That right there was a conundrum.

"I was thinking about that last night," Eric admitted. He'd been silently praying, from the moment his head hit the pillow, as he always did before he fell asleep. "Picture popped in my head, clear as can be. Like a movie. Man, it was so clear...it felt like..."

What was the right word?

"...like a vision," Eric said. That was it. There was no better way to explain it.

"You mean a dream? Never known you to have...*visions.*" Ryan said the word cautiously, like he didn't believe him.

"Not visions, plural," corrected Eric. "Just one. One in my whole life. Ain't so crazy for me to have just one little picture in my head from God, is it?"

Ryan shrugged.

"It happened to folks in the Bible, right?" Eric asked. He wasn't sure why he wanted Ryan to understand how important it was to him, for what he'd seen to be from God—for it to be *real.*

"I guess it don't matter if it was a vision or a dream either way," Ryan conceded. "What'd you see?" He paused, as if unsure of his wording. "Or... um...what were you dreaming about?"

"It was me, and a girl—I mean, a *woman*—and she was holding a little baby. And the girl was looking at me with these warm, brown eyes. Best thing I've ever seen." Eric smiled.

Maybe he'd fallen asleep sooner than he'd thought, and it was just a dream, after all.

But it had felt so real. It felt...*true.* As if God had answered his desperate prayers for healing with this vision, to comfort him.

"Well, a wife and a baby," Ryan said, looking relieved. "That's doable. At least you weren't having visions about winning the Kentucky Derby or something. I thought you were gonna say something crazy."

"It *is* crazy," Eric muttered.

Ryan didn't know, and it wasn't his fault for not knowing—it was Eric's.

"Why do you want me to get married so bad, anyway?" Eric kept a steady pace to their hike, keeping up with his big brother.

Ryan shrugged, and Eric dropped it. He was happy for him. Ryan had found himself a good woman, and they lived just a few miles from Bear Creek Saddle Ranch, which Eric co-owned with his best friends. But he saw his friends at the ranch a lot more often than he saw his own brother.

"I got some good news," Ryan said suddenly, interrupting Eric's thoughts. "Maybe it even has something to do with your, um…vision." He laughed.

"What's up?"

Ryan grinned. "Tiff's pregnant."

"Oh, wow, man, that's awesome," Eric exclaimed. He patted Ryan's back with a hearty thud, and grinned back at him. "You're gonna be a dad. That's crazy."

A tiny slip of jealousy crossed Eric's mind before he shoved it away, clearing his mind of anything other than happy thoughts. What if the baby in his vision was meant to symbolize Ryan's child, not his own?

Couldn't be. Eric knew what God had shown him. It was his own wife and baby.

"And you're gonna be an uncle," Ryan added.

"Wow. That's nuts."

An uncle… Maybe being an uncle would be enough for him. He could be a really good uncle, take his nephew (or niece) out camping and teaching him (or her) how to fish, that kind of thing.

Would that be enough?

Sure...maybe. For a while.

"When's she due?" Eric asked.

"It's still early. We haven't told everyone yet, 'cause she's still in the first trimester. We'll have a summer baby." Ryan couldn't seem to stop smiling.

God, let me be purely happy for him, without being sad for myself. It ain't right. Take that feeling away, Lord, if you can.

Well—of course God could. The question Eric had to answer for himself was, was he ready to stop the pity-party?

Maybe not quite yet. Ryan didn't even know.

Man.

"Sooner you get married, man," Ryan was saying, "sooner you can get to work on bringin' a little cousin into the world for my kid. Just like what you saw, man. They can grow up together, like we did."

"Yeah," Eric replied.

They hiked in silence for a few long minutes.

"I didn't mean to push you," Ryan said, breaking the silence. "I get it. Just 'cause I married Tiff when I was your age, doesn't mean *you're* ready to settle down."

"Ain't any girls in town who'd want to marry me, anyhow," Eric said. He tried to keep his voice casual. As if it didn't matter.

Even though it did.

Ryan stopped in his tracks. "Are you kidding me, bro? You're all set, man—you got the ranch, built your own home, an' we can't go anywhere together without girls looking at you more'n once."

"You look just like me." Eric shook his head and gestured to his brother's thick head of dark hair, year-round tan and even the same blue eyes.

"Nah—you look just like *me*," Ryan said, and laughed. "I was here first, remember?"

"Big shoes to fill," Eric said, but he smiled.

They'd gone almost an entire mile further before they stopped to drink some water and enjoy the view for a minute.

"So." Eric took his hat off and wiped the sweat off his brow, before setting it back on his head. "I got something to tell you, too."

"What's up?" Ryan was drinking from his canteen, and a bit of water spilled on his shirt when he spoke. He wiped his mouth with the back of his hand.

"I went to the doctor a few weeks ago," Eric said carefully. Felt good to finally bring it up. Now was as good a time as any.

"You alright?"

Eric could sense the concern in his brother's voice. Their mother was a breast cancer survivor, and knowing cancer ran in their family put them both on edge whenever anyone brought up the subject of doctors.

"No cancer," Eric said quickly. May as well lead with the good news. "But I can't have kids, anyways. That's why the vision shook me up, I guess."

"What?" Ryan looked shocked. "How would you even know that?"

"I thought everything seemed fine. Everything in working order. But the doctor found internal scar tissue. He thinks it's from a real old injury when I was kid. I can think of more than one that could've done me in."

"Scar tissue." Ryan frowned. They started walking again, but he'd slowed his pace.

"Yup. Inside, blocking…um…man, I don't want to get all detailed and medical, all right? But I ain't got no swimmers."

"Nothing comes out when—"

Eric bit the inside of his cheek to keep from growling at his brother. Zach, his best friend who owned the ranch with him, had asked him nearly the exact same question.

"How many other ways can I say *I thought everything was fine?*" Eric said in exasperation. "No issues I would've known about with a doggone microscope, all right? It's a problem you can't see with your eyes. Either way—it don't matter how long I'm married for, I ain't gonna get my wife pregnant. You got it now?"

Ryan was silent. "I'm sorry, man. How'd you, uh…find out?"

"Doc found the scar tissue, thought it might be something cancer or whatnot 'cause of mom's medical history, and when they did the imaging he figured it out. So he tested um…you know, with the microscope. This…this ain't a problem that's going away. Surgery's kinda a risky option."

"But it's an option?"

"If I'm willing to risk losing my ability to have marital relations at all, I guess," Eric explained. "And I ain't willing."

"Don't blame ya," Ryan said, shuddering as if the mere thought had given him the chills. "Maybe you can adopt."

"Yeah, maybe…"

It wasn't a bad idea. Not that a guy could compare kids to dogs, but if Eric could love Boomer as much as he did, and Boomer was a whole different species, how much more would he love a kid, even if they weren't related by blood?

"Maybe," Eric repeated, brighter this time. "Yeah."

"Maybe you'll even find a woman with kids of her own already.

They're not all off the market, you know."

"That's true." Eric gave his brother a quick smile. Ryan was good at saying the right thing to make him feel better. Always had been.

There could still be the right girl for him out there, somewhere. *Lord, please drop her right in my lap where I can't miss her.*

* * *

Two crammed flights later, with a short layover in Denver, Lindsay found herself in Spokane, Washington—only a couple of hours drive over the border into Bear Creek Saddle, Idaho. There wasn't even an airport in north Idaho for her to go to, as she'd discovered when she got to JFK and rushed to the counter with the crumpled hundred-dollar bills in her hand.

She hadn't texted her sister, which was at best, dumb, and at worst, rude, but what if her sister told her she wasn't ready for guests just yet, and that the invite was really meant to be for a few days or a week from now? In this case, it would be better to ask for forgiveness rather than permission.

Finally, she got the courage to text her sister, even though it was after ten P.M. Either way, Lindsay would be hanging around the airport for a while. That was fine. She could spend the night there if she had to.

Wasn't like she had anywhere else to spend the night, anyway.

It was entirely possible Megan wouldn't see the text until the morning. At some point, Megan would have to come over and pick her up from the airport. The cost for a cab all the way to Bear Creek Saddle from Spokane would be more than she had left after buying the plane ticket.

"*Surprise!*" she texted to Megan's cell. "*I'm here, at Spokane*

International. I know it's late and last minute."

It took a few minutes as Lindsay stared at her texts, waiting for a response, but then her phone rang instead.

"Lindsay?" her sister asked when Lindsay picked up the phone. "Are you really in Spokane?"

"Yup! I...have a lot to talk to you about."

"Everything okay?"

Well, she had her health, even if that health included an unplanned pregnancy. "Yes," Lindsay replied convincingly. "I just need a ride to your place."

Her sister half-laughed, half-groaned. "Hang on."

Lindsay waited until Megan came back on the line.

"You're in luck," Megan said. "Zach's friend, Eric, is out in Liberty Lake at the vet with his dog. He can swing by and pick you up when he's done."

"He's at the vet at this hour? Is his dog all right?"

"I hope so," Megan said. "Zach said he got into a scuffle with a goat. The dog—not Eric."

"As one does," Lindsay murmured. "I mean—that's great. Not great about the dog, of course. Great about the ride. Can you give him my number? I'll wait in the baggage terminal for him. Tell him to take his time and make sure his dog's okay—I'm in no rush."

"Will do, Linds. Can't believe you're actually here! I'll make up a bed for you."

Baggage claim was nearly empty after the people from her flight got their bags and left. She checked on her phone to see how far Liberty Lake was from Spokane. Not too far. They were both in Washington state, for one thing. That was lucky.

Thank You, Lord.

She hoped this guy Eric wasn't too put-out by picking her up. He was probably worried about his pet, to have driven hours to an emergency vet in the middle of the night. His name seemed very familiar.

Best man.

That was it. Eric would be Zach's best man in the wedding. Lindsay remembered now. She would walk down the aisle with him, since she was going to be the maid of honor.

Well, this would be a strange way to meet him, but they would have met eventually at the wedding, anyway.

It was only an hour later when her phone buzzed with a new message alert.

"This is Eric—Zach and Megan's friend. I'm here for you."

She grinned. It had been a long, difficult day, and she couldn't wait to sit back and ride to her sister's place. Lindsay stood, hefting her purse over her shoulder—her only bag.

Across the terminal stood a tall, handsome man with broad shoulders and a brown cowboy hat. Could that be him?

He caught her staring and touched the rim of his hat, as if to say "hello." Or maybe to say, "I see you looking at me."

"Are you Eric—"

"Lindsay?" the man asked at the same time.

"Yes." She smiled as he walked over to her.

"Wow. You really do look just like her," Eric said. "Shorter, and shorter hair, like she said...are you her twin or something?"

Lindsay laughed. It was a compliment, as far as she was concerned. "Her big sister. I'm here early to help plan the wedding."

"That's great," Eric said, his face breaking into a smile that looked completely genuine. "She talks about you all the time. Are you the big-time banking exec from New York City?"

"That's me," Lindsay said, with a light-hearted laugh. "Um, well…actually, I'm not working at the moment. So I've got plenty of time to help her out with the wedding and everything. I'll probably be here for a while."

"I'll grab your bags," he offered, looking behind her.

"Um, no bags. Just me." She shrugged, as if that was totally not weird at all. "I can borrow Megan's clothes. We're the same size, she's just a few inches taller. Not fair, I know, especially since I'm supposed to be the big sister."

Ugh. She was rambling. She couldn't help it—he was too good-looking. Those blue of eyes of his contrasting against his olive skin and dark hair. Amazing. It was making her nervous.

"Okay." He nodded, but she could've sworn he'd looked at her strangely.

Which made sense, of course. Who travels across America without so much as a toothbrush or a change of socks?

"How's your dog?" she asked.

"Boomer's all right," Eric said, slowing his long strides so she could keep up. "He won't be messing with the goats again anytime soon, that's for sure. Got a good long scrape on his side, got some stitches."

"Poor guy," Lindsay said. She loved dogs, though she rarely had the chance to interact with any. Her building didn't allow pets, and none of her friends had dogs. The only ones she saw where when she walked in Central Park and visited the dog park. "What kind of dog is he?"

"Airedale Terrier. Big guy. Bark is much worse than his bite."

"Good to know."

"Good for the goats, too."

They got to Eric's truck, a big black pickup with what looked like a sad and sedated Boomer laying in the backseat.

Boomer barked when Eric opened the door for her.

"Go back to sleep," Eric said. "It's just Megan's sister."

That seemed to be good enough for the dog, who obeyed, promptly resting his big furry head on the bench seat.

"Let me help you up." Eric offered Lindsay his large, calloused hand, and she took it gratefully.

"Thanks," she said, using his hand for leverage to climb up into the seat. She was used to taking the subway everywhere, and occasionally cabs or Uber. Not many people in New York City had big work trucks like Eric's.

He waited until she was settled and buckled in before he went around to the driver's side. How chivalrous. Completely unlike Grant, who didn't even offer to accompany her to the clinic for what could've been the biggest, most awful event of her life...even though it was his baby, too.

Well, not anymore, it wasn't. As far as she was concerned, Grant gave up his paternity the moment he'd paid her to permanently get rid of it.

"Wasn't expecting Megan's call tonight. This a surprise visit?" Eric asked, staring straight ahead at the road.

"Sort of. Megan invited me, but I didn't tell her I went to the airport immediately after she called." Lindsay laughed, as if it were all in fun.

There was no reason to tell more to this complete stranger, even if he was her brother-in-law-to-be's childhood best friend.

"You own the ranch with Zach, right?" she asked, to jog her

memory.

"Yes indeed. Me, Zach, Chris and Jay." He didn't look at her as he spoke, but it seemed to be more a result of keeping his eyes on the road and less about shyness.

She couldn't imagine such a big, handsome man being shy. He'd taken his hat off in the truck, and set it on the console between them. Dark tendrils swept across his forehead, and he ran his fingers through them to push his hair back.

"Did you always want to be a rancher?"

She didn't know what exactly to ask, or what to say. What did she have in common with this guy, anyway, other than her sister? Country life was vastly different from her life in New York. Ranching and banking were worlds apart. And from what she knew of the group of ranchers at Bear Creek Saddle Ranch, they were good guys who went to church every week and walked the talk.

Not like her. A hypocrite who had essentially prostituted herself for a place to sleep.

God, what have I done? Please, please forgive me.

No matter how many times she had asked God for forgiveness, she kept feeling the urge to ask one more time, as if maybe the first time hadn't stuck. Even knowing the extent of God's grace for those who repented, she was having a hard time with it. Was she good enough to forgive? Did she even deserve to be forgiven?

And now she was bringing an innocent child into this mess. A child who wouldn't have a father in his life. From everything she'd learned after researching online, having a father figure in the home was, statistically, really important for children. Those kids with the good luck to grow up with married parents at home led, in many cases, infinitely more privileged lives. She mourned that loss for her child's sake, if not for hers.

Of course, plenty of people grew up with a single mom as the head of the household, and did perfectly fine. She'd be okay. Her sister had said Zach had grown up without a dad, since he'd abandoned him and his mom when he was young. That was probably more traumatic for a kid than not knowing their father to begin with, right?

Eric shifted his hands on the steering wheel, appearing to be lost in thought. "Yeah, I think I always wanted to be a rancher," he said.

Only moments had passed since she'd asked the question, but his response still shook her out of her reverie.

He didn't expand on his reply. Not one for talking much, it seemed. Or maybe it was just with her.

Well, if there was one thing Lindsay was good at, it was getting people to talk and open up. It was one of her jobs at the bank, to make new clients feel like they were her best friend, so they'd trust her enough to put lots of money in the bank. Even if that was part of the job (people skills, as they said) she did genuinely like meeting new people, and by the end of their meetings, she usually had a real interest in them and hoped for their financial success, whatever that might mean to them.

"Tell me about your ranch," she pressed. "I know nothing about this stuff, and I'm going to be staying there with Megan, so I could really use a primer."

"Not much to say, I suppose," Eric said. "Used to be Bill's ranch, but after Melody passed—" He coughed, as if covering for a break in his voice. *Who was Melody?* "Well, Bill sold us the ranch."

"Did you know her well? I'm sorry for your loss."

"She was a good lady. Really threw Bill for a loop when she died. But he's back on the saddle again—he and Allie—that's his new wife—they own Freddy's Diner in town now. Us guys have been working on that ranch since we were kids ourselves."

"You, Zach, Chris and...?" She paused, prompting him to remind her of all the names. They were all going to be groomsmen. She should know this.

"Jay." Eric nodded and checked something on his dashboard. "Sorry, I gotta fill 'er up. You hungry or anything?"

Starved.

"Only if you are." Lindsay hoped the tone in her voice did not sound especially hungry. She hadn't eaten since the cookies on the plane. And prior to that, she hadn't eaten in the morning before the cab ride. Too nervous, plus she might've needed major sedation.

"I know just the place. Burgers an' gas right over the Idaho state line."

They rode past a big green highway sign that said:

WELCOME TO IDAHO: *WELCOME CENTER 8 MILES*

Not too long after, he pulled off the exit ramp. It was so dark out at night compared to the city. Despite the street lamps, there were entire stretches of road bathed in darkness.

From the backseat, Boomer whined.

"Settle down," Eric said, reaching back toward the dog once he'd pulled in front of the fuel pump in front of the tiny diner/convenience store. "I'll get you one too when we get back." To Lindsay, he simply said, "Stay inside the truck till I get 'er fueled up."

"Yes, *sir*," she said, not bothering to keep the sarcasm from her voice. Why was he ordering her around like she had to listen to him? Were all Idahoan men like that?

If Eric noticed her annoyance at his tone, he didn't act like it. She watched as he swung his long, muscular denim-clad legs out of the truck and jumped to the pavement. The truck jostled as he put the fuel pump in to her side of the vehicle, and for some reason, it felt personal. Like he was jostling her.

What is wrong with me? This guy was doing her a favor. A *big* favor, and on very short notice. She was probably just tired. Exhausted, even.

And famished.

He left the pump in the truck and grabbed the windshield washer, dripping in soapy water.

His thin white T-shirt stretched over his biceps as he reached in front of the truck to get to the windshield. With a jump that really rocked the truck, he hopped up onto the floorboard of the driver's side for easier access.

Lindsay didn't want to stare, but he was so intent on cleaning the bugs off his glass that he didn't seem to notice her at all. So there was no harm in just watching him work, right?

Don't lust. That wasn't even what had gotten her into her current predicament (what had? Pride? Or its opposite, shame?), but it could definitely get her into another bad situation.

At least she couldn't get pregnant twice at the same time. Small comfort.

It was strange—she'd spent her twenty-eight years as a virgin, then lost her virginity only a month ago. But the experience had her looking at men in a completely different way.

Or maybe it was just something about Eric. Any woman would agree he was easy on the eyes. If he wasn't such an Idaho cowboy type, he could've been a model in New York. Did he know that? Or was he completely unaware of his effect on women...on her?

She startled a bit when he got back in the truck. Could he tell she'd been thinking about him that way?

"Didn't mean to scare you," he said. "I gotta move the truck so we can grab some food."

When they parked, he came around to her door even as she was opening it for herself. That was nice. Gentlemanly, even.

"Thank you," she murmured, taking his hand to jump down. But as she did, her foot slipped off the running board on the side of the vehicle, and Eric wrapped his arm around her waist, holding her against him, her legs dangling in the air, a foot above the ground.

It had to be at least a foot, because the way he was holding her, their faces were even. She could see right into his eyes.

Blue eyes.

Amazing, deep blue eyes.

Lindsay turned her head abruptly.

"Sorry 'bout that," he muttered, setting her down on the ground.

"No problem." Her cheeks flushed, and she ran her fingers through her dark brown hair. It was cut shoulder length, much shorter than her sister's.

"Looked like you were gonna slip, there," Eric said. "That's all."

"I get it." She looked over at the small diner, which also appeared to be a convenience store, based on the windows.

But Eric was already walking ahead of her. She ran to catch up. Behind her, in the truck, Boomer barked his disapproval.

"Boomer!" Eric yelled over his shoulder, and the dog quieted. "He still don't get that I'm bringing him back his favorite."

"Hamburger?"

"Yup." Eric held the door for her.

She could get used to this door-holding thing.

"Must be a wonderful vet, for you to travel so far," she noted.

"In a real emergency, if I have to, I take 'im down to Couer d'Alene. But if there's time enough to drive, I'll take him to his regular vet in Liberty Lake. He knows Boomer, and the horses at the ranch, better than any of the other vets 'round here."

There was no hostess to seat them, so they seated themselves. Worn red vinyl booths filled the eating section of the storefront. Eric took the seat facing the door.

A pretty waitress in her early forties, with long blonde hair pulled back in a ponytail, greeted them. "Hi, Eric!" she said. To Lindsay, "and Miss."

Was she still a "miss," and not a "ma'am," as she was so often called in New York? Soon she'd be a mother. Hopefully she would graduate to "ma'am" by then. People had told her she looked young for her age, which her mother used to say would bother her until it flattered her.

What would her mom think of her situation now?

Don't even think about it. If Lindsay hadn't known her mom was in Heaven, then she'd assume she was rolling in her grave, as they say.

"What can I get for ya?" the waitress asked. Based on the flirtatious eyes she was giving Eric, she seemed to be completely infatuated with him.

Poor lady. He had no clue she was interested.

Eric flashed her a smile full of naturally straight, white teeth, and handed her the laminated menu that had been sitting on their table when they got there. "The usual."

"Burger, no pink, no cheese, all the toppings, and fries." She scribbled on her pad. "How 'bout for your girl here?"

His girl?

Eric laughed but didn't correct her assumption.

"I'll have a cheeseburger—medium—lettuce, ketchup and mayo, please," Lindsay said.

"Pink or no pink?" the waitress intoned.

Lindsay looked at Eric in confusion. What did she mean?

"A hamburger with cheese," she repeated to the woman.

"Some pink," Eric interrupted. "Thanks, darlin'."

That got a big smile from the waitress. *Darlin'.*

Maybe this friend of Megan's fiancé was a big flirt, himself. Maybe he was a player, like Grant. Someone who was happy to play the field with no cares, no love, and no conscience regarding the consequences.

Didn't matter how good-looking Eric was, or how close he was to her soon-to-be brother-in-law. Lindsay would have to be careful around him.

She couldn't afford to make any more life-changing mistakes now. No flirting or falling for a man at the drop of a dime. Any decisions she made from here on out wouldn't only affect herself.

Without consciously thinking about it, she laid her hand to rest over her womb.

* * *

When the waitress sat the food down in front of them, Eric

bowed his head. It had been a long night, and he was hungry as a bear, but his burger wasn't going anywhere.

"You say grace, too?" Lindsay asked in apparent surprise. "Do you want to say grace for both of us?"

Why not. He reached his hand out across the table, the way his parents had done with him around the dinner table, and she took it.

Her hand was tiny compared to his, soft and white. It was clear she wasn't into vegetable gardening or anything more than typing, if that. But her skin was so soft, he had to physically restrain himself from running his thumb along her smooth knuckles.

When Megan had asked him to pick up her sister at the airport, she'd told him to look for a girl who looked just like her, but shorter, with shorter hair. The description was apt.

Unlike his friend's fiancée, thought, Lindsay had brown eyes. *Warm* brown eyes. And…if possible…she was even more beautiful.

Not that it mattered. A trendy New Yorker who didn't know a cow from a potato wouldn't want anything to do with a guy like him, anyway.

And even if she did, the relationship would end before it could begin. Because he wasn't going to get married and ruin some poor girl's life with his own problems.

"Lord," Eric said, gripping Lindsay's hand, "thank You for this food. Please bless it to our bodies, and please fix Boomer up quick. Maybe keep him away from the goats, if that's Your will, Lord."

He paused, and added a silent prayer of his own: *Please God, if that vision was for real, let me know what to do with it. Why does this Lindsay girl have brown eyes?*

"In Jesus' name we pray," Lindsay added quietly. "Amen."

It had to be a coincidence, those beautiful brown eyes of hers. Or was it?

* * *

Lindsay turned off her cell phone—something she'd never done before. If she'd been at a movie or in a meeting, she'd just turn it to vibrate, instead. But the only person who mattered in the world was right in front of her now, in this rustic log cabin in the mountains of northern Idaho. Forget the distractions of social media, emails or texts. She had her sister. And thank God for that.

"I know," her sister Megan was saying as she placed two mugs of hot decaffeinated coffee in front of them, "Bear Creek Saddle was a bit of a culture shock for me, too, when I first left Manhattan. It's a different world out here." Megan smiled. "In a good way."

Lindsay nodded, running her hand along the smooth grain of the wooden dining table. Her fingers itched to move, to do something, without having a phone to fiddle with. Would her sister ask her? Did she already know, was it written all over her face?

"I couldn't believe it when you called me last night from the airport," Megan said. "I mean, obviously I really wanted you to come out here, not just for my wedding, but so we can hang out. But I figured it would be tough to get you away from that bank for more than a day and a half, much less an entire month before we tie the knot."

Lindsay winced. That was as good of an opening as any.

"The bank let me go," Lindsay said. "I mean, they didn't just let me go on this trip...they—they fired me."

"Oh no!" A few drops of coffee splashed over the edge of Megan's coffee cup as she moved it from her lips. "When was that?

Yesterday? Tell me everything." She shook her head in disbelief. "You know what? Forget them. God has something better for you, He always does. Who needs them, am I right?"

"Yeah." Lindsay hoped her sister was right, that this was all just part of God's bigger plan for her…but if that was the case, then maybe His plan was to turn her into the female Job. Megan didn't even know the half of it yet.

"The silver lining is," Megan said, "you can stay with me as long as you want now. We'll stay here in Zach's house, and Zach will stay in the practice-cabin—I mean, guest cabin—out back."

"I can't kick a man out of his own home," Lindsay said.

"Oh please, he'll be fine. It's only four weeks till the wedding, at which point—"

"I'll have to leave, obviously." Lindsay took a sip of her coffee. "I understand." What was different about it? Real cream, instead of artificially flavored creamer?

"Nooo, I was going to say, that's when you move into the guest cabin, and get on your feet again. You can stay as long as you need."

Tears unexpectedly welled in Lindsay's eyes, and she laughed in surprise.

"I have zero idea why I'm crying. Must be tired. That's really nice of you, Meg. You have no idea." She tilted her head back so the tears wouldn't fall, and smiled. "Thank you. I mean it."

Megan reached out and took Lindsay's hand. "Of course. Can you tell me what happened? That's really messed up of them to fire you after, what, five years with them? That's forever these days."

"I know. But they have a policy about not allowing banking executives in charge of people's accounts to have significant non-student-loan debt, and um…"

Do not cry. Do not cry.

"You don't have debt, though, right?" Megan asked.

"I do now." Lindsay laughed nervously, but it wasn't funny. Nothing about this was funny. "Kind of a crazy story."

Megan leaned forward across the table from her, as if to remind her they had all the time in the world. Lindsay wasn't going to be able to avoid telling her much longer, anyway. It had been hard enough keeping it from her since Megan had run off to Idaho.

"It's not like you to get into debt," Megan said. "Or to lose a job. What's going on?"

"Do you remember that story about Bernie Madoff that was in the news awhile back?" Lindsay didn't wait for her sister to respond. Of course she hadn't—it wouldn't have been on her radar back then. "He had this whole Ponzi scheme, where big money investors would invest in his hedge fund. But the hedge fund wasn't real…whenever his investors wanted to take out some of their money, Madoff would give them money from new investors. He got away with it for years, until—"

"I want to hear about *you*, Lindsay, not some scandal," Megan interrupted.

"This is about me," she said quietly. "I fell for the same thing. Not with Madoff, but a very similar scam. I didn't know. I lost all of my inheritance from Mom."

Megan gasped, then covered her mouth. "Please tell me you're joking. You're just trying to freak me out."

"When have I ever done that?" Lindsay sighed. "I had taken out money to supplement my income at the bank. But the money I took out wasn't really investment income, like I thought. It was some other poor guy's money. And now I have to pay that all back."

"Wait." Megan pushed her chair back and stood, pacing the hardwood floor. Everything was wood in the cabin, from the floors to the walls to the ceiling to the counter tops, table and chairs. "So not only did you lose all your savings, but you owe money now, too? How much?"

Lindsay's stomach sank. She didn't want to tell her. But her sister had to know. Lindsay had kept her in the dark long enough, and sunlight was the best disinfectant.

"Twenty-five grand." Lindsay laughed weakly. "I didn't know. I thought it was mine. I didn't...know."

"You just had to have the designer clothes, those expensive purses and shoes," Megan shot back.

"Whoa, why are you angry with me? I'm the victim here."

"I'm sorry," Megan said. "But if you didn't have such an expensive lifestyle, you wouldn't have taken out so much cash, and you wouldn't be in so much debt, and you wouldn't have lost your job."

Lindsay stared at the table. It wasn't fun getting a lecture from the same girl she had taught how to apply eye-shadow just ten years prior. "I suppose you're right. But the joke's on me, because I had to sell all that stuff to make rent. And now I don't even have the thrift-store clothes I bought to replace it all."

Megan took a deep breath and sat back down, pulling her chair to the table with a scraping sound across the floorboards. "You've been able to pay your extravagant rent just from selling your clothes?"

"And purses. And shoes. But only for one month. You know how much an apartment on the Upper West Side costs."

"So you're good till the end of this month?"

Lindsay shook her head. "This happened months ago. I've been sleeping on friend's couches ever since."

"You should have told me," Megan said. "Why didn't you? How could you keep this from me all this time?"

"I'm sorry," Lindsay said, for what felt like the hundredth time. You were so far away, and dealing with your own issues. You didn't need to hear about mine."

"That's what sisters are for, though…"

Lindsay gave her sister a half-smile, her coffee all but forgotten on the table top. "I'm just so glad you're here for me now," she said. "Can I really stay here?"

"Of course."

"My friends ditched me." Lindsay didn't like the petulant sound in her words. She shook her head, and tried again. "I mean, I don't blame them. I couldn't go shopping with them anymore, or go out to lunch, or to the theater. None of the things we used to do together. They couldn't cover my lunch bill forever. I get it."

Megan scoffed. "No way, that's not right. What they should have done is started planning things to do that don't cost money. Whatever happened to meeting up in Central Park for a picnic? Or having coffee at someone's apartment? Or watching a movie on TV together?"

"They don't want to do stuff like that. And we did hang out a bit when I was at their places, sleeping over. After a week or so, they'd end up politely asking me when I was moving on." Lindsay swallowed hard, determined to keep her voice from cracking. "I went through all my friends, Megan. Every single girlfriend I had let me stay with them, until they didn't. I couldn't get a new job that would pay my bills. I was getting more money from my unemployment checks than I'd get from taking on any of the jobs that were available to me. And then that ran out. Obviously."

What she didn't say was that she'd tried to get an entry-level job, just something, anything, and had been rejected for being "overqualified." Three times. They didn't want to pay to train someone who would leave the moment something better came along, which, theoretically, it would.

"I'm so sorry," Megan said. "I don't know what to say, other than I still can't believe this happened to you."

Lindsay steeled herself for the final bit of truth she had to tell her sister. The one Big Thing she'd kept secret since she'd found out.

God, give me the words to say.

"I did something stupid," Lindsay said. "I went against everything I was taught, everything I told you to do, even. I feel like a total hypocrite."

"What do you mean?"

Her sister was five years younger than her, and while Lindsay knew Megan wasn't going to be a virgin on her wedding night, thanks to a long live-in relationship prior to her moving out to Idaho, Megan had finally come around and was waiting with Zach for their wedding to consummate their relationship.

Lindsay, at twenty-eight years old, had maintained her virginity. All through high-school, all through college, and through various boyfriends (who would usually dump her after she wouldn't sleep with them several months into the relationship). And yet, here she was.

God, give me the words, please. I need You.

"I didn't have any women friends left to stay with," Lindsay said slowly. "I was too proud to call you. I'm sorry. One of the guys I knew from work, you probably don't remember him from my birthday party a few years back—Grant Bowland—he offered to let me stay with him."

"I understand," Megan said. "I mean, I stayed in Zach's guest cabin when I first moved here. To be fair, you kinda freaked out on me when I told you I was taking a stranger up on his offer."

"Because I *knew* that when a man asks you to stay with him, ninety percent of the time, his motivations aren't pure. You lucked into a good guy. I didn't."

"Oh my goodness, did he hurt you?" Megan squeaked. Her knuckles, gripping her coffee mug, where white. Maybe the mug would shatter in her tight hold.

"No, no." Lindsay sighed. "It was my choice. I felt…indebted to him. He was letting me stay with him, buying all my food, taking me out to dinner and paying, offering to use his contacts in banking to find me another job. He even hinted that if it worked out with us, he'd pay off my debt. But it was all just a manipulation to get me to sleep with him. And…it worked."

Megan nodded. "I get it. Kinda reminds me of Todd." Todd was her ex-boyfriend, and a real piece of work.

Tell her.

"I got pregnant, Meg."

Megan cocked her head, her eyes wide. "I think I misheard you. Say that again?"

"Grant said he didn't want a relationship with me, not for real. That he definitely didn't want a baby now. I mean, he's thirty-five, so you'd think he'd be ready to settle down, but no. Seems like he wants to play the field for another decade or so, then find some young trophy wife to marry. He gave me five hundred dollars to…take care of things."

Megan stilled. "Did you?" Her face was blank, impassive. As if she was trying so hard not to judge, and yet was waiting for the worst answer.

"No."

Her sister exhaled. Lindsay hadn't even realized Megan had been holding her breath. "Thank God."

"You called me and invited me to come here when I was in the cab on the way to the women's clinic. I didn't want to risk going back to Grant's for my things, so I just went directly to the airport instead. I used the money he wanted me to use for the abortion, to fly here."

She almost expected Megan to chide her for taking his money, but instead, Megan leaned back in her chair with a smirk. "Good."

Lindsay grinned. "Thanks. I mean it, Meg. Thank you for understanding."

"Wait a minute, so this means…I'm going to be an auntie?" Megan asked. "For real?"

"Yes!" Lindsay patted her womb. "I don't know if my baby is a boy or girl, but I keep getting nauseated, so I think it's healthy, either way."

"I heard lemonade is good for that. Do you want some?" Megan was already standing and on her way to the fridge.

"Sure!" Lindsay's heartrate settled. She wasn't going to be kicked out for getting pregnant outside of marriage, it didn't even look like Megan was going to scold her about it. She seemed just relieved Lindsay was keeping the baby. "Hey, don't tell anyone about it just yet, okay? I'm not even at eight weeks. I want people here to get to know me before they find out I'm preggo."

Megan slid an icy glass of hand-squeezed lemonade in front of her. "You got it. I have to tell Zach, though. I tell him everything. But he knows how to keep a secret that's not his to tell."

Lindsay nodded. That made sense. Now that Megan was engaged to be married, she couldn't expect her to keep anything from her husband-to-be.

"Let's talk about your wedding," Lindsay said. Now that she'd confessed it all, she felt a burden had lifted. Finally. It hadn't been nearly as bad as she'd built it up in her mind to be. "I'm going to plan the best wedding for you and Zach, ever."

As they sat across from each other, discussing color schemes, themes, and budgets, Lindsay finally let herself relax a bit. Yes, she was far away from the only home she'd ever known. Yes, she was going to have a difficult time being a single mother in a small, conservative town. But she had her family, and family mattered most of all.

"I have an idea…" Megan took a sip of her coffee and grinned.

"The last time you gave me that look, we both ended up getting grounded for two weeks."

"It's not *that* crazy, not really," Megan said, shrugging off the reference to the time they'd "borrowed" their mom's car as teenagers.

Lindsay smiled. "All right, lay it on me. What's it going to be? Destination wedding on a mountain top? The bridesmaids all have to enter on horseback?"

"Nope. Much simpler. I want a double wedding," Megan said. "With *you* as the other bride. Let's get you hitched before this baby is born!"

Lindsay laughed and shook her head. "That's more impossible than getting me to climb to the top of a mountain for your vows."

"Nothing's impossible. I just so happen to know three very eligible, very handsome bachelors."

"Like...Eric Hunt?" Lindsay paused. The memory of his arm around her waist when she slipped out of his truck brought heat to her cheeks.

Megan smiled. "You might just be perfect for him."

"Not in my condition," Lindsay reminded her.

"*Exactly* in your condition." Megan grinned, and God help her, Lindsay couldn't help but to smile back, even though she had no idea why.

* * *

Want to keep reading?

Search for my name, Shoshanna Gabriel,
at your favorite book retailer,
and find the rest of the Bear Creek Saddle Series!

Pick up a book and visit Bear Creek Saddle, Idaho,
anytime—
you're always welcome HOME.

GOD BLESS!

♥Shoshanna Gabriel